The Gilligham Collection

CLEAN REGENCY ROMANCE

THE LADY SERIES

DAISY LANDISH

Editing by Rachael Lammie
Cover art by CharmingPixyArt

BEACHES AND TRAILS
PUBLISHING

About the Author

Daisy Landish is a romance and contemporary fiction author living in the UK, whose clean and sweet novellas have tugged at readers' heartstrings across the pond and beyond. When she's not writing love stories, Daisy spends her time reading, hiking at dawn, and riding into the sunset on her horse, Rosebud.

www.daisylandishromance.com

Also by Daisy Landish

Clean Regency Romance

The Lady Series - The Allington Collection

The Lady Series - The Gillingham Collection

The Lady Series - The Blackmore Collection

The Lady Series - The Norrington Collection

Clean Contemporary Romance

Maplewood Grove Series

Love on Spruce Island

Second Chance

Cherry Tree Island

The Wedding Trio

Extra Credit

Counting on the Cowboy

Focusing on the Cowboy

Mistletoe Magic

Grounded at Christmas

Cozy Mysteries

Sophie Brooks Mysteries

Jane and Kennedy Daniels Mysteries

Pine Grove Mysteries

Annie Archer Paranormal Mysteries

Wilma Wade Holiday Mysteries

Mike and Maddie Mysteries

Mystic Moonhaven Mysteries

Sweater Weather: Cozy Mysteries for Fall

Summer Vibes: Cozy Mysteries for Summer

Let it Snow: Cozy Mysteries for Winter

Spring Break: Cozy Mysteries for Spring

Rescuing The Lady

THE LADY SERIES BOOK SEVEN

Chapter One

Eloise Gillingham could be accused of many things, but she would never be accused of not fully enjoying life. She loved life, and she always brought her love of life to wherever she went and whomever she was with. She loathed the winter because it was so colourless and stark, and she could often be heard huffing and puffing through the drafty halls of her father's grand home whenever she was cooped up for any lengthy period of time indoors.

Spring was always Eloise's favourite time of the year when the flowers came out and the colours of nature popped. She could often be seen running down the hills with her long blonde hair flying behind her, running as if trying to catch up with something elusive, just beyond her grasp. All of this created much exasperation on the part of Eloise's governess, Miss Catherine Tomlins, who'd been tasked with running after her wayward charge, often failing to catch up.

Eloise found pleasure in everything. Even in the French lessons she was subjected to in preparation for being a 'proper' lady, a role she had prepared for and had been reminded of over and over again for the whole sixteen, nearly seventeen, years of her life thus far. Since her mother's death, Eloise and her three younger sisters Penelope, Virginia, and Anna, and her brother, Andrew, had been effectively raised by their governess, their heartbroken father never having remarried.

Mama and Papa's marriage had been a marriage borne out of convenience that grew into one of love. For the first ten years of Eloise's life,
she had been privileged to witness her parent's great fondness for each
other first-hand. When her dear mother had died six years ago, Eloise
had only just turned ten, while Penelope had been eight, Virginia six and
Anna four.

Mama had died giving birth to Andrew. In her own way, Mama had
fulfilled the great duty of every English wife, to give her husband a son
and heir to continue the family legacy. However, the fulfilment of that
duty had come at a very great cost. Mama's death had been hard on all of
them as a family. Time healed all wounds, and eventually, they had
learned to move on and be whole again. All except Papa, who seemed so
lost in his grief, so much so that he could barely look at Andrew, even
now, six years later.

Not everything was maudlin though, by any stretch of the imagination. The sorrowing family had their share of good times growing up.
Now, Eloise was just about to celebrate her seventeenth birthday and
she was finally coming out. In just one month, she and her friend,
Evelyn Chatsworth, would both be presented at court. The girls had
shared long excited discussions about the event and what it might mean
for them going forward. They both knew that it was the grand event of
every notable English girl's life. And while the prospect thrilled them, it
was all somewhat daunting, even terrifying, especially for Eloise who
was expected to navigate these perilous waters without a mother to steer
her through safely. Not that she was facing the season without any
support whatsoever. Lady Chatsworth had already seen too much of
Eloise's wardrobe and was prepared to shepherd both girls throughout
the season. Even so, Eloise dreamed about her presentation night after
night. Sometimes the debutante ball would be everything she had ever
dreamed of. Sometimes, it would be a disaster.

Raising herself up from her pillow after one such night of fitful
sleep, Eloise yawned and stretched, deciding to get out of bed early and
face the day rather than try to rest further.

"Well, it shouldn't be so hard," she consoled herself. In last night's
dream, the presentation had been disastrous where Eloise had tripped

and fallen flat on her face. "Men have certainly done tougher things than stand before a sovereign to proclaim they were now ripe for marriage."

She rang for her maid, Polly, so that she could dress and prepare herself for the series of lessons that would follow throughout the course of the day.

Polly helped Eloise into her corset, pulling the cords tightly while her mistress held the bedpost firmly for support. "Polly, do you think me ready for my presentation?" Eloise mused, as her maid deftly tied the ribbons and helped her with her gown.

"Aye, my lady. I reckon you can cope with any challenge that comes your way."

Eloise smiled fondly, certain that she could do no wrong in Polly's eyes. Theirs was an unusual relationship, being friends more so than mistress and servant.

Despite arising early, Eloise took her precious time preparing herself that morning, but she eventually had to trudge her way to her classroom where her governess, Miss Tomlins, was waiting for her, looking impatiently at the clock. "Good morning, Miss Tomlins," she greeted the woman with a curtsey, hoping to look more awake than she felt.

"Oh, good morning, my dear. How fare ye this fair day?" her governess replied breezily.

They both laughed at Miss Tomlins' weak attempt at humour and settled in for the day. They went through several French verbs and some arithmetic before they settled down for a fifteen-minute break.

"Just a month more before the grand event of the season," Miss Tomlins observed.

"Oh, don't remind me, I feel so nervous, I fear that I might faint before the Queen and all her ladies."

"Don't be silly, child. You are going to make a most marvellous debutante. You are so beautiful, just like your mother, God rest her soul. And I daresay, you will be bound to catch the eye of a handsome Duke within a week." Miss Tomlins sighed. "Imagine! You will be a Duchess and live in an even grander house than this one and live happily ever after."

"Oh, you and your fairy tales, Miss Tomlins. I want that too, provided I do not obliterate the said Duke's toes with my bad dancing first," Eloise added with a grin.

Miss Tomlins' eyes were now as round as saucers. "I know full well you have been taking dancing lessons all these years!"

Eloise made a face. "Oh, you know full well how far from London we are. The dancing I have been taught would have been more appropriate in my mother's day. I have yet to be introduced into the mysteries of the waltz, or any other type of dancing I wish to do, anyway."

"The waltz *is* becoming more accepted," Miss Tomlins said with a frown. "It is quite likely you shall encounter it in London. We must get you a teacher at once because you must not embarrass the Gillingham name. I will put the matter before your father later today."

They laughed together while they discussed some more about practising for the ball before finally returning to their lessons. Three more hours were spent on philosophy, music, and history before retiring for the day.

After such a long day, Eloise wanted nothing more than to sleep. But she was requested by her father to make an appearance at dinner, and so make an appearance she must. Which also meant dressing for it too. She rang for Polly again to attend her for the preparations. As Polly brushed Eloise's long blonde hair, Eloise wondered to herself silently why the English must be so rigid and set in their ways. As far as she was concerned, she would wear her most comfortable clothes to the dining room, put her feet up on the table, and eat with her fingers like the Americans. Or at least, that's what she had been told.

She pictured doing those very things in front of her father and his stiff friends and started laughing so hard that Polly had to put down her brush and wait for the giggles to cease. It took some time. Eloise silently imagined Lord Aldridge choking on an olive, and Lady Pelbrook simply dying of shock at such an ungainly sight.

Polly smiled, shaking her head. She bent over the ribbons to sort through which one would best match Eloise's dress, that she might use to tie back the girl's hair. "Pray tell, my lady, what has put you in such a merry state?" she asked as she extracted a green satin ribbon from the rest.

"Oh, Polly, if you could only peer into my mind and see what I see there sometimes, I should think you would laugh enough for all of London."

Polly braided the ribbon into Eloise's hair, her fingers flying. "Tell me, my lady. Oh, I should love to hear it."

"And I would love to tell it, but I fear we must not keep my father waiting or he will have another one of his fits."

Polly straightened from her task and bid her mistress to stand. She'd chosen the green silk dress that set off Eloise's complexion so beautifully and had artfully arranged her hair in the latest fashion.

Eloise gasped when she looked at herself in the mirror, "is this just dinner with my father, or is the King himself invited? My! I look so grand."

"Oh, just rehearsing for the future, my lady," Polly replied carelessly, though her smile was enigmatic.

Eloise descended the stairs, passing several oil paintings of frowning ancestors and giving each one a playful smile as she passed, as though to try and make them smile. She paused at her father's portrait though, lingering for a moment as she studied his serious countenance. Her smile was perhaps wistful as she considered the rock he had been for her and her siblings since Mama's death. She was always told she had inherited his keen mind and sharp instincts and she had always felt very proud whenever she was told this. She was very fond of her father indeed. It was just such a shame he was now more like a shadow of himself without Mama around. She had heard it said that behind every great man there is a great woman. She wondered at the truth of these words now.

Lord Gillingham did not have the same start in life that most of his peers had been privileged to have. Although he'd inherited the viscountcy, he'd also inherited a great deal of debt from his father and had worked very hard to ensure that he secured the wealth to protect the Gillingham name. He'd done this most successfully, but the war had taken its toll on the coffers and the remade Gillingham fortune was now no longer as secure as it once had been.

Eloise was not ignorant of this fact. She suspected Lord Gillingham was now getting desperate. Even today he was pacing the dining room, thinking and thinking on his legacy and ideas on how to keep the estate afloat in such desperate times. So much so he hadn't even heard his eldest child enter the room. This troubled her. Of late, he had been murmuring phrases such as, "It is the way of things" and "marrying a man of means is not such a bad thing." Such words had left Eloise with the uneasy feeling that her upcoming season had much weight riding upon it, as though she must carry the family's burden. While this was not uncommon in England, she was unsure how she felt about going into matrimony with such an outlook.

"Papa..." Eloise called, jerking the Lord out of his deep reverie.

"M'dear, come, come," he said. Papa pulled out a chair for her before taking his seat. Eloise noted the absence of her siblings at the dinner table but did not comment, concluding that Papa simply wanted to quietly discuss her coming out with her. Her stomach twisted nervously.

"So, my dear, what have you been doing today?"

"Nothing much beyond the usual lessons. Papa," she toyed with a spoon while she thought about how to raise the topic of her coming out. "I am greatly anticipating the next month, and quite frankly, I just want it to be over and done with."

There. She had expressed her trepidation.

"I understand, my dear." He smiled fondly. "I'm so proud of you. You've grown into a most delightful... and beautiful... young woman." Unexpected tears started gathering at the corners of his eyes. "Your mother would have been so very proud."

Eloise tried to control an unladylike sniffling, her heart swelling with love for her father. "Oh, Papa, I wish I could always be your little girl."

"You always will be, my dear." He nodded, dashing at the tears he fought so hard not to show. "You always will be."

Eloise and her father had dinner together and conversed on a number of insignificant matters. After a while, Lord Gillingham cleared his throat and held Eloise's hand. His eyes became more serious. "My dear, do you remember what I always told you about the Gillingham name?"

"Yes, Papa. You always said that honour to the family name and the family legacy must come first, regardless of our feelings and the circumstances."

"Well, you are just coming of age, and the fates have decided to place the burden of the Gillingham name on you now."

Eloise's eyes widened, she could not for the life of her understand what the honour of the Gillingham name had to do with her when she was not even of age yet. Her fears resurfaced.

"What do you need me to do, Papa?"

"It's nothing so serious, my dear," her father replied. "Certainly nothing which has not been done before."

Eloise, who was now visibly perplexed, shifted to the end of her chair and leaned in.

"I just want you to remember that it is our duty to make sacrifices for our family. And our family name."

Papa then explained what was on his mind. It happened that the Duke of Richmond had approached Lord Gillingham with an offer of marriage for Eloise. In exchange for his daughter's hand in marriage, the Duke promised to finance Lord Gillingham and restore the dwindling coffers of the Gillingham Estate. Lord Gillingham had been elated when he received the offer. He knew the Duke by reputation and comforted himself with the fact that even if the marriage was devoid of love, his daughter would be well cared for. Besides, he had no doubt she could grow to love her spouse just as he had grown to love his. Such was often the way with English marriages of convenience.

Eloise didn't know what to say to all of this. So she said nothing. She didn't know the Duke of Richmond. They had never met that she could recall. Apparently, Papa had shown the Duke her likeness on a miniature portrait, and the Duke had been quite taken by her picture. Maybe he was a nice man. Maybe he was even handsome, but Eloise would have liked to have had some say in who her husband was to be. Like all girls, she had dreams of a love match and now Papa had snatched that opportunity away from her.

The dinner continued in silence. Eloise, her mind preoccupied, politely nodded and smiled at everything her father said, only asking that she be excused when he was finished. She did not quite trust herself to speak. She dragged herself upstairs to her room on trembling legs, feeling as if she might faint at any moment. This was far worse than she had expected. From the sound of it, she might not even enjoy a full season in London before the matter would be settled.

She decided against ringing for Polly that night and just crawled under the bedcovers and had a good cry. She was aware that her whole life was about to change and she had absolutely no power to stop it. She knew she had a duty to her family and that she had to fulfil that duty. This was her destiny and she would embrace it. Tomorrow, she would find some backbone from somewhere and live up to the Gillingham name. Tonight, however, she was just another young girl, with fantasies of love and romance.

Downstairs, Lord Edward Gillingham sat down at his desk with his head in his hands, knowing his free-spirited daughter well enough to surmise that, right now, she would be sobbing her heart out. Though she would obey her father, she might still baulk unexpectedly, and that made him distinctly uncomfortable. Even if such a marriage was the English way, it was no easy thing to give up the idea of a love match for something more practical, as he well knew. He had been in a similar position once, and while he had come to love his wife dearly, it was not the case initially. It had taken time for those feelings to grow.

Right now, however, the Duke of Richmond had something the Lord really needed; money. He knew he had to be firm and not give in to Eloise's delicate tears. The very future of the Gillingham Estate relied upon the union. He must ensure that it happened, no matter what his daughter's, and his own, personal feelings were about the matter. He felt a proper bounder sacrificing his daughter in this way, but he rationalised it by thinking about Penelope, Virginia, and Anna whose own futures could only be secured if Eloise made this match. There was also little Andrew, who would one day inherit the estate.

The Duke of Richmond had agreed to do without a dowry but he might not be so lucky with the other girls' husbands. Lord Gillingham had to take whatever fortune that fate decided to hand him and his family whenever it was handed him. In other words, he had to seize every opportunity while it was hot and not be overly sentimental of idylls of love. He was a shrewd enough businessman to know that. Love didn't pay the bills.

In the meantime, the debutante ball was almost upon them and he just wanted to do what tradition required and present his daughter properly. After that, his goal was to see Eloise safely wed to the Duke of Richmond and see the Gillingham coffers full again to ensure the future of his whole family.

Chapter Two

I t was the night of the debutante ball and the whole household knew it, from the servants to Eloise's sisters. It seemed everyone was somehow participating in Eloise's first ball. Her dear friend Evelyn had sneaked in to visit her earlier in the day. They had held each other crying, and sighed and told each other that they were going to be fine and make grand matches in their first season. Eloise didn't dare tell her friend she was already promised to the Duke of Richmond whom she still hadn't met, as he was away on business.

Later, as Eloise dressed, she watched Penelope and Anna who were seated on her bed giggling and whispering in low voices. They were so little, dreaming it was all a charade.

"Oh, I wish Eloise will marry a prince. Then I can be the sister to a princess," Penelope said.

Anna sighed dreamily. "That would be so grand."

Her sisters would know the reality soon enough when this night was safely past. Papa was keen for the nuptials to happen as soon as possible.

By this point, Eloise had been fussed over and primped and petted till she couldn't bear it anymore. She just wanted the night to be over and done with, at least the fussing part. Inwardly, she was about to explode. This was supposed to be her first dance, her introduction to the gentlemen of the ton. She should have been caught up in the grandeur of it all. Instead, it was almost too much for her. Nerves led her to want nothing more than to laugh hysterically. It was a wonder she could suppress the feelings at all.

When she giggled for the umpteenth time, Polly had to ask what she was thinking. Eloise, unable to come out and say what was on her mind to her dear maid. She instead turned towards her little sisters with a smile, engaging the youngsters in a game where they had to guess what was thinking. After several wild conjectures, Eloise caught her sisters in a hug and laughed, sending the girls from the room so she could finish dressing for the ball.

The moment they were gone, she turned toward her maid in dismay. "Oh, Polly, I think I'm going to burst. I hope I don't vomit on some gentleman's shoes from all this excitement."

"You'll be fine, my lady. You will be the belle of the ball!"

Eloise giggled again as Polly adjusted the flounces on her dress before stepping back in satisfaction.

She sat down in front of the mirror and Polly went to work on her hair, artfully arranging it in the latest fashion. Eloise was to wear the family diamonds that night and Polly helped her to clasp the necklace around her porcelain neck. When she raised her face to look at the mirror, Polly gasped. "You look so beautiful, so refined."

Eloise looked and tried to see what her maid described. She only saw innocence, a tremulous hope in her eyes so arresting that it gave her pause. Eloise didn't know she could look this way.

"You look like a vision," the maid whispered. "Just like the portrait of your mother in the hall."

It was at times like this that Eloise missed her mother, Maude, so acutely she wanted to cry. She wished more than anything she could have her dear Mama with her in that moment. Mama would have known exactly what to say to alleviate the fears Eloise had, and more importantly, how to bolster her confidence.

Eloise cast away such thoughts and stepped out of the room, ready to find her father. That they might leave for the ball together.

As she descended, she saw her father waiting at the foot of the spiral staircase. He struggled to speak when he saw her. "Why, my dear, you look just like your mother."

Tears filled Eloise's eyes. They stepped out of the grand hall and climbed into the carriage. The ride to London was smooth, and they got to the ball in good time.

When they got to the ball, Eloise did all she could to stop her jaw from dropping to the floor. She had never encountered such an ostentatious display in all her life. She had thought the Gillingham Estate was quite enormous, but this place was grander than grand.

Eloise's father took her arm and escorted her into the ballroom. They were duly announced and ushered in. Eloise was faced with a hundred ladies in dresses, each more beautiful than the last. Candles set like diamonds in crystal chandeliers. More importantly, she passed by so many dashingly handsome young men that she thought she would swoon.

Lord Gillingham introduced her to the young men who were brave enough to approach her in these first moments. They fawned over her and bowed. She, in turn, curtsied appropriately, making good use of Miss Tomlins' lessons over the years.

"Good evening, Lord Gillingham," a deep voice said beside her.

"Oh, Barrington, fancy seeing you here. I thought you were away at school," Papa replied.

Eloise barely breathed. Something about this voice struck a chord deep within her. Barrington? She was unsure of the name, but the voice was so arresting, she found herself not quite daring to look.

"I have completed my studies at Cambridge, sir."

"Good for you. Oh, I want to introduce my daughter to you, Lady Eloise Gillingham. Eloise... meet Lord Barrington."

Eloise turned gracefully around, lifting her eyes to see the most handsome man she'd ever laid eyes on. He was quite tall, square-jawed with a dash of red in his brown hair.

Lord Jackson Barrington turned and bowed. "A pleasure, my lady." The handsome young man took her hand and kissed it and Eloise blushed prettily. "May I have this dance?"

Indeed, the dance was starting. Eloise took Jackson's hand and followed him to the dance floor. They took their positions and the dance promptly began.

"How do you know my father?" Eloise spoke without thinking, then drew in a sharp breath when she realized what a faux pas she had just made. A lady simply didn't speak first. It was unheard of. "I am sorry..."

"Oh, don't apologise. I believe ladies have a mind worth cultivating. I rather welcome questions," Jackson grinned wide as they moved gracefully around the ballroom.

"I should say you have a quite unusual attitude, my lord, but I am most pleased to hear it."

The young man was refreshing. Handsome too. But though her heart was fluttering, she could not allow herself to like him. She was promised to the Duke of Richmond, whomever he was. This was just for show after all, and that made Eloise sad. In other times, she'd have allowed herself to grow excited by this handsome stranger's presence. More excited than she already was, despite trying not to be.

They danced for a few more minutes before Jackson said, "We met at the club. He and my father are acquainted."

Eloise nodded politely. She was endeavouring to find something interesting to say, but this avenue of conversation seemed to have nothing more to offer. "Do you keep a house in London, Lord Barrington?" she asked finally.

"Jackson, please," he insisted. "Every time someone calls me Lord Barrington, I turn around expecting to see my father."

Eloise shyly looked up and their eyes met. There was a real warmth beyond the young Lord's intelligent gaze. Hunger too. It was the look of a man for a woman, as though he would never let Eloise go. It was a look she didn't understand entirely, but she relished in it.

"Then, you may call me Eloise," she offered, feeling daring for allowing such familiarity.

They made small talk for a few more minutes before the dance ended. They bowed and curtsied respectively and broke apart. Jackson occasionally looked over his shoulder at the beautiful girl as she returned to her father. Eloise curiously met his gaze from across the room.

Later, Jackson spotted Lord Gillingham in a dark corner of the room and approached him.

"Lord Gillingham, your daughter is most delightful. For someone so young, she certainly knows her mind."

Lord Gillingham smiled uneasily. "You can admire her, but bear in mind that she is already spoken for."

"You certainly don't waste any time..." Jackson shook his head, unable to quite believe it. "But it is a shame my Lord, a real shame. I find that she has spirit, something lacking in many of the young ladies who are only interested in the gowns they wear and their jewellery they use as lures to draw in the unwary."

"Well, see to it that you do not get near her 'spirit', else, you might find yourself at the edge of my sword." Lord Gillingham guffawed and turned away.

"What makes you certain that you would win?" Jackson said with a roar of laughter as he walked away from Lord Gillingham, aware though that many a truth was spoken in jest.

Two weeks later, Lord Jackson Barrington woke up in a distinctly ambitious mood. He decided to not let such a fine day go to waste and planned to seize the opportunity to call on Lord Gillingham and his family. It was much more Eloise he wanted to call on, as in truth, he'd been able to think of little else but her since the ball.

Perhaps her father could be persuaded to let her find a more suitable match, he mused. He'd heard whispers from his valet, Victor, that Eloise was engaged to the Duke of Richmond no less. He couldn't believe that Lord Gillingham would really want his daughter married off to such a balding fat, good-for-nothing womaniser. In short, the Duke of Richmond was rumoured to be quite a collector of vices and hardly the appropriate match for a young lady of such delicacy and breeding.

"Victor!" he called. "Saddle my horse. 'Tis a fine day for a ride."

Jackson leapt on his horse and set out for the Gillingham Estate. As he neared, he paused to appreciate the scenery. He thought of his own family's estate and the day he would inherit it. Though he inwardly hoped it wouldn't be for many years to come. He supposed he was unique in this wish. Unlike many English sons, he actually liked his father, and they shared a very good relationship.

Eloise was sitting on a swing in the garden. She was so engrossed in the book she was reading that she did not notice Jackson until he was almost in front of her.

"Good afternoon, Lord Barrington," she said, a little flustered at his appearance for he cut a very fine figure in his riding breeches and boots.

"Jackson, remember? Good afternoon, my lady, fare thee well?"

"Very well, thank you," she replied. "And it's Eloise, remember?" She grinned cheekily. "Are you lost? It hardly seems proper for you to be wandering in the garden when I suspect you are expected at the house?"

"I wanted a few minutes to appreciate nature," he said humorously, "I do hope you take no offence."

Eloise smiled while assuring him that it was all right. Jackson offered his arm to escort her back into the house and she took it. They both walked leisurely, each one absorbed in their own thoughts and quite taken by each others' proximity.

The butler, Gibbons, opened the door and ushered them in.

"We have a visitor... Where's Papa?" Eloise asked.

"His Lordship is in the library," Gibbons replied. "He has another visitor in with him."

Eloise led Jackson to the library and knocked delicately before entering.

"Papa..." she started, before she raised her eyes to meet that of Papa's other visitor, a man in his late forties. He was a most unattractive sort, with a large paunch and shiny bald head that glistened in much the same way his sweaty fingers did while holding his sherry. "My apologies, sir. Good day to you," she said.

"Good day, Eloise. It's lovely to see you," the man replied. "You're even more beautiful than your picture." He smiled at her warmly, like he already knew her.

Eloise frowned. He'd been very familiar with her. But she had no idea who he was.

Her father coughed uncomfortably, looking from one to the other, shuffling from foot to foot. Eloise frowned again. Surely this couldn't be–?

"Eloise, meet the Duke of Richmond."

Eloise fainted on the spot.

~

Eloise awoke to Miss Tomlins kneeling over her, fanning her face rapidly. Someone had lifted her to the settee, which only made the whole incident that much more appalling. Eloise sat up quickly, surprised to see a concerned Jackson kneeling by her side.

"I think she needs some air," Jackson said. "It is very stuffy in here."

"Quite," grimaced Miss Tomlins. "Very stuffy indeed." She gave the Duke of Richmond a barbed look.

Both of them knew the real reason why Eloise had fainted.

"I can take her out for a ride in a short while, but I have a little business first," the Duke coughed looking askance at Eloise's father.

"She needs air. Now!" Jackson insisted.

Eloise felt quite dizzy and sick to her stomach. She began to plan ways to slip out of the room. Sadly, none could be achieved without creating a scene.

Jackson saluted. "If I could be at your disposal, Sirs–" He offered the crook of his arm to Eloise, that he might assist her in standing. "I will take her out for some air while you gentleman see to your affairs."

An uncomfortable period of long awkward silence passed between them before Lord Gillingham waved him off dismissively. "Go then." But his eyes gave a look to say, *don't try anything, my eyes are upon you.*

Jackson cleared his throat and nodded. Jackson looked as though he could still not quite comprehend how the Viscount could possibly give his daughter to the fat, balding Duke. Yes, he was a Duke after all, but some things were just not done.

He escorted Eloise outside. She left with relief, especially as soon they were both walking in the fragrant kitchen garden, her hand tucked into the crook of his elbow, with Miss Tomlins several steps behind.

It was a beautiful day, and the garden was in full bloom, but neither Eloise's nor Jackson's thoughts were on that.

"I suppose I should say congratulations on your impending nuptials," Jackson stammered. "I have heard the Duke is a very wealthy man. You will want for nothing in your life together."

Eloise's face went even whiter. She thought she was going to be sick. She was hoping it was somehow a bad dream and maybe the man in the library with Papa was another Duke of Richmond than the one she had been promised to. Marriages of convenience were one thing, but marriage to someone like him? It was preposterous! Surely, they weren't that poor that she had to marry this creature.

The thought was too much. Eloise started sniffling. "But how could Papa do this to me? How? I thought he had at least some affection for me."

Jackson had become awkward in the extreme. Nonetheless, he kept murmuring words of comfort and encouragement. She looked so small and fragile, and he realised with a start, he wanted nothing else but to protect her and that he actually deeply felt something for her. He knew, at that moment, that if he had the power, he would marry her even if she did not feel anything for him either, that it were just to spare her the horror of being the Duke of Richmond's wife.

They spent a few more minutes in the kitchen garden, most of which was spent trying to get Eloise composed enough to go back inside. Miss Tomlins tried to catch Eloise's eye but Eloise stiffly and resolutely stared at the beds of edible herbs as though the sight was the most fascinating thing she had ever seen.

They walked back slowly towards the house. "I cannot go back inside." Eloise gulped back tears, shaking her head.

Jackson was watching her minutely all the while. "You must," he said. His eyes fixed with hers. Without actually saying any words, his look promised her he would try to fix this.

Jackson took his leave and Eloise ran upstairs. Miss Tomlins followed her and sat on the end of her bed while Eloise wept wretchedly.

"Talk to me, child," Miss Tomlins pleaded.

Eloise cried harder and clung to her sheets.

Miss Tomlins encouraged her and told her she was not married yet and still had the time to change her father's mind. He was after all a man, and men were known to change their minds now and then.

"Do you really think so?" Eloise whispered hoarsely.

Miss Tomlins nodded. "Indeed I do."

Eloise sat up with a new resolve, to get her father to change his mind.

Dinner that evening was a stilted affair. The mood was dour and Eloise's father and two of her sisters, Penelope and Anna, tried their best to cheer her up with no avail. Andrew just stared at her and poked out his tongue when she looked his way.

"Whatever ails you my dear?" her father finally asked. "You have barely touched your plate."

"Can I speak to you, Papa? After dinner?"

When the tense meal finally concluded, Eloise and her father proceeded to the library and sat.

"Why have you promised me to the old, fat Duke of Richmond?" Eloise demanded, already looking on the verge of tears again.

"You know why. We had this conversation last month and you agreed–"

Papa could not maintain eye contact with her. It was clear he was ashamed of his decision. That he stood by it still was baffling to Eloise.

"Before I knew he was three times my age and fat and bald and just awful–" Eloise choked back a sob. "I thought he may be at least nearer my age! How could you, Papa? How?! I didn't want to believe it at first. I thought, surely, my dear father would not subject me to a miserable existence, but you care about money and titles more than my own happiness."

Eloise was crying now but Lord Gillingham's face remained an implacable mask. The child was young, full of the naïve idealism of youth, she was yet to understand how things really worked.

"We all must make sacrifices for the family legacy." Lord Gillingham coughed again. "I'm sorry if this isn't what you wanted but you are already promised to the Duke and you *will* marry him and become a Duchess. That is the last I will say on the matter!"

"Never, Papa, I will NOT marry him!" Eloise turned on her heel and fled from the room.

She went up to her room and rang for Polly, got ready for bed, and climbed under the covers. Her sleep was fitful at best, and she kept waking up at intervals throughout the night.

Morning did not ease Eloise's pain, instead, it only seemed to heighten it. Eloise woke up tired, dejected, and depressed. It took her a gargantuan effort to get out of bed and ring for Polly. When the maid arrived, things were no better. Even Polly was caught up in the melancholy and dourness.

Eloise excused herself from breakfast and sat in her room, thinking about the hard task her life would be, should she marry the Duke. She knew, however, that she had little choice in the matter unless another reputable, and wealthy, gentleman were to ask for her hand instead. The only other option that came to her mind was Lord Barrington, but how was she to proposition a man? It was unheard of, preposterous even.

A knock on the door startled her out of her reverie and she looked up to see Miss Tomlins walk into her room.

"Your things are here, child."

"What things?" she asked.

"Your wedding attire, from the modiste and the milliner."

"I'm certain I shall be miserable," Eloise said, shuddering at the thought of her upcoming nuptials. "Has Papa told you that I am to marry the Duke?"

"Of course."

Eloise burst into another fit of tears. She was hysterical at this point and Miss Tomlins had to take her into her arms. "Oh, child, I'm so sorry this isn't as you wish. I wish I knew what to do to prevent this terrible fate."

Eloise hiccupped between her tears, "I think I shall have to speak to father again, I must try to make him see reason."

She rose with determination, stiffened her spine, and stalked out of the room. She marched straight to her father's study and knocked.

"Come in," a gruff voice answered.

Eloise entered and attempted to stare her father down. She announced shakily that she was not going to marry the Duke. Her

21

father told her in clear terms that yes, she would, and she better get used to the idea. Eloise left the study in another fit of tears, and with a pounding headache.

Meanwhile, Miss Tomlins thought long and hard about Eloise's situation. Her thoughts landed on the sunny kitchen garden and the pair of young adults wandering through. She knew she could get a message to Lord Barrington, currently in residence at Sunningdale Manor. Miss Tomlins did not want Eloise to be subjected to a miserable life married to the old Duke. She knew, without a doubt, that Jackson would be a suitable match for the dear girl, even if he wouldn't inherit his family's Earldom for years to come.

Jackson was enjoying a leisurely chat with his best friend, Lord Henry Allington, when the message from Miss Tomlins was delivered by the butler. He read the note and kept still. For he knew that he must find a way to offer for beautiful Eloise. Without title, income, or even a home to call his own, there was no way Gillingham would even consider his offer.

"You should ask my brother for assistance," suggested Henry. "Perhaps he could provide funds to entice Lord Gillingham, which you'll reimburse when you inherit."

Henry's brother was none other than the Earl of Sunningdale, married to Jackson's sister Josephina. Jackson was loath to ask for such a large favour, but he knew his father would not part with the funds needed to make a suitable offer.

As he'd always been close with Josephina, he approached her first. The irony was not lost on him. He had gone to Josephina on a similar errand all these years before. At the time, Henry had been the victim of a bully, and Jackson had come to his aid. The drama had ultimately led to the love match between Josephina and Frederick.

"Of course, we'll help," was Josephina's response. When they took the matter to the Earl, he agreed wholeheartedly.

"I'll even provide you with a home until you inherit the title. The steward for one of my smaller Estates has perished and I haven't found another to replace him yet. Would you be willing to step in?"

"Yes, of course. I would be honoured," replied Jackson, touched by the Earl's generosity.

"I'm afraid it's not quite as grand as the Barrington Estate, but it will provide the hands-on experience necessary for estate management," said the Earl.

"I'm sure it will do nicely, wherever it is. Thank you very much, Frederick," replied Jackson, clasping his brother-in-law's hand. Josephina rose and embraced them both.

"I can't wait to meet this enchanting creature!" she said.

Chapter Three

Jackson sat in his carriage by the corner, anticipating Eloise's arrival. Since receiving her governess's missive, he had been on edge. Even his horses had started feeling his anticipation and he tried to quiet them, and himself, down. He really couldn't understand why he was feeling this way. He had faced his share of challenges, yet, the thought of this sweet seventeen-year-old girl had him quaking in his boots. How was it he was so taken with her?

Eloise, on her part, wasn't faring much better. She was at the modiste, and was having a terrible time staying still. She quaked with anticipation of what was to come, and Madame Beaufort almost stuck the needle in her twice due to her fidgeting. At last, the torture was over, and she could go to meet Jackson.

Miss Tomlins discreetly walked behind Eloise and she struggled to keep a normal pace as they walked away from the house. It was not long before she saw a carriage approaching. Eloise stopped and climbed inside the carriage, glad to see Jackson was inside, waiting for her. They looked at each other and Eloise smiled shyly.

"I find that you frequently inhabit my thoughts and I don't want to put a stop to it. I am quite taken with you, my darling Eloise," Jackson said.

Eloise blushed prettily and affirmed that she too, indeed, had feelings for Jackson.

Jackson knew on the spot that he would never forget this day. He could conquer the world. He felt ten feet tall.

Eloise found herself worrying suddenly about what would happen next. Her smile faltered and she looked so sad, Jackson inquired what was wrong. Eloise explained that the only way for Jackson to free her from her father's promise to the Duke was to speak to her father and ask for her hand instead.

Jackson accepted this suggestion readily and promised to seek an audience with her father in the coming week. They both spoke for a few more minutes, during which Jackson confessed his love again for Eloise. She, in turn, affirmed her love for him too. When Lord Barrington left the carriage, a beaming smile was upon his face.

The Duke of Richmond, however, had been secretly spying on Eloise in the past week in order to come up with some chivalrous plan to make her fall in love with him. He saw the whole situation for what it was and decided, right there, to hasten his wedding to Eloise.

The next day, Jackson was out riding when his valet rode out to meet him in the fields. Jackson opened the note Victor brought to see that his father's steward, Mr. Smith, had requested his immediate return to the family's country estate in Norfolk to deal with an urgent matter.

Jackson silently cursed to himself, as he had a meeting arranged with Eloise's father later that afternoon. He told Victor to deliver a message to Lord Gillingham, explaining his absence and apologising for the sudden change in plans. He also asked that a stable boy saddle another fresh horse, that he might leave for Norwich at once.

As it was already midday before he set out, he arrived at the estate late at night, by which time it was too late to rouse Smith. Jackson went to bed with the expectation that he would speak to him on the morrow.

The next morning, Jackson awoke early and sought out Mr. Smith on the Norfolk Estate. He was not a little surprised when he discovered that the steward had never sent for him. While trying to determine who would play such trickery, he realised, with a sickening feeling, that it was all likely a ruse to get him away from Eloise.

He jumped on his horse and furiously galloped back home, realising even as he was doing so, time was most likely against him, and the Duke of Richmond would get his wicked way.

Eloise was both excited and jittery. She tried to calm her nerves, ever conscious of the knowledge that, in a few minutes, Jackson would arrive to plead his case to her father. They both waited silently but it became painfully clear after nearly an hour of waiting that Jackson would not show up for their meeting and there was no note of apology.

This devastated Eloise but she kept insisting to her father that Lord Barrington would match the Duke's offer. Without an actual offer, however, Lord Gillingham insisted that the agreement with the Duke must be honoured. He stomped out of the room declaring that Jackson was obviously a cad and a bounder to make such promises to a young girl and not show up.

Nobody knew that Victor had been bribed by the vile Duke not to deliver the note to Lord Gillingham, just as he had been bribed to deliver the fake Norfolk note to Jackson.

Later that day, the Duke came to call and informed Lord Gillingham, in no uncertain terms, that the wedding would take place the next day and that Penelope, Eloise's closest sister in age, would be her attendant. He insisted that the Viscount either accept his decision or forget about the whole arrangement.

Lord Gillingham, visibly displeased by the turn of events, tried to sway the Duke with the argument that the nuptials were taking place too quickly, but the Duke was having none of it. He would either be wed to Eloise the next day, or he went elsewhere with his money. The wedding was therefore speedily arranged.

Chapter Four

E ven with the brightness of the spring day, Eloise had never felt more depressed. She went through all the motions of preparing for the wedding like a curious observer removed from her own body. She was stunned at Jackson's betrayal and even more devastated that she would actually be marrying the fat, old Duke.

Miss Tomlins tried and tried to cheer her up but Eloise, her face whiter than her wedding dress, looked as though she was attending her own funeral.

Polly fussed and primped and tried to get her to be excited about the wedding, but Eloise only concentrated on not shedding bitter, heavy tears, lest she shame her family by making an unseemly display.

They got to the church and her father walked her down the aisle in grim silence. If she hadn't been hanging on his arm, she didn't think she would have made it, as her legs were so weak. Was this what it felt like to be facing the gallows? She spotted the Duke's heavy bald bulk waiting at the end of the aisle and tried her best not to retch.

They finally got to the end of the aisle and her father offered her hand to the Duke. As angry as she was with her father, she still tried to hold on to his hand, pleading with Papa with her eyes, *please don't hand me over to that vile man.* He still had the power to stop this. But Lord

Gillingham only bent to give her a kiss on the cheek and stalked resolutely to his seat.

In that moment, Eloise knew she was doomed. Dazed, Eloise said her vows and although she had to be corrected about four times, the priest eventually pronounced them as man and wife. Eloise had officially become the Duchess of Richmond.

There had been no time to organise a grand wedding breakfast after the ceremony, as everything had been arranged so hastily. Eloise felt relieved, as she burned with shame. She wouldn't have coped with her friend's pitiful glances, in any case.

The Duke announced his honeymoon plans to Eloise, telling her and her family that they were to leave on a trip to France immediately. Eloise, who had actually been having nightmares about the upcoming consummation of their vows, was relieved at the delay and she nodded her assent to the proposed journey.

They promptly set out for Dover. Lord Gillingham, visibly upset, looked so sad. He did not know what to do. His darling daughter was no longer his. The thought of how scared she might be and how alone she must feel made him uneasy. But tolerate it she must. It was the English way. She was still so young and had never travelled further than London. Now, to go all alone with a strange man to a foreign land, would be so hard on her. He wished things could be different.

Meanwhile, Jackson urged his mount on, eager to get to the estate before Eloise was taken from him forever. He arrived and asked for Lord Gillingham, only to be told by the butler that the Lord had no desire to see him, as his daughter was wed just yesterday. She was now the Duchess of Richmond.

"In fact...," the butler stated matter-of-factly, "the Duchess had already left for her honeymoon in the south of France."

Jackson, visibly dejected, not to mention devastated at the news, trudged wearily home. He knew Eloise must think the worst of him, but he did not know how to see her or even begin to make amends. He acknowledged that it might be a little too late for them and wondered, mournfully, if he would ever find another like her.

Eloise too was miserable. She refused to meet the Duke's eyes and frankly, just wished he would leave her alone. They stopped at an inn and Eloise's eyes widened in horror as they were led to a bed-chamber upstairs.

To her surprise, the Duke excused himself almost immediately. "I have some urgent business, my dear. I will be back in a short while."

"Take your time, Your Grace," she answered, relieved to be away from him. Eloise stared listlessly around the shabby room while thinking of Miss Tomlins and her sisters, even her annoying little brother. Right now she even missed her father, angry as she was with him. She lay down on the bed, and closed her eyes, exhausted.

The Duke of Richmond, used to getting what he wanted, walked briskly around the corner and stopped when he saw who he was looking for. "Sligo, my good man, I hope all is as we want it."

"Aye, my Lord. 'Tis as it should be."

The Duke tossed a pouch of coins to the man with the shrunken eyes and whistled as he went back to the inn. It so happened that the Duke, intending to increase his chances of gaining favour with his new bride, decided to try the path of chivalry. He had it all pre-planned. The man, Sligo, would 'abduct' his new bride, and he would swoop in to save the day, thus becoming a hero in her eyes. The problem with this plan, however, was that Sligo wasn't the most honest of men. He had received half the money from the Duke with the promise that he would receive the rest on completion of the assignment. But he had no intention of completing the assignment. He had other, more nefarious, plans for the beautiful Eloise.

Eloise was rudely awakened by a strange man shaking her roughly. She attempted to scream but was cut off by a hand over her mouth. She gagged on some vile potion and was blindfolded before she could even gather her wits about her. She felt herself being picked up and deposited in a carriage that immediately set in motion. Instead of following the Duke's agreement and setting out towards Dover to board a French vessel, Sligo headed to the *New World Rose*, sailing for New York in the Americas.

The Duke laughed heartily as he boarded the *Lucretia* for France, "'Tis a fine day to fall in love," he said to himself and started to whistle. He moved from cabin to cabin and after two trips around the ship, realised with horror that his new wife and her abductor were nowhere to be found. He thought long and hard on what to do and decided to head back to London at the next port and enlist his new father-in-law's help.

He rehearsed a concocted story of how his new wife was taken from the inn without his knowledge and headed back to meet a livid Lord Gillingham who vowed, after learning of the Duke's foolery from his butler, to kill the Duke. With veins throbbing in his neck, he challenged the Duke to a duel.

The next morning, the Duke of Richmond and Eloise's gallant father met at dawn for a fight to the death. Due to the Duke's girth and coupled with his lack of physical exercise, it didn't take long. It was over within seconds, with the Duke lying dead by gunshot. Other than their seconds, no other witnesses were present and, considering the circumstances, no one was inclined to fetch the Magistrate.

Lord Gillingham sent his footman, and every other man, out to Dover to search for his daughter, while he doubled back towards London. He was aggrieved, dejected, and very much regretful he had ever thought the Duke a viable prospect for his darling eldest daughter. He only hoped she was still alive. He would give up every ha'penny he had just to have her back now.

Chapter Five

Eloise felt like she was in the very heart of hell itself, the abyss that she had always heard about. In the days and weeks of their passage across to America, she was kept prisoner in her abductor's cabin. Sligo very rarely left her side, trying to see to her every need. He tried to put up a front of kindness, but his eyes were cunning and malevolent, and she knew that he wouldn't hesitate to use her for his own selfish purposes. He scared her to no end, but she tried hard to hide her fear, lest he use it against her.

Eloise had never been to sea, so she suffered from a vicious bout of seasickness and her days were kept busy by her illness. She was so weak and tired, and she felt miserable all the time. She couldn't eat or keep down any food and nothing she did made her seasickness any better.

By the third week, however, Eloise began to show signs of improvement. She began to eat again and keep food down. She actually felt better. She learned that they were only three days away from New York and she wondered weakly what her abductor planned to do with her once they got to the city.

They finally docked in the harbour on a bright sunny afternoon. Eloise had long since lost track of the days and she didn't know what day or time it was by the time they made it to the dock. She was just glad to glimpse a view of dry land again.

After giving her another sleeping draught, Sligo transported Eloise to a hotel in a shady part of the city. He left her to sleep it off while he went to meet with a partner in a nearby bar. The two men came to an agreement that Eloise should be sold to the American fellow for a tidy sum, since it wasn't often they got an unsullied virgin to sell in the underground slave market.

Sligo was over the moon at the sum he was going to make from the sale and it took everything to keep from guffawing in delight. Maybe, finally, his days of doing dirty, odd jobs were over. He could buy a house or travel the world and hunt for treasure. He felt at that moment that the world was truly at his feet.

Meanwhile, Eloise yawned and stretched, trying to get her bearings. Opening her eyes lazily, she abruptly sat up and tried to gauge her surroundings. She was surprised to find herself alone because, in time past, her abductor had never left her for more than a few minutes.

She got up and went down the hallway to a proper toilet and even found a washbasin. She then deduced that the establishment must be a hotel. She might be unable to change into any clean clothes, but at least she was able to wash somewhat. For the first time in forever she felt clean, improving her spirits considerably. At least until she got a look at herself.

She saw a mirror and looked in it, gasping at the reflection she saw. She looked so haggard, so unkempt and uncared for. Of course, now was not the time for vanity. She had to get out, quickly, before her captor came back. With no one in sight, she went down the stairs, and walked out of the hotel as though she were a normal person. Surprisingly, no one noticed her departure.

As soon as she made it to the street, she walked to the nearest shop and went inside. The owner of the haberdashery looked Eloise over snootily before asking her, "How can I be of assistance?"

Eloise didn't know what to say or where to start. She only knew she needed help. She knew that she looked a right mess and her story sounded so far-fetched, however, she didn't have a choice, but to confide in this stranger. She implored the lady to help her and told her that once she was able to return to England, she would ensure that her father would reimburse her for all the expenses, and then some.

Unexpectedly, the owner of the shop, Miss Mary Atwood, laughed aloud, which surprised Eloise to no end. She told Eloise that she should no longer worry about anything. She would take care of her, and she would even send word to her father in England via some friends who are going back to the Old Country in two days' time.

Eloise was extremely happy and relieved to hear that Miss Atwood would be able to help. She was, however, still worried about her abductor finding her after he went searching for her. Miss Atwood assured her that she had nothing to worry about. She knew the hotel owner, she said, and would ensure that he hear about the situation to take the necessary action to eject the abductor from his establishment.

"We don't care much about these sorts of men who take young women into slavery, even here," Miss Atwood told Eloise. Eloise breathed a sigh of relief, she knew that she was safe, at least for now.

After that, the good Miss Atwood ensured that Eloise remained well-hidden in the back room of her shop until nightfall. When night fell, she took the young woman home with her to a very comfortable apartment just outside of the merchants' neighbourhood. She poured a bath for a delighted Eloise and offered her some clean garments to wear. The two women shared a meal of bread, milk, and a stew of potatoes and chicken. They chatted for a while and Eloise narrated her whole sorry story to Miss Atwood.

"For someone so young, you sure have had your own share of troubles," Miss Atwood enthused. "What of your husband?"

Eloise shrugged, smiled faintly, and told her that, for now, she was just glad to be safe and away from her abductor. She would worry about the vile Duke of Richmond later.

That night, Eloise, weary from all her ordeal, knelt by her bed and uttered a tearful prayer. "Dear Lord, thank you for rescuing me from the grip of wicked men and for sending the kind Miss Atwood to me. Please, help me to get back to my home and my family in Jesus' name. Amen."

Confident that she was heard by her Lord, she crawled under the covers and had the best sleep she had had in a long, long while.

Chapter Six

Sligo walked merrily, kicking stones and pebbles along the path. He had a hard life, but he knew that his hard days were finally coming to an end. Time and time again, the gods of fortune had eluded him and turned their ears away from his plea for wealth, but now, he was most certain that good fortune was finally upon him.

He admitted to himself, that when the fat Duke came to him for help regarding his bride, he thought the Duke had gone mad. He couldn't, for the life of himself, understand why a man of his stature would go to such lengths to win the affections of a woman. He wasn't sure he would ever return those affections if he were the woman in question. After much thought, however, he knew he had found the ticket to wealth, disguised as a young, unsullied 17-year-old girl with aristocratic blood in her veins.

Here, she was being sold to the highest bidder and no one would think to look for her in New York. As far as he knew, Eloise had no relatives in America. He whistled 'God save the Queen' heartily and even gave alms to some beggars who were by the sidewalk.

Sligo was about enter the hotel when he jerked to a sudden stop, realising he had forgotten to bar the door. He ran up the stairs, silently cursing his luck and whatever made him drink so much. He hoped fervently that the lass was still asleep. He broke out in a run, curses spewing from his mouth, and he got to the door to find it slightly ajar.

He started to sweat profusely. He nudged the door open slowly, with the toe of his boot, and gasped in surprise when he was pulled abruptly into the room.

"Please, don't hurt me!" he cried out.

He was seized roughly by the collar and marched straight out of the hotel. Sligo was so roughed up that he couldn't see well. But at one point, he started seeing the mooring pier get closer and closer. He was plunged into the freezing river by the muscled men who told him, albeit forcefully, that if he ever came back to the neighbourhood, they'd drown him.

Sligo was certain that he would die, his lungs were burning and twice, he felt his breath leaving his body. He held on for dear life, pleading with the powers that be that the men would not decide to kill him and feed his body to the fishes. He must have been heard because the men left him there after a few kicks and shoves, with him silently cursing and panting and raging under his breath, lest they decide to come back to finish what they started.

Through his tears of pain, he realised that his trip from England had been for nought with deep anguish. The passage for two hadn't been cheap and the only thing he could do at the pier was to weep openly, bitterly regretting the choices which had led him here.

Three weeks later.

Lord Gillingham placed the letter back on his desk with a deep sigh of relief and gratitude. Ever since Eloise went missing, he had not been himself. He kept seeing his late wife's face in his mind and picturing her acute disappointment in him. Just the other day, he had needed to explain the situation to Penelope, Virginia, Anna, and Andrew and they had all comforted each other and prayed for Eloise's safe return.

When the footman brought the letter earlier that day, he had been elated. The letter had been from Eloise, using a Miss Mary Atwood's address in New York telling him of her whereabouts and assuring him that yes, she was alive and well.

Lord Gillingham, moved almost to tears, vowed silently never to make the same mistake he made with Eloise with his other daughters.

35

He admitted to himself that he owed Eloise a huge apology for all the misery he'd put her through, and he vowed to give it once he was reunited with his daughter.

At Miss Tomlins' request, the Viscount contacted Lord Barrington and told him of the situation. Jackson was stunned to learn of Eloise's abduction but relieved that she was alive and well. He realised that he had merely been existing since her marriage to the Duke. He had been unsure of how to move on with his life, to return to the land of the living. He also admitted to himself that what he felt for Eloise wasn't just infatuation, but a deep-seated, genuine love that would make him readily give up his life if that was required to keep her safe.

Jackson offered to help in any way he could to get Eloise back to him and her family. Lord Gillingham, already overwhelmed with guilt over how he had been planning to barter one of his daughters for the sake of the family legacy, tasked Jackson with fetching his daughter from New York, as he needed to stay home to ensure his other daughters were safe.

Lord Gillingham looked him in the eye. "You have my permission, should you seek to take my daughter's hand in marriage."

Jackson did not need to be asked twice, he immediately agreed, and purchased passage on the *Britannia* from London to New York City. Meanwhile, Lord Gillingham wrote to Miss Atwood thanking her and explaining to keep his daughter in hiding, lest harm befall her again from the hands of Sligo or his cronies. He also told her to inform his daughter that her husband was now dead and she was free, and that he couldn't put into words how sorry he was for everything.

Chapter Seven

The day was bittersweet for Jackson. He had just found out that his beloved was able to be with him again, yet, she was still in much danger. He acknowledged, with a grunt, that she was now very wealthy. Her wealth was of no consequence to him, he didn't even need a dowry, as his family wasn't doing badly with their finances. He just desired to rescue her from whatever danger she was in at present and bring her to London to be his wife, bear his name, and bear his children. He yearned to embrace her and protect her forever. He also felt an intense longing to marry her and make her his Countess.

When he got back home, after speaking with Lord Gillingham, he relayed the circumstances to his parents who readily offered their support in his quest to retrieve his bride-to-be. His mother, known for her propensity for tears, told him to hurry up and come back with her new daughter, while his father simply grunted and slapped him on the back.

"Well done son, Godspeed to you," he said. Jackson, in an uncharacteristic display of open affection, embraced both his parents and told them how lucky he was to have them in his life.

Jackson hastened his plans for travel. He made quick plans to board a ship going to New York to locate Miss Atwood and Eloise. The weeks at sea were not very kind to Jackson either. For although he had been at sea before, he wasn't a true seaman and he suffered severe and intermittent bouts of seasickness.

He finally, gratefully docked on a cold November morning. After storing his luggage, he headed straight to Miss Atwood's. While journeying there, Jackson wondered and imagined how much Eloise may have changed. Did she still love him? By God, he hoped she did. Even if she claimed she didn't, he had all the time in the world to change her mind.

Eloise came out of the shop for air. She was being extremely careful because she didn't know if her abductor was still near, despite Miss Atwood's assurance that he had since been taken care of and would not be showing his face on the streets of New York for a long time to come.

Eloise decided that she could not be too careful. She thought about Jackson every day, wondering if he still loved her. She thought about her father whom she had long since forgiven and wondered if he was really sorry for his actions and when he would come to get her. She thought about Miss Tomlins and her sisters and how much she missed them. She was in this deep reverie when she saw someone who looked like...

"Jackson!"

But it couldn't be, Jackson was far away in London. Surely, she was hallucinating? But she knew she wasn't when she heard her name from the beautiful man's lips.

"Eloise, oh, dear Eloise. How I've missed you so."

Jackson and Eloise were reunited amidst tears and hugs and sniffles. Eloise, giddy with happiness, couldn't believe Jackson had ventured across the ocean for her and her heart swelled with love for him afresh. She remembered their reunion with contentment in her heart. He had rushed over, and taken her in his arms, cradling her for several minutes.

Miss Atwood, having taken on the girl's care, insisted, albeit humorously, on propriety. Eloise laughed at the picture forever etched in her mind, her heart truly full indeed.

As they made plans to travel back home, Jackson and Eloise both realised that they couldn't make the journey without compromising Eloise's reputation. Miss Atwood tried to volunteer as a companion, but was turned down by Eloise who didn't want the woman's haberdashery business to suffer. The couple decided that the only sensible course of action to take was for Eloise and Jackson to get married before they travelled, and so married they got!

Eloise, tired of propriety ruling her life, decided to not undergo the customary year of mourning but instead proceeded to the civil court for a civil ceremony with Miss Atwood as her attendant. It was a beautiful day, one that she and her new husband would always remember.

Mr. and Mrs. Jackson Barrington returned to London with hearts full of love for one another. Sometimes, Jackson would be caught staring at Eloise, and Eloise, when she caught his eyes, would blush prettily. Their days travelling back to London were more bearable because they had each other, even though they both still suffered from seasickness. They both laughed with each other and held each other often, certain that the days ahead could be overcome with them being together.

Epilogue

Six months later...

Jackson and Eloise's arrival back in England had caused no small stir. Her father, much subdued from his recent attempt at meddling in her life, had nothing other to say than to wish her happiness in her new marriage. He also, however, apologised to her tearfully, confessing that he had failed her as a father.

Eloise, well cured of her hero worship of her father, but still very much filled with love for him, tearfully admitted to having forgiven him. She held no hard feelings towards him. To quiet the wagging tongues, Miss Tomlins suggested (insisted) that they have a wedding celebration, where all the people who mattered in society were invited. They set to preparing the grandest ball of the season.

Eloise, who had now moved to the Barrington Estate, had to endure trips to the modiste and the milliners and the seamstresses till she couldn't take it anymore. Jackson fared no better, as he was also frequently conscripted for one thing or the other.

Eloise's three sisters enjoyed their own fair share of primping and fussing, and Anna was so taken with Jackson that she blushed prettily anytime she was near him. Life was good on the Gillingham Estate and in the weeks before the grand wedding reception, Eloise blossomed into a fine picture of womanhood. Everyone who saw her and could openly comment about her beauty made sure they did so. Her hair flourished, her face shone, and her skin glowed. Miss Tomlins could be heard, at one time or another, openly commenting on the fact that Eloise had made her proud.

Eloise also made peace with her father's actions. He had fallen off the pedestal that she had placed him on. And he had lost a part of himself that his beloved late wife would have helped him cling to. But Eloise was sure that time would heal their wounds, and that someday they would have again the easy banter and laughter that had once marked their relationship.

Eloise also gained new parents in the form of Jackson's parents. Immediately upon introducing Eloise to his mother, Jackson noted that they both became thick as thieves. Jackson had to remark, in mock horror, that he had better stay on the straight and narrow, or he would be eviscerated by his two favourite ladies.

Eloise sighed dreamily while staring out her window. Today, she, the widow of the Duke of Richmond, was finally having her wedding reception after facing many trials. Her long blonde hair shone in the sunlight and her veil trailed after her. Her dress was a stunning blue masterpiece that she crafted herself, much to Miss Tomlins's chagrin. Eloise, however, didn't care. She was so happy, so giddy with that happiness that for a moment there, she seemed almost drunk on it.

Finally, she and Jackson were here now and while they had married in a civil ceremony months before, they were going to make a statement to all of England that they were deeply in love and would stay together forever. Never had she been so happy in all her life.

As Eloise stepped down from the carriage at Almack's where the ball was about to commence, she saw the number that had come out to celebrate with them. Maybe there were some gossipmongers or two, but who minded them on such a day? Eloise sighed contentedly. She had never loved her life more than at that moment.

The End

Advocating for The Lady

THE LADY SERIES BOOK EIGHT

Chapter One

Penelope Gillingham was considered, by some, to be a strange young lady. As the second oldest in her family, she was expected to marry soon, something she did not care to do. Of course, she didn't mind settling down at some point in the future. In fact, she desired it, but she wasn't ready for it yet. She was preoccupied with something else. She had far more important things on her mind.

She was a keen abolitionist, endeavouring to end slavery in the British empire. While the slave trade itself had been made illegal not many years before, the practise of slavery still existed within the British Empire and would so unless brave men and women did something to stop it. Her tender heart pained her when she considered what it must mean to have no freedom. It positively infuriated her that anyone, regardless of their creed or colour, could be forced to serve another against their will.

Of course, one day, she would be expected to marry, but not until she could do more to end the suffering of others. Besides, all the eligible men she had been introduced to were so infuriatingly tedious. There seemed absolutely nothing behind their ears. Such a union would hardly be a true meeting of minds.

In the meantime, she was greatly influenced by the on-fire evangelical Methodist preachers rife through the abolitionist movement. Penelope Gillingham regularly subscribed to Mr. William Wilberforce's pamphlets. She did what she could, being a woman, to fight the grave injustice, writing letters and attending talks regarding the subject whenever possible.

While somewhat sympathetic to her cause, her father, Lord Gillingham, ignored her efforts, suspecting she would grow out of her youthful idealism soon enough when she realised the way of the world. Of course, a large part of him always wanted to cushion her from reality. What parent wanted to see their beloved child shipwrecked on the cold hard reality of life? For now, Lord Gillingham would do all he could do to protect his second oldest daughter from this stark reality. Meanwhile, he quietly sought her a suitable match so she could be forever cushioned from the more dreadful aspects of society.

To his way of thinking, it would not be hard to convince his wayward daughter to settle down. She enjoyed several more maidenly pursuits of other young ladies her age. Penelope took great pride in her sewing and painting. She loved reading and was well-versed in the ways of society.

But Penelope was still very much her own person in many ways. She greatly enjoyed riding her horse for hours, giving little regard for inclement weather, or murmurs from the town that she was something of a hoyden. After her mother died in childbirth giving birth to her brother, Andrew, Penelope sought solace in taking increasingly longer rides. Penelope was now an accomplished horsewoman. She had a beautiful white mare that she would take for long canters across the rolling Sussex Downs to escape her younger siblings for a while. She loved them dearly, of course, but it was good to get away from Papa's estate and clear her head.

On this particular day, however, her family was away visiting some incredibly tedious relative - a very distant relative, a cousin of a cousin or something like that. Until that morning, Penelope had long assumed this particular relative was dead. She'd begged off from familial duty, using the invention of a sudden headache to gain her freedom for the afternoon. After all, Penelope had a new horse to try out, and what better cure for a headache, imaginary or otherwise, than fresh air.

As it turned out, Bob, a rather spirited chestnut brown gelding, happened to be one of those horses who loved to give his rider a hard time. Perhaps, she thought ruefully, as she watched him gallop for home without her, *perhaps this is his reaction to being given such an unprepossessing name.*

Penelope cursed in an unladylike manner as she watched Bob gallop away from her, rather gleefully it seemed, his hooves kicking up great clods of dirt. This was the second time that day she had landed, rather ignominiously, upon her backside, sitting in soft, damp grass a few miles from her home.

She picked herself up and dusted herself off. Thankfully, Bob had no idea where 'home' was, being rather new to the area, and had been heading into a copse of woods she knew to be rather dense. In all likelihood, he hadn't gotten far, and she wouldn't have to hike all the way back to the manor on foot.

She took a step into the small, wooded area where she had seen him disappear and came to an abrupt halt when she realized someone had gotten there before her. A dark-haired man raised his hand towards the snorting horse, elegant fingers stretched to catch the dangling reins.

"Whoa there," the man said to Bob. "Whoa."

After tossing its head several times, the horse calmed down, his mane a cascade of silk that rippled over his own neck. These movements became less and less vigorous the more the man spoke.

"Shhh." The stranger murmured words, Penelope couldn't hear, something which caused Bob to settle, ears twitching, but quiescent and calm.

The man looked up when a twig snapped underfoot, as Penelope brushed through the scrub. He shot her a quick smile and lifted the reins in his hand towards her. "Good afternoon. Yours, I take it?"

She smiled ruefully, gesturing down at her riding attire, stained with green grass, knowing full well she had leaves and twigs in her hair. "You guess right, Sir."

She could not understand why the man's dark eyes stared at her with such fascination, as if he had never seen a lady before. Another time and place, she would have thought his gaze insolent, but today, she did not mind it. Something about him made her want him to look at her. However, for once, she wished she was in her prettiest organza dress with puffed sleeves, with her hair put up properly in ribbons with a crown of flowers, not the awful mess she was now. She was sure that she must look a terrible fright.

Penelope moved closer and looked him up and down, quite frankly, the very way he had just examined her. He was a handsome man with a rugged jawline, the slash of his mouth, now in a captivated smile. He stood still for her perusal, as though he didn't mind, waiting in silence, as though amused by her observation.

She felt her cheeks burn a little as she approached to take Bob's reins from the man's large hands. Still, she liked the way he caressed the horse, murmuring calming words. The man was a magician with the animal. For a fleeting moment, Penelope wondered what it would feel like to be touched by the man and a delicious thrill she was not accustomed to ran through her body.

"Thank you," she murmured, her hand brushing lightly against his. "You have a great way with horses."

"He's a beautiful creature," he smiled, yet he was looking at her all the while he spoke.

"I... well..." she fumbled for words, then smiled. "You should see my mare."

"Oh?"

"I should say the finest horse in the whole of Sussex." She brushed a stray hair from her cheek and gazed at him with her eyes focused, still wondering why he stared at her so. "Not near so difficult as this animal is proving to be."

"No doubt." He cocked his head and examined her closely as though trying to place her. "I thought I knew everyone from around here, but it appears I was very mistaken."

She extended her gloved hand. "Lady Penelope Gillingham."

He took her hand briefly. "Duke Mark Thompson." He patted Bob's flank. "I just returned home from the Continent."

"Charmed." Her lashes fluttered briefly. And she was, although she was not about to admit just how much. She was sure her eyes gave her away, however.

"May I walk with you home, Lady Gillingham? Or shall you ride him back?"

Unafraid of Bob, Penelope had been inclined to ride him home before the offer, but this was now a far more seductive offer. She would much rather walk.

"It is many miles that way," she pointed westwards.

"Time enough for us to become better acquainted then."

She cocked her head to the side, attempting to decipher his thoughts. "Indeed, your Grace."

He grinned wide. "It is a beautiful day."

Her eyes narrowed. Was he talking about the sunshine? Penelope could not be sure.

She took the reins and guided Bob, who was the calmest Penelope had ever seen him, as they walked the winding country lanes leading back to her father's estate.

The Duke seemed inclined to talk. "Lady Gillingham–"

"Oh, call me Penelope, please," she begged, feeling quite daring as she pushed a stray lock of hair from her cheek. Why she said it, she wasn't sure. Something about the day, about being alone together, made her feel as though the conventions could be ignored.

"Of course, Penelope. Then you must call me Mark."

"Mark," she smiled. It had a good ring to it. A strong manly name. An honest one.

From the look on his face, he liked the sound of his name rolling off her tongue.

"Penelope... So what brings you out today, here of all places, on this magnificent boy? And why not the mare, the one you say is the finest in all of Sussex? I do not doubt she is a beauty. For a lady like yourself, it would only be fitting."

Her dark eyelashes flickered, and she smiled at his flattery. She reached up to ruffle Bob's mane. "I felt like an adventure today. Bob is a newcomer to our stable, and I wondered what kind of ride he would give me. I soon enough found out. I fancy he doesn't like me at all, so he threw me at the first opportunity...Twice, in fact."

She wrinkled her pretty nose.

The Duke roared with laughter, flashing a row of perfectly white teeth. "It is not that. He is just young and stubborn, has a mind of his own. He just needs to be trained properly. I am surprised your groom did not warn you he is rather green. He is a fine animal."

Penelope laughed. There was no doubt the Duke knew horses. "He did, actually, but I assured him I was up for the challenge." She rather liked that he had not scolded her for riding the animal or in any way suggested she should perhaps stick to more ladylike pursuits.

He turned to her. "A mind of one's own is very important in life, don't you think?"

She looked at him in surprise. His comment was very much in line with her own thinking. "Absolutely, Your Grace— Mark." Penelope nodded again, wondering if he would speak in such a way if he truly knew her mind. Her sister, Eloise, regularly told her she was too opinionated and wilful. So did Papa, but he was a father and inclined to be rather stuffy, especially regarding his daughters.

"Tell me about your family," he then asked, as if reading her mind.

"Today, they are visiting distant relations," she said. "Incredibly tedious ones, as it happens."

"Aren't most relatives tedious?" He winked. "Particularly old aunts with dour expressions, reeking of *eau de cologne* or scented lavender." His nose wrinkled playfully.

The corners of Penelope's lips twitched, and she found herself smiling despite herself, her eyes twinkling with mirth. "I see you have those kinds of relatives too."

"I believe it comes with being aristocratic, Penelope." He leaned in to whisper in a conspiratorial manner, "They usually have little lap dogs too."

"Oh, don't they just!"

They rounded the last bend in the lane, where hedgerows fell away to reveal her father's house standing majestically on a small hill. Its bath stone facade gleamed warm and golden in the late afternoon sun.

However, just now, Penelope wished her father's house was another five miles away. She didn't want this moment to end. She somehow knew the Duke felt the same.

"This is me now.... Thank you so much for walking me home, Your Grace."

"You are very welcome, Lady Gillingham. May I at least walk you to the door?"

She shook her head, only too aware of the questions that would be raised if she showed up in the company of a gentleman with no chaperone. Such a thing would invite scandal. "There is really no need. But thank you..." she hesitated. "I realise I didn't actually ask you, but where do you live? I thought I knew everyone around here."

He blushed shyly, pointing from back whence they came. "Oh, I would guess it to be no more than a dozen miles in that direction. A little less, perhaps. I am visiting the area and am not quite sure of distances just yet. My afternoon walk has turned out to be a touch more ambitious than I had anticipated."

Penelope gasped. "But it will be nightfall by the time you return home!"

"Then I shall have to run, will I not?" he grinned and tipped his top hat to her. "I hope to see you again, Lady Penelope Gillingham."

"That would be quite...nice. I would like that very much, Your Grace!" she murmured, a little flustered but well pleased with his interest.

She then turned, walking away with the docile horse plodding along by her side. When she looked back, she saw the Duke still gazing after her with a silly smile on his face.

He was not the only one smiling.

Chapter Two

When her family came back from wherever people go visit tedious relatives, Penelope was itching to tell them all about her encounter with the Duke. Too excited to keep the whole experience to herself, that evening at dinner was when she made her big announcement.

"While you were all away visiting Lord and Lady Smythe, something rather lovely happened." She smiled enigmatically at her father and siblings, her tone immediately grabbing everyone's attention.

They looked at her, willing her to go on. Papa put down his fork and gazed at her. It was rare to see his daughter so excited.

"I met someone. A very fine young man who is visiting Alfriston Manor. A Duke by the name of Mark Thompson."

Papa smiled. Clearly, he wanted to applaud his daughter for making such a catch. "That would make him the Duke of Roxbury, I believe. I do remember the family well. They often visited when he was a boy. Though I suspect he is not much of a boy now. He must be in his twenties. But then everyone seems like a boy to me now... So he is back from his travels? I had not realised. They are a lovely family. Quite well off. The house belonged to his mother's family, I believe. I do hope he's thinking about staying."

Penelope blushed, feeling a little indignant. "I hardly see where how well off they are is pertinent," she said with a sniff. "It is him that I rather like. He and I seem very well suited."

Papa nodded, relieved. Perhaps his wilful daughter would not remain a spinster after all. Her dedication to the abolitionist movement had become quite worrying of late. "In that case, you should ask him to dinner and have him meet us all."

She smiled at Papa. "That would be wonderful!"

"A Duke!" Andrew exclaimed and tittered, only to be slapped sharply by his sister, Virginia, under the table.

Anna, the next oldest, smiled, ignoring the teasing of their brother entirely. "Does that mean you will be a Duchess if you marry him, Penelope?"

"Well, yes, I suppose it would. It seems rather soon to be discussing such things, though, seeing as he and I have only just met." Not that Penelope had not thought about marrying him already. Oh, she had thought about it constantly all evening, wondering too as every hour passed, whether the Duke had made it back home yet. She rather hoped he had found a place to hire a horse at the very least, that he not be forced to walk so far to get home.

She brushed the thought aside. He was a Duke. She had no doubt he had been able to secure transportation at the nearby village. In the meantime, it was better to focus on what was important: whether or not she had just met a man worthy of her hand in marriage.

Selecting her own husband greatly appealed to Penelope, rather than having it all arranged for her by others. Not that she had been inclined to consider marriage yet in any case. Still, the Duke had made that prospect suddenly attractive. She hadn't been able to think of anything else since laying eyes on him. *Duchess Penelope Thompson.* She rather fancied how that sounded. It had a certain ring to it.

Before going to bed, she wrote a letter to Mark.

My Lord Duke

You might call upon me tomorrow afternoon at 4 pm if you so desire. I would like to see you again very much.

Sincerely,

Penelope

She handed the letter to her maid, Millicent. Then, satisfied the letter would be in his hands soon, she lay down ready for romantic dreams of the handsome Duke to fill her mind. There was something about him that made her long to see him again. The soonest possible time. She hoped he would meet her as she had invited. In the meantime, her imagination would have to do.

~

The following afternoon was a beautiful warm day. A gentle breeze ruffled Penelope's blonde curls as she waited in the garden for her caller.

She was wearing her favourite dress, the sunshine yellow matching the colour of her hair, tucked beneath a white bonnet with a yellow ribbon, all set off with a pair of white gloves with a little daisy embroidered on their wrists.

She heard the crunch of coach wheels on the dusty gravel and spun around to see the Duke's landau coming up the drive.

The Duke was met by one of the servants at the house, who directed him around to the gardens. Penelope glanced quickly at her maid as the Duke approached. They had discussed this beforehand. The maid was meant as a chaperone but had agreed to fain a deep interest in her book, to give the young couple some time alone. Sure enough, Millicent pulled a book from her sewing basket at the Duke's approach and opened the cover with a sly smile.

Of course, Penelope would have much rather met the Duke upon her own, but if this was the best she could do, then so be it. She would make the most of things. After all, one could not create a scandal.

Penelope smiled wide as he approached. His answering smile grew wider with each step. "Thank you for coming," she murmured, extending a gloved hand.

He took her extended fingers in his own and bent over to lay a gentle kiss upon the back of her hand. "How could I resist your invitation? You look... a picture, Penelope."

"Thank you," she murmured, likewise examining his green waistcoat and frock coat over fawn breeches tucked into deerskin boots. She liked what she saw. "Mark."

He guided her over to where water burbled across the stones of a tiny brook that wandered through the garden, finding a shady spot beneath a weeping willow tree where a bench was tucked. It was the perfect seat, in plain view of her chaperone, but far enough away that any conversation they had might not be overheard. He gestured that she sit down, fussing over her, making sure she was comfortable before joining her. Only then did he remove his top hat, the weather being far too warm for that formality.

"You'll forgive me. My feet are a little sore." He grinned.

Penelope giggled, feeling a little guilty. "Truly, you did not walk all that way!"

"It was not quite so far as I supposed. All the same, I hardly noticed the distance."

She blushed and fussed with her skirts, tucking them more carefully around her so they did not blow up in the breeze." I would not be surprised if your shoes were quite worn out."

He roared with laughter. "I will let you in on a little secret. I do have other pairs."

They sat beneath the shade of the weeping willow tree, enjoying the sound of the gentle flow of the waters of the babbling brook. Penelope was reluctant to break the spell but shyly glanced up at him every now and then to meet his warm brown eyes every time.

"You are incredibly beautiful. I know it is not exactly the proper thing to say on so short an acquaintance, but I cannot help but speak my mind. Damn the proper way of things! I have never seen anyone as beautiful as you in the whole of Sussex. Nor anywhere in England, I say!"

If she had thought she was blushing before, it had nothing on the scarlet which flamed into her cheeks now at such a declaration. "You jest with me, Sir."

His voice was throaty, deep. "No. I have seen beautiful women in my time. Of course, I have. But there is something about you. I don't know what it is–"

".... My exquisite riding skills?"

He slapped his thigh and roared with laughter, a deep rumbling laugh. "Yes, I should say that is exactly what it is."

So uproarious was he that Millicent glanced up from her reading.

Seeing all was well, she soon returned to her book while Penelope blushed and tried to think of what to say.

"So, tell me, Mark, how do you engage your time now that you are done travelling?" She peered at him with curiosity.

He shrugged as his warm eyes met hers again. "Nothing so unusual. Reading, writing... I play a little violin. Rather badly, I hasten to add. What about you, when you are not riding stubborn geldings or cantering across the South Downs on beautiful mares?"

"I play the pianoforte. As you have already confessed to being musical, I wonder if you play as well?"

"Terribly. I can manage a recognizable tune, but not much beyond that." He mimed playing an instrument using only one finger and smiled at her. "And only if the tune is nothing rapid. I can manage a waltz if pressed."

She chuckled. "I am sure you are not that bad." She leaned back to study the blue sky between the leaves, allowing silence to fill the space between them again. It was a good silence, of the companionable variety. For the first time in her life, Penelope felt contented and able to fully relax in the company of a man. She rather liked the feeling.

Together, they watched the wind rustle through the garden, sending the heads of the roses bobbing as though the flowers themselves wished they could get up and dance. For a moment, she wondered whether to tell him about her political interests, but then thought better of it. She didn't want to spoil the magic of the moment.

The Duke mopped his brow. It was a hot day even beneath the tree, and Penelope felt stifled in her layers of clothes and petticoats, especially as the wind seemed to be dying down since they sat down.

"It is hot today," she sympathised.

"Indeed."

After a few moments, she had an idea. She gestured toward the brook. "Have you ever considered wading, Duke?"

It was a daring suggestion. In truth, she could picture it in her mind. She would shed slippers and stockings alike, running into the water the way she had as a child, the Duke following. They would splash each other until they were breathless with laughter.

She turned to face him. "Come, it is so beautiful." She started to rise.

He rose with her, catching her hand before she could go more than a step. "My lady, I do not think it would be wise. Nor would your chaperone approve."

She turned to face him, noting for the first time the strength in his hands, the elegant tapering of each finger. Funny how a hand could possess so much character. How lovely it was to be held in such a way. His fingers twined with hers, intimately locking in an embrace she found herself yearning for instinctively. She wanted him to hold her in other ways, and it flustered her.

It lasted a minute. Maybe more. In the end, reluctantly, he had to let go. His breathing seemed quicker, his eyes dark with an expression she couldn't define, as he drew his hand back.

There were no words spoken, but everything was shared. Her breath caught in her throat as she struggled to know what to say.

"Penelope." Her name was a sigh upon his lips.

She shivered, no longer warm.

He leaned down and pressed his lips on the back of her hand, leaving a soft imprint upon her glove.

"Oh, Mark!" She knew from that moment on, there would never be any other man for her.

Chapter Three

A rather frustrated Penelope watched the Duke's landau rolling towards the house as the footmen brought it back around. She was sure she looked fairly bedraggled, having spent all day in the sun and wind, and yet she did not care. She shook out her skirts, hoping the movement would restore her appearance, at least somewhat, and grinned wide.

He sat opposite her, still giving her that amazing look. His hair had tumbled over his forehead, and his jacket was torn at the cuff from when he'd tried to pick her a bouquet from her garden. Their time together had led to a certain playfulness. She might have been somewhat guilty of leading him astray. Theirs had not been the most dignified of calls, but it had been fun.

"I must look a frightful state!" she exclaimed, feeling quite exhausted.

"You look utterly beautiful," he murmured.

And Penelope knew he meant it.

He took her back inside her father's house, his expression regretful, as though he too hated to see their time together come to an end.

"I expect I owe my maid many thanks for her...."

"Avid interest in reading?" he asked with a laugh. "I daresay she read the same page a hundred times in her efforts to offer us some privacy."

"You will come again?" she asked, fearful now that their afternoon was over that he might not call again.

"Of course!"

He spoke with such heartiness that there was no need to fear. Still, she had a reticence to see the day end. Oh, but she hated for him to go. To have him leave him now after such a delightful afternoon felt too sad for words. "Will you come for dinner tonight?" she asked impulsively. "Papa said you may–"

He raised an interested eyebrow. "You spoke of me already to your father?"

She blushed. "Well... yes. I DID get his permission for you to call." She grinned impishly.

"This is true. You have told him good things about me then?"

"Only good things, I assure you, Your Grace!" She grinned again, "So, tonight at eight?"

"Try keeping me away... Goodbye, Penelope."

He hesitated before reaching to hold her hand again, placing another kiss upon the back of her glove. He hurried, lest anybody see them.

"Goodbye, Mark. See you tonight."

Penelope counted off the minutes until Mark arrived that evening. She excitedly told Papa that she had seen the Duke again. He had accepted the dinner invitation, omitting to mention anything about just how unrefined their call had been.

Only her maid, Millicent, had bore witness to their childish antics. The poor woman had been beside herself to keep from laughing when the Duke had nearly taken a header in the flower bed, trying to attain the perfect rose. Of course, she would never tell. Millicent had already been sworn to secrecy. Millicent, her maid since childhood, was good with secrets, and she could be trusted. Penelope loved her dearly.

Upon the Duke's arrival that evening, he was given a grand house tour just before dinner. Papa discreetly allowed Penelope to do the guided tour, happy for the magnificently-matched pair to bond over their time together.

Penelope gazed at a portrait of one of her ancestors looking sternly down over the hall. "My Great Great Grandfather, I believe. Richard Gillingham. Related to Richard the Lionhearted."

Mark whistled, impressed. "Is that where the title came from? The crusades?"

"I suspect so. Yours?"

"I suspect so," He wrinkled his nose then smiled. "Actually, I know so."

He hesitated, "My family has certain expectations of me. They wanted me to continue the great family tradition of joining the army and serving the King. They wanted me... expected me... to be someone I am not. In truth, my father never really knew anything about me."

She sighed, understanding perfectly even though she did not know the full details. "I understand that. My father... he has his own expectations of me."

He grinned and winked at her. "It comes from being in the aristocracy. That and the smelly old aunt bit."

She chuckled. "But of course."

The dinner bell rang, signalling the end of their conversation. They were approaching the stairs that spiralled down to the sweeping reception hall. He offered her his arm as they slowly descended the stairs, her petticoats rustling with each step they made.

He glanced at her with admiration in his eyes. She looked at him shyly, enjoying the attention and still wondering at it. Everything felt too wonderful like she'd fallen into a dream. "It is strange I did not see you around here before. I go riding often enough. Though you said you had been travelling, and father implied your family does not use this house often."

"I was on the Continent until very recently," he said with a smile. "To be honest, I only thought to visit the house because my mother was concerned about how it was being taken care of. I am sorry now my family has not spent more time here. I might have met you sooner."

"Had I not chosen to ride Bob, I would have never met you at all."

"Good old Bob." He smiled. "I shall forever be in your horse's debt."

They reached the marble reception hall. He let go of her arm, and she twirled down the long corridor that led to the dining room as though she were dancing. She was just too happy to be still.

"You did say you were abroad, Sir... pray, what were you doing there? On the Continent, I mean?"

He hesitated. "I was involved in activities my father and I never saw eye to eye on. He felt a gentleman had no place in such dealings."

She spun on her heel. He had her undivided interest. "How exciting! Do go on."

He coughed, suddenly awkward. "Well, I am involved in the emancipation movement–"

Her hand clapped to her mouth. "But so am I! I eagerly read all of Mr. Wilberforce's pamphlets–"

The Duke seemed startled and then much relieved. "But that is who I was working for overseas...spreading the message abroad. That is such a relief, Penelope, because I could not bear it if you were the kind of dunderhead who thought nothing of these poor people's plight, or worse still, supported slavery."

"On the contrary, Sir!" Penelope's heart raced within her, and she grinned. "I am all for abolishing slavery altogether! The English Empire has no business allowing slavery in any of their territories. It must be stopped!" This man was a dream come true. An abolitionist!

"Penelope–" Mark stopped dead in the hall. His voice was low, deep. "What would you say if I were to ask you to marry me? I know we have only just met, but when you know you know. And what I know is that I am hopelessly smitten with you – and something tells me you may feel the same way. You and I, we share the same goals, the same mind perhaps... and certainly the same heart–"

Penelope flung her arms around him, not caring who might see. "I would say yes!" She then hesitated. "... You are asking me, right? Not just asking me a hypothetical question?"

The Duke roared with laughter. "I suppose I am, but I really ought to ask for your father's permission. There are certain protocols which must be followed...."

Penelope smiled wide. How could Papa possibly object to her marrying a Duke in line to inherit such a fabulously large inheritance as his? Even Papa could not find a better match for her in the whole of Sussex, no, the whole of England! It was strange how such a short while ago she had been well pleased to have the best mare in all of England. In a matter of days, she had learned how much more there was to life. How much more she might have. The Duke was the best suitor in all of England.

It was a dream come true.

Chapter Four

E very day for the rest of that magical week, Penelope woke up with a big smile on her face. Not one thing could bring down her mood. Not even her bratty little brother, Andrew, who was terribly annoying, as little brothers were wont to be.

Her whole world was brighter now, with her handsome Duke in it. Nothing would stop the pair of them. Together, they could take on the world! She knew that as much as she knew anything.

Everything was blissful until one afternoon, her maid, Millicent, went and found her at the pianoforte practising some dreadfully tedious scales. But practise she must, to keep up the finger speed and agility.

"Lady Gillingham, your gentleman, is here to see you," Millicent announced.

Penelope turned, and her smile widened at the sight of the handsome Duke. Her wonderful betrothed, because of course Papa had given his permission right away for them to marry. Papa was probably already calculating the pound's sterling the Duke likely had in holdings at his bank. At least he thought the Duke was more than a suitable match for his daughter.

Penelope's smile quickly faded when noticing the expression on Mark's face. He seemed bewildered, lost even.

The maid left, closing the door quickly behind her.

"Mark, whatever is the matter?" She gently closed the lid of the pianoforte and pivoted around on her piano stool to watch the Duke pace up and down the room. "Will you stop walking up and down? You are making me quite dizzy!" she cried, perturbed.

Mark collapsed into an armchair and mopped his brow, even though it was not hot in the room, as this side of the house saw little sun. "My family has invested heavily in a company... somewhat like the East India Company... and several of their ships were sunk at sea in high winds off the Bahamas, causing the company to go bankrupt overnight."

She frowned. "*Somewhat* like the East India Company?" She paused, frowning, as she considered what this meant. "Do you mean slave ships? Then I say good riddance to those ships and that dreadful company if it has gone out of business! Of course, it is a terrible business if any slave drowned as a consequence of this calamity but--"

The Duke sighed. "Well, yes. But... I don't think you understand the implications." He hesitated, not knowing how to break the news. "You understand I don't agree with it, but I can't help who my family is?"

She nodded, though, in truth, she found this entire confession troubling. Deep down, she knew these things mattered. "Of course. Just as I cannot help mine."

She noticed how pale and fidgety Mark was. "But why are you not glad the company has gone?... So your family has lost a little on the investment—"

"No, Penelope, you don't understand. They lost *everything*. I have no inheritance now! Nor do I have an estate. Even the house I am visiting now will have to be sold. They lost absolutely everything. It is wiped out. All of it is gone. It will be going to pay my father's creditors."

Penelope gasped, and the room seemed to swim around her.

His voice now seemed muffled. "Your father won't want you with me. The truth is, I cannot provide for you at the moment."

Her perfect world had been shattered overnight. "What... what does this mean for us? Money is not something that matters, not when we have each other... I still love you.... I – I will always love you."

"Just as I do you, my sweet, darling girl. But I'm going to get a job and make an honest living. I have already made enquiries. I can tutor for a family I know - the Cranleys." He looked up at her. "It doesn't pay much, but it is honest money and is better than blood money."

A tutor. Penelope nodded. Perhaps all was not lost. Of course, tutoring was not exactly the same as a title. She had no idea how much such a job would pay, but surely the situation would be temporary. Entire estates did not just disappear over one poor investment. Things would surely right themselves in time.

"Penelope. Please, I beg you, wait for me, sweet girl. I know it is asking an awful lot of you, but I cannot imagine being with anyone else after meeting you..." His eyes pleaded with hers, desperate and love-filled "... ever."

She nodded, her eyes reflecting his. How did she even have a choice when her heart was already his? Of course, she would wait. She caught a glimpse of her reflection in his eyes. "I feel the same. I will always wait for you. One day, I know we shall marry."

He nodded, relieved.

Chapter Five

The Duke immediately secured employment as a tutor for the nearby Cranley family, just as he said he would. Lord and Lady Cranley had a sickly son, Frederick, who needed help with his Latin and Geometry. They were pleased to help out the unfortunate Duke, who they had always been rather fond of. They were able to give him somewhere to live along with a small income. Mark's parents had moved in with one of their own dreadful aunts, but at least they were not homeless.

In the meantime, the Duke could not continue his travels to the Continent in support of the abolitionist movement, due to no longer having the means to pay his own way. However, he attended the abolitionist meetings when and wherever possible. Lord and Lady Cranley were also greatly sympathetic to the movement and allowed him the time off.

The other big plus from attending the meetings was seeing Penelope at many of them. As promised, Penelope was prepared to wait for him, and they sat across from one another at these meetings, occasionally giving each other knowing glances and secret smiles.

Of course, officially, their engagement was off. Still, it was enough for Penelope for now just to be near him in his invigorating presence.

Every day, even from afar, she fell deeper and deeper in love with him, and he with her.

Some of the meetings they attended were strictly for supporters. Others were meetings of public debate where both sides would speak to passionately present their case. At one of these meetings, a tall and lean young man spoke fervently in favour of the slave trade. Penelope's fingernails dug into her palms. She could not believe what she was hearing: a human being actually defending the vile trade!

She had heard these arguments before, of course. Still, there was something about the young man with his shock of blonde, almost white hair that aggravated her more than most of the other slave trade supporters. Was it his zeal for the topic? She had never heard anyone speak so vehemently for the other side before and did not know what to make of this gentleman who spoke so well and could, at the same time, be so terribly wrong in what he said.

Penelope raised her hand to speak. "Sir, the slave trade is dreadful. I cannot fathom how you can possibly support it. The men, women, and children - whole families - suffer enormous cruelty at the hands of their owners."

The man's dark and beady eyes bore into hers. A smile crossed his lean lips as his gaze dropped down to her breasts before returning to her face. His look was insolent. "Of course, you are likely not aware of how the abolitionists warp and bend the truth to suit their purpose. Such things are simply not true, Lady–"

"—Gillingham." she snapped. "Lady Penelope Gillingham."

"… Well, Lady Gillingham. The slaves are not badly treated at all. They are very lucky to be fed and provided with accommodations. Poor people in Africa do not enjoy such luxury. They starve and die from illness brought on by something so simple as mosquito bites. They live as savages without a Christian education–"

"A Christian education?!" She snorted. "What kind of Christian education is it to teach these so-called savages that it is acceptable to enslave another human being? To own whole families of human beings?"

"It appears you are not familiar with Ephesians Chapter 6, Verse 5. 'Slaves obey your masters'." His smile was condescending, even cruel.

"Perhaps you should leave the debating to the schooled and learned men here, Lady Gillingham, those who have minds enough to comprehend the larger matters of the world. The female mind is emotionally-driven, ladies being creatures unable to understand–"

"I may be emotionally driven, but at least I have a heart, Sir! You are an investor in the trade that profits from people's misery! You decide with money, not your heart. There is less of the gospel in you than greed. You are a profiteer and a pirate!"

"That I am." He shrugged, clearly unashamed. "But you could say that too of the cotton mills in the north of this great nation, towns such as those in Lancashire - a miserable existence, I have no doubt, for all those that work there. But I see nobody here seeking to oppose those mills."

Others chuckled in the room, and there were a few titters of 'here, here'.

"And I need not point out, I am sure, to a good Christian woman such as yourself, that Christ Himself said, 'the poor you will always have with you.' I assure you, Lady Gillingham, the slaves are just fine doing what they do. There is no need to worry your pretty little head."

There was a lot of male laughter in the room.

Penelope's chin tilted up. Her eyes flashed. That he would use Scripture to justify his position was not only vile but evil. She rose while stating what needed to be said. "And I don't need to remind you, I suppose, of Christ's words 'do unto others as you would do unto yourself'? Or Saint Paul's words, 'If I have not to love, I am nothing. I am but a clanging bell'? You, Sir, are but a clanging bell."

There was more laughter in the room, but this time with her and not against her.

Disgusted with the whole proceedings, she stormed out of the room, her face flushed and indignant, not wishing to hear another moment of his nonsense.

Mark rushed out the door after her. They walked out behind the town hall, and her breath was fast as he took her in his arms and silenced her fears. She felt weak and shaky from her encounter and hated that she felt that way. But in Mark's strong embrace, she found strength that she could borrow for a time until she was stronger. It felt good to be able to lean on him in this way.

Meanwhile, unbeknown to either of them, the spindly man she had argued with at the meeting, whose name was Lord Nicholas Baker, set out to find out more about Penelope Gillingham. He wasn't used to being stood up to by a woman, especially not in a public venue. At the same time, he'd found their row exciting. She had fire. Spirit. Misguided, perhaps, but alluring. Not only that, her form was very becoming, and he wanted to see more of it, possess it for himself even. And being a man who was accustomed to getting exactly what he wanted, Lord Baker set out to do exactly that.

Chapter Six

The entire Gillingham family were now busily preparing for a long trip to the Continent. They had been invited on an extended trip to Tuscany, hosted by someone whom Lord Gillingham claimed he had met in Florence while on a Grand Tour some years before.

Penelope was excited about the trip, mainly because she had heard Mark would also be there through the Cranley family, whom he was still working for. The Cranleys wintered in the warmer climes due to their son Frederick's weak chest, and of course, Mark, being his tutor, was expected to be there as well. Mark's role in the Cranley family was a blessing to all concerned. For he grew into the boy's mentor while remaining close to Penelope's family estate where he could admire her from a distance.

Penelope didn't know how this amazing synchronicity had occurred, which was now taking her to Italy. Still, she was happy she would get to spend time with the Duke rather than having to wait for his return to England in the Spring. She imagined days in the golden Tuscan winter sun with Mark by her side. Perfect.

Papa met her as she was making her final preparations for the trip. Millicent was squeezing the last of her wardrobe into her trunk. Papa coughed as he made his announcement, "Ah, Penelope! I have some news for you."

He coughed again, and his eyes darted as his hands scratched his wrists. It was Papa's tell that he was anxious.

"What is it, Papa?" she asked, adding another few pretty little things into the tray, which would be fitted neatly into the top of the trunk. At Papa's look, Millicent scuttled off.

"I have found you a good match." Papa's teeth flashed white in a wide grin. "A young gentleman with enough money to provide for you. He has asked particularly for you. He is quite taken with you, so I hear. Smitten, I should say."

She paused in her work, dropping the silk scarf she had been folding. "But Papa. I... but I can't. The Duke– Mark."

Papa sighed. "Penelope, you will need to realise sooner or later that the Thompson boy, good man as he is, will never earn enough by tutoring to provide for you. His fortune is gone for good. His father is ruined. His family had to sell their estate. You know all that. All he has left now is his title."

"But the Duke, one day he will have enough again to provide for me and-" Her voice trailed off. She did not sound as convincing as she'd hoped. Maybe because she was no longer fully convinced herself, which pained her to realise.

"One day? When? When you are old and barren? You are getting to that age where I worry."

"Mark has promised me he will have enough means soon to support me."

Her father snorted. "The Duke speaks lies, or he is an utter nincompoop. His fortune is gone, and so he has lost his chance with you. You are nineteen now. Should you wait much longer, you will be considered on the shelf, a spinster!"

Penelope did not know quite what to say. Of course, her father was exaggerating. She would not be considered a spinster for a few years yet. She had time yet and saw no need to rush. Shouldn't Mark be at least given a proper chance to right things? "Do I not get a say whether he has lost his chance or not?"

Papa shook his head. His face was expressionless.

Of course not. Penelope gritted her teeth, knowing full well how useless this argument was. "Who is this man who has been asking after me?" she finally asked very quietly.

"Lord Nicholas Baker."

Penelope frowned, wondering which young man of the ton he might be. "I am not familiar with his name."

"It is of no consequence. He knows yours well enough."

So, her father expected her to marry a stranger then? Furious now, she slammed the lid to her trunk with a bang and turned to face her father fully. "Does it not matter to you at all that I am in love with another man?"

Papa shrugged. "The arrangements have been made. You have already been promised to him. You will want for nothing. Lord Baker is even richer than your Duke was–"

"I will want for nothing except for love!" Penelope trembled from head to toe, her cheeks hot and flushed. "Have you learned nothing from Eloise, Papa? You promised the rest of us girls would not have to go through what she did because of your...your meddling!"

Papa looked stung. He sighed deeply. "That was different! The man I chose for her was considerably older. Not at all handsome. This man. Lord Baker. He is young. From what I understand, the ladies consider him quite comely. It is not the same thing as Eloise at all. No, no, no. I will not have that said! It is not the same at all!"

She bit her lip, blinking back tears. There was clearly nothing further to say. As he left the room, she considered the horror of being married to anyone other than her Duke. She hoped this stranger Papa had struck a deal with wouldn't want her when he got to know her. She could wait for the Duke a while longer and hope against all hope that he - or love - or both - would find a way out of this predicament, where currently she saw none.

Of course, things did not turn out this way.

Penelope was shocked when she stepped onto the ship and saw the man she was to marry. Lord Nicholas Baker, unbelievably, was the man who had ridiculed her at the meeting. He grinned wide upon seeing her, his eyes darting again to her breasts and the rest of her delicate figure before coming to settle upon her face. Furious, she refused to so much as look at him the whole crossing. She just couldn't. She didn't care how rude she appeared.

Everything had been arranged behind her back, she discovered, and her father had already struck a deal that the pair were to be married in Florence. To be stuck with someone as wretched as him even on the voyage to Italy pained Penelope. The thought that she might be stuck with Lord Baker for life was overwhelming. She felt trapped.

It was some consolation, strange as it sounded, that she was violently sick on the voyage. She was not one well-suited to prolonged voyages by water. At least this gave her an excuse to spend the entire trip in her cabin, hoping that somehow the Duke would find a way to come for her and rescue her when they arrived in Italy. Therefore, she counted the days until she could see her Duke again, praying their love would find a way. It was the only thing that had kept her from throwing herself overboard.

Chapter Seven

One week had passed since Penelope had arrived in the beautiful Tuscan countryside, but she had not seen the Duke once, not even from a great distance. It hurt Penelope to be left alone in such a manner. She was convinced that he would make every effort to do so if he wanted to see her. To her, his silence, and the way he stayed away, left her feeling like he had abandoned her entirely. Especially since the Cranley's castle was in the same beautiful district as the Gillinghams' rented villa.

Meanwhile, preparations for her forthcoming church wedding to Nicholas were underway in Florence. Her sisters Eloise, Virginia, and Anna, caught her up in a whirl of excitement and activity. At the same time, Andrew remained his bratty little self, seemingly going out of his way to annoy her.

One night, Penelope had escaped to her room. She was reading by candlelight when she heard the clattering of a stone against her window. She started, then she curiously opened the window and peered outside. *It had better not be Andrew playing tricks,* she thought.

Then she saw him. She saw her Duke, barely able to stand upright, out in the garden below. He looked up as he heard the window latch go before leaning against the stucco wall, as his legs buckled beneath him.

She rushed out, grabbing a shawl on the way, as the nights here had a slight chill this time of year. She hadn't seen her Duke for ages, and it had broken her heart. And now he was here, illuminated by the moonlight, a tragic figure of grief and remorse.

He was also blindingly drunk.

"Penelope," he groaned. "Congratulations on your forthcoming nuptials. I came to say Godspeed and farewell."

"Never say farewell to me!" she urged him and pulled him close to her. "You fool. You get drunk when instead you could have been kissing me!"

He resisted her, and then he was weak again in her arms. "I am yours, hopelessly ever yours."

She sighed, sinking down next to him, equal parts disgusted and impressed. He had, after all, gotten himself into this state because of her. "Oh Mark, what are we to do?"

"All I know is that if I have not you to love, I am nothing. I am but a clanging bell."

He looked at her again as if suddenly stone-cold sober. It was too much for her.

They both wept.

He stroked her face tenderly. "Penelope... We need to end this. You are marrying another man soon. I cannot be a party to adultery."

Her eyes filled with tears. "But you told me to wait for you."

"I did say that, yes I did, and I meant it. But now I am telling you to carry on with your life. I cannot provide for you. Marry Lord Baker... have a life, a home, children while you can–" He hesitated, his chest heaving. "I realise now I can never earn what I need to provide for you. We cannot be."

"But we are! I want you! I love you." Her eyes searched his face, pleading with him.

He closed his eyes, his expression pained. "I know... But it cannot be. Another lifetime, perhaps, but not this one. Darling girl. Go... carry on with your life, but it cannot have me in it."

He got back onto his feet and reeled away from her. He did not look back. She tightened the shawl around herself and watched him stumble away into the night, her heart breaking within her breast. Only when he was out of sight did she steal back inside. Safe in the privacy of her room, she threw herself onto her bed and wept bitterly. She cried until morning and renewed her weeping upon rising.

~

She didn't come out of her room for two days. And when she did finally come out, it was only because she realised, sooner or later, that she must. She could not subsist on trays sent to her room forever. Not that she felt hungry or thirsty. Life had suddenly lost all taste and joy. The rolling golden Tuscan hills now only seemed grey to her.

As if in a trance, she prepared for her wedding day. She was a lamb before the slaughter, but she no longer cared. She and Nicholas had barely shared more than a few sentences, but he frequently came to dinner, only to stare at her breasts. She took to wearing a fichu to make him stop, but he looked anyway as if he could undress her with his eyes.

If he thought she would be more communicative with him after the wedding, he had another thing coming.

Dawn finally broke over Florence on the day of the wedding. Church bells rang out as though announcing the grand event. While weddings in their class were typically small, attended only by family, her father had insisted upon making this a true Florentine occasion with everyone from high society being there.

It was a lavish occasion, with only the best of everything, with no expense being spared. After the church wedding, a grand ball was planned for the evening.

As Penelope walked down the aisle, she wore a beautiful white silk gown with puffed sleeves and white gloves to match. She also wore an exquisite lace veil to cover her head, her blonde curls only just visible peeking through. Papa had arranged for the dress from a Florentine dressmaker, insisting the seamstresses work day and night to have it ready in time. It had cost him an arm and a leg, but he said so be it. It was his daughter's wedding.

Others gasped and said she looked divine if she didn't look so darn miserable. 'She could at least smile at her own wedding,' others whispered.

Nicholas wore a richly embroidered red waistcoat over a white linen shirt, with a silk cravat. He wore a black-tailed jacket in the same colour as his breeches.

He was a handsome enough man but an oaf, a monster who made money from other people's misery. She wondered how he could not see her misery. Did he think her expression would improve over time? The future stretched out before her, one bleak and terrible day following another. Penelope was sure she would never smile again.

As the organ chords played, she walked down the aisle, her arm wrapped in Papa's, her eyes met the Duke's. Of course, she should have expected he would be there with the Cranleys. His face was impassive.

Papa, proud as punch, presented her to Lord Baker. The vows were read, and the wedding ring placed upon her finger. It was all a surreal whirl around her, as if it was all happening to someone else.

There were cheers and laughter as everyone toasted the bride and groom, but Penelope barely heard them. She was with a man who was against her beliefs and who would never be the love of her life.

After all, she was not with her Duke.

Chapter Eight

Penelope, feeling sick about the thought of the wedding night, wished that night's ball would go on forever, even though she was not enjoying one minute of it.

Of course, her beloved Duke was there with the Cranleys. Penelope had to bite back her tears of unhappiness as she swirled around in Lord Baker's arms, regularly sharing glances with an evidently pained Mark.

"Your new husband is very handsome," her sister, Lady Eloise Barrington, murmured.

Eloise was so lucky to be in love with her husband, Jackson. But their love had not been a smooth road. Perhaps, Penelope thought, it was to be the same for her and the Duke. *Did true love always win?* She couldn't help but wonder. But how could that be when she was now married to someone else?

Penelope stared at the oaf she must now call her husband. He was swilling down yet another glass of champagne. She supposed he was handsome, as handsome men went, but she also knew just how ugly he was inside.

"What a frightful prig."

"Oh, Penelope." Eloise squeezed her hand. "You simply must not be like that."

"Oh?" she raised an irritated eyebrow. "How must I be? Grinning and bearing it?! If I were a boy, I would not have to endure this nonsense!" She wiped a hot tear from her cheek and bit her lip to keep from saying something she might regret later.

The only consolation Penelope could take from the night was that Nicholas got so drunk he could do absolutely nothing to consummate the marriage and fell asleep in his dressing room, falling into a chair and immediately snoring like a pig.

Penelope had left him there in all his fancy dress, ran to her room, and bolted the door, relieved to be alone.

The next morning, Penelope winced as she dressed in her plainest outfit, dreading greeting the day as the new Lady Baker. She gritted her teeth as she descended each step of the sweeping marble staircase, counting them off one by one.

Nicholas was dressed and sitting upright at the breakfast table, drinking a cup of tea. Light streamed in from the window behind him, making his shock of blonde hair look even whiter.

"Good morning, my dear."

"Good morning, husband. Are you well?"

"I have something of a headache, but I trust it shall soon depart. I am sorry about last night–" his voice trailed off.

"Not at all. Don't be sorry." It would have been rude to show how relieved she felt, and much as she hated her new husband, she was not generally rude. She slipped into a seat at the breakfast table in a chair across from him to be safely out of his reach. Maybe he would take that as a hint.

Lord Baker took another gulp of his tea. "However, I am afraid I have more bad news."

"Oh?" Penelope raised an inquisitive eyebrow. She could hardly bear looking at him.

He picked up a letter and stared at her. "This was delivered earlier this morning. There is no easy way of saying this, my dear, but I have been called away on urgent business."

"Oh," was all that Penelope could say, inwardly cheering.

"Yes, I am sure you will be disappointed, but we will have to have our honeymoon some other time."

"Where have you been called to, Husband?"

"My business partner's sugar plantations in Jamaica. I will not bore you with all the details, particularly as I know you likely wouldn't approve anyway. But business matters are not for women to comprehend in any case." He coughed and took another gulp of tea. "But to cut a long story short, I must go there at once. I am the only one who can sort matters out safely if I do not wish to lose a fortune."

"Jamaica, but that will take you away for many months!" Penelope tried to hide the immense joy she was feeling. It would be rude to smile, but surely Lord Baker could see the happiness in her eyes, she thought. Surely, he must, as her heart was now singing like a bird.

"Indeed. Of course, you could come with me. Jamaica is a beautiful country."

"I do not travel well..." she reminded him, hoping she did not sound too eager.

Thankfully he only nodded, not unduly concerned. "I recall how sick you were just crossing the Channel."

Penelope nodded vigorously, never happier that she had such bad seasickness. It ran in the family. Eloise was always sick as a dog at sea too.

"What a shame, Husband," Penelope said disingenuously.

Lord Baker seemed blissfully ignorant to her lie. He pecked her on the cheek. "I must be going straight away. I have instructed my servants to assist you in learning your way around while I am gone. I expect you will be able to manage things here without too much trouble. I will write, of course—"

The new Lady Baker nodded. "I understand perfectly."

So it was, Lord Baker set sail for Jamaica without any more ado, and Penelope headed back to England to become the new Lady of Shillington Manor.

Chapter Nine

T he new Lady Baker had been back in England for some months now and had settled into a kind of routine in the sprawling Surrey mansion Nicholas owned. Shillington was only twenty miles away from her sister, Eloise and her husband, Jackson.

Nicholas' parents were dead, and being the only son, the manor was all his. It was a beautiful place, tastefully and elegantly furnished. The family's great wealth revealed in even the tiniest of details, such as the intricate carving on the architrave and the gold gilt on the doorknobs.

However, Penelope could not but help wonder at the Lord's sneering ancestors depicted on the dust-laden gilt-framed canvases hanging in the huge hall. She wondered whether their fortunes had also been made from the slave trade. As it happened, the butler, Jarvis, told her that was not at all the case. Most of the family money had been made in breeding horses.

Lord Nicholas Baker's involvement with the slave trade was only very recent, since his father's death. It was but a minor part of his much wider portfolio of investments. That gave Penelope some relief as she hated the thought of living a luxurious life at the expense of the weak and downtrodden.

Today, Penelope was perched on the piano stool, her attention clearly on her sister, Eloise. The latter was holding up two plates from unmatching sets.

"What do you think about the rose pattern, Penelope? It is rather fashionable, I daresay. But then I am somewhat taken by the willow pattern too."

Penelope spoke in a dull monotone, her face showing no interest. "They are both equally nice, I suppose."

Eloise snorted, quite exasperated with her younger sister. "You really must make an effort as the new lady of the manor."

"Must I?!" Penelope got up, her cheeks pinking as she raised her voice. Moments passed, and then she walked over to the window, not looking once at the plates. She calmed herself and still stared out the window, her voice suddenly becoming forcibly gay and bright. "Then the rose pattern we shall have!"

She lifted the pianoforte lid to play her scales.

Eloise made a note. "Have you heard from Nicholas?"

"Yes, I got a letter saying all was well."

Penelope just wished she could say the same for herself.

With her husband away, she had continued to attend the abolitionist meetings, catching occasional glances at Mark, who could barely look at her. But she knew he loved her. Still, she could see it in his eyes. And that was the only thing that kept her going.

It was one of those spring mornings where the whole garden felt fresh. The clean and dew-laden air even tasted fragrant on the tip of Penelope's tongue, and the heady smell of grass and bluebells mixed in one intoxicating combination.

Penelope inhaled but found little pleasure in the scent, just as she took no pleasure in anything else at any time she was away from the Duke. She could not recall the last time she had smiled.

She meandered along the path, taking her time with her morning stroll in the garden. She walked out of habit not pleasure, returning to the house by way of the kitchen garden when she was greeted by her husband's manservant, Jarvis. Jarvis' face was flushed, and he was panting slightly.

"My Lady," he gasped. "I have urgent news."

Penelope noticed his eyes were red-rimmed, and he looked like he had been crying.

Penelope started. "What on earth is it, Jarvis?"

He gestured towards the house. "I think you had better go inside and sit down first, my Lady."

Penelope tensed. Was something wrong with her sister, Eloise? Or Papa, perhaps? Or Virginia or Anna? Or even Andrew? Bratty as he was, she loved the tyke. "Oh heavens, Jarvis, out with it!"

"Very well, if you say so, my Lady," Jarvis gulped. "It is his Lordship, my Lady. His ship was travelling back from Jamaica–" He gulped, and his eyes suddenly could not meet hers.

"Jarvis, please, you are scaring me!"

"His ship–" he stuttered again, and his voice then broke up. His thumb went to the corners of his eyes to wipe away tears that were forming there. "His ship–" he began again.

Penelope turned around, gently put her hand on his, and faced him. Her eyes locked with his. "What about his ship?" But inside, she already knew the answer.

"His ship was caught in unexpected storms and went down with all loss of life. His Lordship is dead, my Lady. His body was found washed ashore in Boston Bay. He is most definitely... There is no hope–" Jarvis's voice faltered.

Penelope didn't know why, but her legs suddenly gave away beneath her, and she burst into a fit of tears. Jarvis joined her as he knelt down beside her and gestured for the footman to quickly come to help her back inside.

Her servants all assumed she was distraught at the news of her new husband's death. A broken-hearted young widow who had not even had the chance to honeymoon with him was tragic indeed. It would have been cold and callous to tell them it wasn't at all that. It was the great shock of it all.

She was finally free. Free...and immensely wealthy. She was also without the need of a man to rescue her from a life of poverty. And in that one moment, all she could think of was her Duke.

She and Mark could finally be together.

Chapter Ten

The next few weeks were a whirlwind of arrangements that were made for her husband's funeral. Everyone who was anyone was there, exchanging sympathetic glances. Still, the title tattles remarked that Penelope looked happier than on the day of the wedding. Which was true. She did.

The Duke did not attend the funeral. It was perhaps just as well.

Meanwhile, Penelope investigated the Lord's business dealings, insisting his accountant tell her all, even though she was a woman. At first, Penelope was inclined to sell that terrible company. Then, to the accountant's great surprise, she instead asked him to buy out the other partners involved in the Jamaica plantation.

The accountant was even more surprised when she immediately instructed that every slave there was to be released with no forfeit. Only those who wished to remain at the plantation should do so, but this time as free men being paid a fair wage.

The London-based accountant was quite exasperated with her and said it was simply no way to do business. She was being emotional and must think in the long term.

"I am thinking in the long term," she insisted.

When leaving the Highgate firm of accountants, she bumped into the Duke. Her heart leapt in her chest at the sight of him, looking as handsome as she remembered, if not more so.

"I heard you were to be here today," he smiled.

Penelope frowned. How? Then she realised people talked, especially about women doing business in Jamaica. The London-gossip circle was small.

"Tell me, how are you?" she asked. She had thought of him constantly over the months since Nicholas' death, but it would not have been proper to go to him, as much as she wanted to. Therefore, she had not even sent him so much as a note.

"I am well. And all the better for seeing you." He could not look away from her lips. "I need to speak with you about something at once. It cannot wait a minute longer!"

"Yes? What?" she whispered.

"Walk with me." He offered her his arm, and they walked towards Penelope's waiting landau.

"Penelope," he gulped. "I know I am not a man of means, but what I have is yours, and that is my heart. I have loved you since the moment I saw you, and I know I will always love you." He turned to her, his brown eyes dilated, full of love. "Will you marry me?"

She said nothing and stared at him, tears streaking down her face.

He presented a sapphire ring he had spent every last penny he had saved up over his time tutoring. It was not the grandest of rings, but it was *his* ring. Slowly, he put it on her trembling hand.

"Will you have this poor man who has nothing but his love to give you?" he asked.

"Yes!" she gasped. For that was more than enough, but she could not finish the thought, for her lips were on his, and he was kissing her urgently.

Epilogue

T hey were married the following Spring. This time, Penelope was smiling the widest she had ever smiled as she became the new Duchess Thompson.

She looked radiant as she walked down the aisle. Her dress was entirely different from the one worn at her Florentine wedding, being instead of a beautiful primrose blue with puffed sleeves and matching blue slippers.

Pulling the landau to and from the wedding had to be dear Bob, who turned out to be better suited as a carriage horse than one for riding. The horse even had his own blue ribbons to match Penelope's dress and shoes, seeing as he was the one responsible for her meeting the Duke in the first place.

Her fingers intertwined with her Duke's, the new Duchess Thompson sighed with happiness as Bob set off from the church. In the streets, people waved at them as they passed. Inwardly, Penelope thanked her lucky stars she had ridden Bob that fateful day instead of her usual mare.

Life was truly something to look forward to again. After an extended honeymoon, they would dedicate every spare moment to fighting the slave trade. Damn the proper way of things! They both knew however hopeless things looked, things could change. They would work together to make sure that they did.

The End

Catching The Lady

THE LADY SERIES BOOK NINE

Prologue

"Braithwaite!" Lord Belson sped through the front entranceway to embrace his young friend. "So good to see you at last!"

Viscount Phineas Braithwaite stepped aside for the footmen scurrying into the house carrying his luggage. "Belson." He returned the enthusiastic embrace and clasped the older man's shoulders to match grins. "Thank you so very much for having me. I shall try to not be a burden."

"Nonsense! You would not be a burden if you tried. My home is honoured to have you in it. But you are considerably later than I expected."

"Yes," Braithwaite nodded while focusing on something far away. "Please forgive me; I was delayed by several hours, something to do with an obstruction on the road ahead from what I understand. Apparently, an entire flock of sheep had decided to congregate and would not be moved."

"Oh, good heavens." Belson grinned at the thought. "I would have thought that sheep would run at the approach of a carriage."

"Apparently, they did." Braithwaite shrugged. "From what I understand, however, no two of them could agree on which direction to run and heading back towards the horses is somehow acceptable when running *from* the carriages. It was at least an hour of panicking sheep, swearing herdsmen, and one overworked dog."

"Oh, dreadful." Belson's barely contained laughter belied the dreadfulness of it. He slapped his young friend's back and led him into the house. "However, I fear that I must be as dreadful a host. I was hoping that you would have a chance to freshen up and you could join me, but I received a note from my banker. Something he suggests needs my immediate attention. I have my doubts; the man is notorious for being somewhat trigger-happy when an opportunity arises. Still, I suppose I should attend him."

"Do not trouble yourself on my account, old friend. After the mutton on the way here, I need to stretch my legs and enjoy the autumn air. Do not keep the man who holds the purse strings waiting."

Belson grasped his shoulder and gave it a friendly shake. "I shall return within the hour, and I will make it up to you."

Braithwaite found himself alone in the entranceway with Belson's butler patiently waiting. The footmen had taken the bags somewhere into the depths of the house. The carriage he had hired from the station was gone. He heard the horse's hooves and knew that Belson had gone.

"Sir," the butler seemed to have an uncanny ability to speak without any visible sign of movement. There was a ventriloquist at a party in Braithwaite's youth who would have envied the butler's reticence to allow not so much as a twitch to his lips as he spoke. "Would you care to be shown to your rooms?"

The prospect of a hot bath and a quick nap after being folded into the train's seats for much too long was tempting. He already felt stiff and sore as it was; forced inactivity would surely cramp his muscles even worse. What the body called for was a good stretch and some fresh air.

"I think I should like to stroll the gardens if that is acceptable."

"Certainly, sir." The butler bent at the waist and waved a hand toward the rear of the house. "This way. Would you like some tea while you are there?"

"Thank you, no." Braithwaite shook his head. "The journey was quite tiresome. All I really need is a little solitude and some quiet country air."

"Excellent, sir." The butler indicated a set of French doors at the end of the library. "Just through there, sir, I believe you'll find the path clearly marked."

Braithwaite gave a perfunctory bow in acknowledgement and headed toward the sunlit exit. *Path? We'll see about that.*

Chapter One

The October skies were unaccountably blue. A few light clouds bumped against each other in the breeze, but the sun held domain as the last of summer drained away. Virginia Gillingham adjusted her shawl and tried to decide whether she should laugh or be shocked at her friend's words.

"He will be old," Madeline du Campion clearly enjoyed tormenting her sister, Selina. "And scaly. And he'll have hair growing out of his nose!"

"Madeline!" Selina snapped, "that is *quite* enough." She turned to Virginia with the look of exasperation that only a young lady with a younger sister could manage. "Honestly. Father isn't even looking in earnest for suitors, yet that is all that this one," she shot a glare at her little sister, "can speak of anymore. And each manifestation of my 'future groom' is more monstrous than the last."

Though she loved the young girl, it was a repeated taunt and grew quite tiresome. Madeline had obviously scored some minor victory with her sister. Still, she was young enough to not understand that there was a limit to teasing.

"I have to agree," Virginia told the girl gently, "and I might remind you that you are not far behind your sister, and your father will soon be looking for a suitable match for *you*."

Madeline made a face at that, and Selina jumped at the opportunity. "And he'll be old and fat." She paused a moment and added hastily, "and sweaty. With blubbery lips and no hair!"

Instead of succumbing to her own medicine, as it were, Madeline seemed to take the description and consider it. A look of utter confusion crossed her face, and she turned to her sister, all innocence and bewilderment. "Why would Papa arrange a marriage with Uncle Marchard?"

Selina sighed and turned to Virginia. "She has a valid point. I had not realised it, but that is Uncle Mark to a tea." They broke into giggles, even though such things were undoubtedly unladylike. One of the benefits of running off to "play" in the woods was being able to be as unladylike as they chose. It was also a chance to escape from her younger siblings, trapped in the schoolroom doing their lessons.

"You are so lucky." Selina put her hand towards Virginia. "Your father will no doubt let you marry whomever you will, as your sisters did."

"They both made good matches." Virginia sobered quickly. If this was some slight against her sisters' husbands...

"Of course, they did. I had not meant to imply they did any less."

"But married for *love*." Madeline interrupted her sister with a heavy sigh. "It would be like something out of a story."

"I suppose you may be correct...." Virginia stroked the long grass under her as though it were the fur of a particularly shaggy dog.

"I certainly am!" Selina snorted. Her sister looked at her in complete shock, and the three of them began another round of scandalous giggles.

"I'm just...I'm not ready yet. To marry, I mean. I want to do so much before then. I don't want to marry, have children, grow old, and lock myself somewhere in a dowager house, watching the world through a window. I know I *must* marry, but...."

"Well, you certainly do not wish to become a *spinster*?" Madeline hissed the word as though its name could cause it to pass. Selina watched with widened eyes.

"Of course not." Virginia snapped. "I just am not ready. Not yet."

In the ensuing silence, Selina's grin turned positively predatory. "I know what will keep you from becoming too ladylike too fast." She paused for effect. "A dare!"

"What sort of 'dare'?" Madeline sat back on her heels. Virginia could see the girl was dubious but had no intention of ostracising herself from the others.

"Oh! I have the most delicious idea," Virginia looked at Selina for a moment and saw that her friend's smile matched her own. She turned back to the younger sister and made the dare as tempting as possible. "Our cook has made some small cakes for dessert this evening. I dare you to steal one from the kitchens. Besides, our little picnic could use more snacks."

Madeline returned the grin, and all three girls rose and ran back to the house. It felt good to run, to feel the wind in her face and the rolling grass under her feet. Virginia was supposed to be a young lady, but just for today, she was still the girl she'd always been. She had a week until her birthday, after all, and coming out was just around the corner. But none of those things had happened *yet*, which made all the difference.

They stopped at the door to the kitchens and hid behind a stack of firewood meant to fuel the great ovens. At their urging, Madeline slipped in through the service entrance and vanished.

"It hardly seems much of a dare," Selina whispered. "We are guests. Are we not allowed in the kitchens if we so desire?"

"That is why it is the perfect dare for your sister," Virginia giggled. "At the very worst, Cook will scold her for ruining dinner, but Cook is a good woman, and I think she always makes a little extra when she bakes, just for stealing."

Selina covered her mouth to stifle the laugh. "Does this mean that you have a larcenous history?"

Virginia grinned back openly. "Only with cakes. Sometimes bread. Once with tarts, but I *did* get into trouble over those." She let loose a giggle she could no longer suppress. "How was I to know they were planned for Mother's tea?" She paused to consider this. "Perhaps if I hadn't taken quite so *many*...."

Selina laughed and clamped her hand over her mouth to stifle the sound. As they watched, the door opened again. Madeline fled the kitchen as though the hounds of hell were on her tail. Virginia spotted the old cook's face peering out through a crack in the door. The kindly old woman was smiling in a patronising way. Virginia resisted the urge to wave to Cook, but that would have given the game away.

"Your turn." Selina challenged her little sister around a mouthful of cake.

"Fine." The girl wiped her mouth with the back of her hand. Virginia grinned at the motion. "I dare you..." she stared at her older sister, "to steal a letter from the governess's table."

"Miss Albright?" Virginia sucked in a deep breath. This might be taking things too far, but if it was only a letter, the woman was constantly in correspondence with so many people; what difference would it make?

"Dare you." Madeline thrust her chin out. Selina stood at once and ran into the house, the others following her. There was no reason to slip into the main rooms and sneak past where the adults were visiting. Still, the action added to the drama of breaking and entering, theft, and their thrilling mischiefs. Hiding from a footman revealed themselves to an upstairs maid who only smiled and curtsied. They walked just then, like proper young ladies, until the maid was out of sight, then ran down the long hallway to the small room Virginia's governess had claimed as an office.

Miss Albright was, for once, not in her study. Her desk was neatly organised. Virginia stood in the hallway and kept watch while Selina strode into the room as bold as shined brass, snatched a piece of foolscap, and ran back to where the girls were hiding. They turned and pelted down the hallway to an alcove where they could be unnoticed long enough to read the treasure Selina had procured.

They crowded around Selina, gawking at the flowing letters that graced the missive.

"And what do we have here?" Virginia jumped at the all too familiar voice; Madeline let out a squeak of surprise Virginia wouldn't have believed possible to create with a human throat. Miss Albright had snuck up on them and now glared at the three girls, arms crossed and giving them a look that promised there would be trouble aplenty.

"Just a letter, Miss." Virginia tried to sound as innocent as she was able.

The young governess raised a single eyebrow and lightly tapped her foot. "While you may be on the cuff of your adulthood, I can assure you that you have not yet achieved it, and until that time, I am still in charge of your affairs." She turned to Madeline and Selina, "and as for the two of you, I have allowed Virginia this time away from her final lessons thinking your time together is also part of her preparation for adulthood. I wonder now if I have chosen her company well when you seem as childish as she."

"We are both being presented this season." Madeline protested, but Selina hushed her.

"So," Miss Albright took a deep breath, ignoring the interruption, "if there is a correspondence, perhaps we should all hear it. Please read it out loud."

"Miss Albright, I hardly think...." Virginia tried to forestall any further discussion.

"Now, please!" The governess barked.

Virginia tried to send a mental message to Selina, praying her best friend would make up some innocuous message from a great-aunt or distant cousin. Selina seemed to be unable to comply with the governess's orders. Madeline tore the foolscap from her sister's hand to Virginia's horror. She began reading the letter word for word in a clear, loud voice.

"My dearest, how I miss you and the long walks into the garden. I see you in clear memory laughing on the swing with the sun in your hair and your feet flying...."

"HOW DARE YOU?" Miss Albright tore the letter from the girl's hand so rapidly it was a wonder Madeline had fingerprints left. "Why I aught...." Whatever it was, the woman was lost in indignant sputtering. Virginia bolted for the front door, the other two girls in hot pursuit, none of them quite able to suppress their giggles.

"GET BACK HERE!" The woman's cries were lost to the sounds of birds and the wind over open fields.

"Won't you get into trouble?" Selina called out as they ran across the grounds and towards the wall that separated them from the neighbour's garden.

"I *am* in trouble," Virginia allowed, "but I would rather face censure later when we have finished the dares."

"Well...I shall have to think of a good one then." Selina gasped, as they all touched the stone divider between properties. She looked up, and Virginia followed her gaze. In the light of the afternoon sun, the apples on Lord Belson's trees looked bright and round. The gardener had obviously missed a few when he pulled the rest from the branches. Understandable, as these were at the top of the tree and would be difficult to see from the other side. One incredibly round and bright one caught the sun as though it were a prize, ripe for the taking.

"We need an apple." Selina grinned. Virginia eyed the wall and the tree and hitched up her skirts.

Chapter Two

V irginia pressed against the rough bark and heaved herself upward. The apple dangled above her, and she fancied herself as Eve reaching for the forbidden fruit for a moment. Of course, that particular tale had no happy ending, now did it?

She ruthlessly pushed the story from her thoughts and tried to replace it with something more heroic. No matter how she tried, she could not replace the image of the apple in her mind with a grail or golden fleece. Nonetheless, her prize was literally at the tip of her fingers, but it evaded her grasp agonisingly. She only needed another inch, perhaps less.

She stretched her leg, flexed her ankle against the bole that held her, and reached as far as possible. A part of her realised that, should someone happen by, they would have more than an ample view of her ankles, awkwardly arranged as she tangled through the branches. But the house was a fair distance away, and she had seen Lord Belson ride out an hour ago. Besides, the gardener was a cantankerous old man who had little to no tolerance for man nor beast. Virginia couldn't possibly be blamed if a young ankle caused the old man to die of apoplexy.

The apple bobbled on her fingertips; her thumb could not grasp the peel. She heard gasps from the gardens on the other side of the fence as she stretched just a little more. A half-inch further was all she needed.

Her shoulder was beginning to ache, and she could feel the ball of her foot slipping on the bark. Her other foot tried to steady her, but that was at the expense of another inch. To secure her prize, she had to put the other foot on the bole that gave her reach at the cost of stability. Her hand closed around the base of the apple.

"What delightful fruit these trees grow."

A voice, a man's voice, called from below. Virginia turned and looked down, expecting to see the old gardener. Still, the movement caused the friction between her foot and the bark to transfer sideways, and her foot slipped off the branch. Her hand gave the apple a single last slap as she fell from the tree, clutching branches to ease her fall, and landed at its base. Her skirts flounced up, baring both ankles and a fair portion of white stocking. She smoothed them down again quickly, covering herself, but she couldn't miss the expression on the man's face. He offered his hand as consolation for the lost apple.

This was no elderly curmudgeon with gardening shears. Instead, she had exposed her calf to this young man who stood over her, dressed like a gentleman, his grin showing more than just amusement; he seemed pleased to have seen her, especially the parts her fall inadvertently showed. She felt the warmth of blood as she blushed and tried to scramble to her feet.

"What were you doing up there?" He seemed more bemused than upset. Somehow, that seemed worse.

"Nothing," Virginia replied more hotly than she had intended. The apple rolled from the branch and landed in her lap in the ensuing silence.

The young gentleman roared with laughter. "It would seem the tree has offered you a truce." He obviously thought it the height of humour. Virginia found her footing and grasped the apple, fighting an unladylike urge to throw it at the lout.

"I beg your pardon." She tried to sound affronted. Sometimes the best defence was to take offence. "I do not believe we have been introduced!" Unfortunately, her ire seemed to cause greater amusement. She drew herself upright before the handsome stranger.

"I daresay falling from a tree and landing at one's feet is an introduction. I doubt that Belson would begrudge the loss of a single apple considering the effort you spent on the procurement. Though, I daresay that I would not have chosen you as a child. You look old enough to have achieved adulthood, though your actions belie that assessment."

"How dare you?" Virginia knew she should storm off, but the only way to return to her father's house was through the gardens and around the retaining wall or to climb the wall in front of this...this...horrible man. Neither option would have proven her status as a near-adult. Nor would either option assist in retaining her dignity.

That ship had sailed. However, they both heard the unmistakable sound of her two friends gasping, then suddenly turning tail to run, from the other side of the wall. Cowards.

"I *am* of age, sir." Virginia snapped. She spoke loudly to help drown out the sound of her former compatriots. It was true enough. A matter of hours, really. Hardly any time at all before she would officially be so.

"Young ladies 'of age' are rarely found in trees," the young man admonished. "Or so I am often told. Though I can imagine if they were, such trees would be planted in profusion across the English countryside."

Virginia clenched her fist around the apple. Throwing it at the young man's head was ill-advised. Still, she was only barely able to constrain that action by reminding herself that he would certainly take that as proof of her inability to act maturely. Of course, such an impulse was, by definition, childish.

There was a moment when the choice hung in the balance.

"Please, keep the apple."

"That is so very generous of you, sir, considering this is not your tree," she snarled at him.

"Nor is it yours, though you already gave yourself permission to take its yield, so why should I not also allow you to take that which is not mine to give? Is that not the way of children? Adults act with responsibility."

There was a twinkle in his eye that spoke of amusement and censure. The blush was travelling down her neck. She could feel the heat. She gaped a moment and realised there was nothing more to say. She could hardly maintain her adulthood while acting childishly, a trait he pointed out. "I happen to admire irresponsible behaviour, but when you reach adulthood, you'll find fewer and fewer who will accept such. Even from one so pretty as you are."

Virginia shoved the apple into a pocket of her apron and spun on one heel. She didn't want to risk being spotted alone in the garden with a young man, admittedly, a *handsome* young man. Such a thing could be scandalous enough to alienate her on the eve of her coming out and embarrass her family. The alternative was to crawl over the fence, exposing her backside to the rake, beyond her ability.

Back straight, head high, she strolled from the garden as though it were hers, as if the flowers bloomed for her and the sun was there because she was. It was little enough, but it was a salve for her battered ego.

Blast the man.

Blast the man!

Good looks, merry laugh, and all.

Chapter Three

"Virginia, stop that." Eloise sounded at whit's end. "It only prolongs the fitting if you fuss so. Truly, if you have such aversion to being fitted for your coming out gown, then sit still. It will go that much quicker."

Virginia tried. She willed herself to be still, stand like a perfect dressmaker's dummy and not fuss or heave her breast or grind her teeth or any of the other things her oldest sister called her on so far. It wasn't easy. She had already been through the agony of corsets and lace and billowing skirts for Selina and Madeline's mutual coming out ball. The fact that Madeline was a full year younger than her sister was unusual, to say the least. But then Selina had been quite ill last year and had missed what was planned initially as her coming out.

You would think a dual coming might have caused some resentments, but the girls seemed pleased enough to share their event, unusual though it was.

Virginia understood that. It would be wonderful to have someone take the pressure off her upcoming ball. Perhaps she could even point to a sister when being poked and prodded while having one's middle section squeezed off and air-restricted by whalebone. In truth, Virginia was becoming more and more certain her new corset was built of cast iron.

But rather than worry about what Madeline and Selina were doing, Virginia should have been more concerned about her own. After all, it was her forthcoming ball, and it wasn't about to be called off, even if she had to show up in petticoats and wrapped in a sheet. She gritted her teeth, careful not to grind them, and closed her eyes as the dressmaker pulled, poked, and prodded until she reached some unfathomable perfection.

Fittings, so her sister informed her, was something adults had to do. Virginia couldn't tell if that was a backhanded way of saying that Virginia was far from adulthood or a demonstration of her recent actions, for she had been caught sneaking out of the neighbour's gardens. Thankfully, no one had seen her escort, who had lingered under the trees. There would have been scandal aplenty, regardless of her age and circumstance.

I am adult enough now, though, she thought with some satisfaction. Her birthday and come and gone with a suitable acknowledgement of the day. This particular dress fitting is one of her presents. Right now, the dress she was being fitted for did not feel much like a gift.

Adulthood. What a strange thing to be one thing one moment and then quite another, simply by virtue of a date upon the calendar. She certainly felt no different. Still, she fought to find the words to say, to speak up in her defence, as the modiste stuck pins through the hem of her dress in a hundred places. Virginia was again admonished to stand still.

Maybe it would forever be difficult to find the right words. It had been the same with the strange young man in Belson's garden. She had not spoken well then either. She scrunched her eyes tightly as if the pressure could rid her mind of the image. That dreadful superior look, those flashing eyes. He had laughed at her. So smug. So...so...

"VIRGINIA!" Eloise gasped. Virginia opened her eyes to see the delicate lace she was entrusted to hold now crumpled into a ball in her fist. She mumbled an apology and tried to smooth it, but the dressmaker only pursed her lips and patiently took it from her and lay it aside.

"I swear," Eloise muttered, "I have never seen anyone so rabidly opposed to getting a new dress. You are only expected to wear it for a night. Surely you can manage that much?"

"I...I am sorry...I hope I have not destroyed it." She glanced uneasily at the dressmaker. Virginia suddenly realised she did not know the woman's name, though she had been introduced, and it was the second time she'd posed for the woman.

"If it is ruined, she will bill father for the difference." Eloise sighed again before the woman could answer. She shook her head and waved Virginia off. "Go on, get ready for dinner. Father will have something to say to you, I think. He wants to be sure you understand how to behave."

"I *know* how to behave." Virginia carefully slipped out of the dress, avoiding being skewered by the small pins holding the cloth together.

"Of course you do." Eloise shook her head and retrieved the ruined lace to examine it for herself. She turned toward the dressmaker, shaking her head regretfully over the crushed edging which would look so fine along the bodice. "It is a lovely gown. Are you sure it can be ready in time for the ball?"

Virginia did not wait to hear the end of the conversation but dashed into her rooms to change. Father was a wonderful man, but he insisted on punctuality at the dinner table. The lace certainly was not her fault and could surely be pressed again. If it had not been for that self-righteous and annoying man in the garden, she would not have crushed the lace at all.

Funny how he had been haunting her thought for days now.

"Stop it." She faced herself in the looking glass. "You have your coming-out ball, your two best friends have had theirs, and you are still lost on some random stranger in a garden more than a week past the incident. What foolishness!" She gripped the dresser until her knuckles turned white.

After a moment, her posture reasserted itself, and she was able to stare coldly into her reflection. She wore her dignity like a cloak. She had probably looked much the same way when she stalked out of that garden, after that...that man...

"STOP IT!" The face in the mirror looked grim and determined. Father would never accept that much tenacity at dinner. She found a smile somewhere and wore it instead.

The dinner bell rang.

~

"...and keep in mind, an essential part of your introduction to society is laying the groundwork for a good match. Your actions at the ball will determine a great deal of your suitability." Her father smeared butter on his bread, the knife flowing like a sword over the helpless bread. Virginia couldn't keep her eyes off the bun.

"Father..." Eloise said softly.

"Jackson will be here for the ball, yes?" Lord Gillingham asked his eldest daughter.

"Yes, of course, he should be on his way out from the estate soon and plans to be here late tonight."

"Good." Lord Gillingham returned his attention to his bread, but his conversation was directed to Virginia. "Jackson is a good example, a good match for Eloise." He brought the bread to his mouth and tore a piece of the bun off with his teeth. Virginia felt sudden empathy for the bun. She refrained from mentioning her father's initial reluctance on the subject of Jackson Barrington.

"You must behave like a proper young lady. The ball is about you, and all eyes will be on you. The future of your place in the ton, and your future husband, will be largely determined by your actions and attitude."

He tore apart the bun, ripped a small piece with his fingers and popped it into his mouth. Virginia nodded miserably. Her own appetite altogether fled the more this particular conversation wore on.

"Father," Eloise lay a hand on his arm and spoke softly, "the ball isn't for another few days; there are still preparations to make. Perhaps we can allow her these last few days of childhood before we lay such responsibilities on her?"

Responsible. There was what that man said in Belson's garden. The very word. How was she irresponsible? It had been only an apple. Just a lark. What sort of killjoy or stodgy old man in a young man's body would begrudge someone a freshly picked apple? He had her so rattled she never even ate the silly thing. It had sat on her dresser until the maid threw it out, unfit for even the horses.

If she were to be completely honest, it was too much of a reminder of her encounter to eat.

"Virginia!" Her father clanged his plate with a fork. "Cease this wool-gathering. We are discussing this coming out; you need to show some responsibility for...."

"Responsibility?" Virginia burst out. She clamped her teeth shut, but the words would not be contained.

"Responsibility?" She threw her napkin on the table, barely missing her father's plate. "I do not even understand why I must come out when I am delighted staying *in*!" She leapt from her chair and fled the room.

"What the devil was that about?" Her father's confusion followed her into the hall.

Chapter Four

U pon the announcement of her arrival, Virginia Gillingham slowly descended the staircase. All eyes of the ton gathered in her father's house and were trained on her. Their eyes were welcoming, appraising, and critical, all at the same time. It was as though she were a horse on the auction block, and the crowd had gathered to judge her merits.

By walking slowly and deliberately, Virginia had neither intended to show off nor keep the focus on her. It was the only safe way to move down steps in her pinching new shoes and flowing skirts that threatened to fold under her soles with each hesitant step.

She felt as though she couldn't breathe, but that was not *entirely* due to the cruelty of the corset her maid had tied, once she was sure there was no place left for Virginia's internal organs. They had moved behind her breasts, which now jutted upward salaciously. She felt more naked in front of all of these people than if they had found her in her shift.

As she reached the bottom of the staircase, the musicians restarted their measures, and the guests began to dance. Eloise smiled and nodded to her, and Virginia felt she had passed a test. There would be more. She stood still for a moment, catching her breath as best as possible, and looked at the ballroom around her. It was magnificent, brightly lit with candles until it appeared the sun had come to rest indoors for her sake.

All of impeccable breeding, Lords and Ladies bowed and nodded to her, and she returned curtsies due to their stations. There were many strangers, but that was the point of the introduction to society, to become acquainted with her peers.

She nearly sobbed in relief when she felt a sharp poke on her back. Rather, it was intended to be a sharp poke, but only the basic pressure could get through the armour of her dress. Behind her, Madeline and Selina grinned foolish grins, and although they were all adults, they were once more three girls playing dress-up.

"This is lovely," Madeline gushed. Her gloved hands took in the company and the setting.

"It really is beautiful." Selina agreed. She clasped her sister's hand in hers and reached for Virginia.

"Thank you both for being here," Virginia whispered. "I do not know that I might survive all this without the two of you."

"Nonsense." Selina shook her head. "We survived it, so will you."

"After all, you survived Miss Albright's wrath, did you not?" Madeline grinned.

Virginia blushed. "Well, it depends on what you consider 'survival'. Father was quite piqued and said I had acted unwisely. While I no longer needed a governess, I still have two siblings who do. All the same, what could he do but accept her rather...indignant resignation?"

Madeline covered her smile, but Selina's eyes grew wide as she looked over Virginia's shoulder. She nudged her friend and nodded her head for Virginia to look.

Virginia turned and nearly fainted on the spot.

"My dear," her father interrupted, "allow me to introduce this young gentleman." Virginia stared into the face of the arrogant fop who had made a fool of her, the face she had not been able to excise from her waking thoughts. Nor from her dreams, for that matter.

There was no reaction other than polite disinterest from her friends. Virginia wondered how they could be so calm. Still, they were behind the wall as she had her encounter, and they would not have seen this particular gentleman before. Any hope that he would have forgotten about her was dashed as that self-satisfied smile crept across his face.

"Lord Braithwaite, may I introduce my daughter, Virginia. This is Lord Braithwaite, a good friend of our neighbour Lord Belson. In fact, Braithwaite is wintering with Belson, I believe, that he might enjoy the London season with him."

Virginia opened her mouth to greet the man and say *anything* to keep him from speaking first. She prayed the young man had sense enough to not mention they had already met. However, before she could manage the words, he smiled at her father and gave a quick bow of his head. "She is as lovely as you said, Sir. I am sure she is the *apple* of your eye." He put just a hint of stress on that word, and Virginia heard the gasps behind her. She didn't know whether it was his voice or the use of the word *apple* that tipped her friends. However, it was clear that they suddenly realised it was the same man who had dressed down Virginia in the garden.

"I wonder, Miss Gillingham, would you do me the honour of a dance? The music is quite compelling."

"She would be delighted." Virginia's father accepted the invitation on her behalf, then turned away. He was already engaged in another conversation, with his daughter safely settled. She watched him leave, with growing horror, and then returned her attention to Lord Braithwaite. She realised, belatedly, that her mouth had been open in shock and surprise for some time.

Before she could utter an apology, Virginia flew into his arms and only retained her footing because of his adroit catch. She turned her head to hiss a silent curse at whichever of her two friends pushed her that hard and with a good enough aim to propel her into the man's grasp. She saw them melt into the crowd just before Lord Braithwaite led her to the dance floor.

Wonderful. Every time she was around him, she looked like a fool. She made an angry resolve to keep her lips shut, thinking if she didn't speak at all, there was nought she could say which would later prove embarrassing. Whether such a plan would work or not remained to be seen.

She tried to divine his thoughts from his expression. But her eyes kept resting on his rugged jaw, and his steely blue gaze that brimmed bright with hidden mischiefs. He really was quite a handsome man, with thick, sandy hair framing his face rather elegantly. He moved like a self-assured tomcat, and she had no doubt he would prove to be an excellent dancer despite his many flaws.

Dance. 'Tis only a few moments upon the dance floor. Nothing more.

To her surprise, she somehow managed to calm down by the time they reached the dance floor. She was calm right up until the moment that she felt his arms around her. They moved into the rhythm of the first few steps. In that instant, she looked up. She immediately saw the mischief in his eyes and knew that this was not going to be "just" another dance after all.

Chapter Five

One dance. Virginia reminded herself that until it became a mantra in her head. *One dance.* She could survive a single dance in his arms. Strong arms that went well with his strong jawline, flashing ice blue eyes, and thick, wavy hair...*stop it*. She swallowed hard, trying to keep her thoughts in check. She reminded herself of her previous encounter with this man and the way he had belittled her, calling her a child. All because she had been climbing a tree.

She closed her eyes for a moment. It was rather childish to reach for that apple on a dare, but wasn't that the point of the game? To delay the inevitable change into adulthood, to *be* a child for a little longer. Perhaps he had reason to chastise her, no matter how it stung. She looked up at him, trying to sort her feelings, and to her horror, she belatedly realised that he had asked her a question and was awaiting an answer.

"Please forgive me, sir; I seem to be overwhelmed by the ball. Or perhaps more, accurately, by the *nature* of the ball. I should say, my coming out. I mean, I have...." She clamped her teeth on the verbiage that threatened to spill out. "Would you mind repeating the question?"

He laughed once and looked over her head at the crowd. "I believe the question has been answered." He turned his grin back to her. "For the official record, I had asked how you were enjoying the ball."

"Oh." She felt the heat rise in her cheeks again. What was it about this man that could make her blush so easily? She focused on the dance to cover the awkward moment. She didn't need to concentrate on her steps; he was an excellent dancer and a strong lead. She only had to keep her feet. He would manage the dance quite well.

She tried to isolate what she was sensing, and in a rush, it came to her. He *smelled* wonderful. She had never paid attention to smells before, not from people anyway. But he smelled of clean soap, freshly laundered clothing, and yet, there was a trace of horse and meadow, even something hinting of sunlight. It was as though he brought the outdoors in with him, and it was intoxicating.

She allowed herself to take a deep breath of the aroma and could not suppress a shiver as he spun her around. It really was quite exciting if she would only let herself enjoy the moment. The ballroom seemed to be whirling around her, sweeping with elegant dresses moving in unison, as the gentlemen led their partners past each other.

She looked up at his face and nearly misstepped. He was looking elsewhere. Intently. Virginia turned her head to see what he was looking at and why that bizarre smile was on his face.

He was staring at a woman. Not just at any woman. This lady, in particular, wore a green dress and was watching Virginia's own partner dance with a look that spoke of pride rather than jealousy. It was the same look a woman might give a man she knew was doing his duty by dancing with the guest of honour. It was an insulting look, for it clearly dismissed Virginia as being beneath her notice as if she indeed were a child playing dress-up.

Virginia returned to the familiar steps as the only rules she could understand in this game. Why had her governess not prepared her for things like this? Why had her sisters ignored this most basic of duties?

Virginia blinked back sudden tears as she swayed and stepped in time to the music. She reminded herself it mattered little if this particular Lord was interested in someone else. She had no interest in *him*. After all, he had been the bane of her existence since they met. She had spent the intervening weeks obsessing with how arrogant and wrong he was. If that was not sufficient proof of her disinterest, what was?

At the same time, she was starting to think her vow of silence for the duration of the dance was foolish and, yes, again, childish. She opened her mouth to speak, floundering to make small talk...

...and the song ended. Virginia stopped opposite her partner, equal parts afraid that Lord Braithwaite would ask her for another turn around the floor later and equally scared he would not.

"Thank you for the dance," he said stiffly and bowed. Virginia curtsied as she had been taught but suddenly realised that her former dance partner had not bowed to her but to her father, who had appeared at her side. Lord Braithwaite did not seem inclined for conversation, for he spun on a heel and made a straight line towards the woman in the green dress.

Oh. So that's it then.

"Daughter..."

Her father seemed inclined to speak. No, he was probably more inclined to criticise, for he had clearly been watching and noticed her silence. Virginia could not bear it, not right now when she was so near tears.

"Please excuse me, father, I need to...."

She didn't define what she needed, leaving him to guess. Instead, she curtseyed and made her way toward the ladies' sitting room, thinking an escape to the necessary would suffice as an excuse. Maybe she could hide there for the rest of the night. Or better still, sneak up to her room and be done with it.

No. Virginia was not so cowardly as that.

Uncertain about what to do, Virginia paused, searching the crowd for her friends. She was standing still at the edge of the dance floor as couples whirled and spun around her. She stood as though she were alone in the world, and the dancers around her took no notice.

This is my ball! It was a strange and almost troublesome thought.

"Lady Gillingham." Virginia jumped at Lord Braithwaite's voice behind her. The woman in the green dress was standing next to him. *Closely* next to him. "May I present Lady Roswell?" He nodded towards the woman beside him, "Lady Roswell, Lady Gillingham, the reason for tonight's festivities."

"Congratulations, my dear," Lady Roswell took Virginia's hand briefly and allowed it to drop. "It is an elegant affair. You must be very proud. I recall my own coming out ball. I was a nervous wreck, but I survived it, and I expect you shall also."

Just how long ago had her coming out ball been? The woman was at least a few years older but still young enough to have the blush of maidenhood, certainly a desirable match for some young Lord. A *certain* young Lord.

"Thank you, I...." Virginia nodded and tried to think of something to say.

"We should perhaps leave the dance floor," Lady Roswell grabbed Lord Braithwaite's sleeve and tugged gently. "We would not want to be in the way."

"Of course." Braithwaite bowed to Virginia and allowed himself to be removed like some errant child, especially given they had not even been on the dance floor but only near it. All the same, he and Lady Roswell vanished into the guests milling around at the side of the dance floor. Virginia looked for an opening between, looking for the easiest way to navigate the press around the edges of the room, and rushed to the punchbowl, seeking something to do which would buy her some time to comport herself.

She told herself firmly that if Lord Braithwaite was happy with that sort of woman, she wished him all the happiness. She could scarcely say what "that sort of woman" meant, but nonetheless, Lady Roswell was... very...

Beautiful. That's the word I was looking for. Beautiful. Virginia kept her gaze firmly on the punchbowl as if it were a scrying glass. She took a deep breath or tried to, but the corset denied her a decent sigh.

"He looked a good dancer." Ah! Selina and Madeline had found her after all. Virginia spun and fought an urge to embrace the sisters. Selina was looking at her with great anticipation, and Madeline seemed about to burst with curiosity.

"Madeline," Virginia lay her mouth next to her friend's ear. "See that woman in the green dress?"

"Oh," Madeline sighed in delight, "she's so pretty. I wish I looked like that."

Though Selina couldn't hear Virginia's words, she followed their looks. "She looks so...sophisticated, so...adult."

"Madeline." Virginia hissed. Both girls jumped at the tone of her voice. "I need you to find out who she is. Her name is Lady Roswell, but I need to know anything you can find out about her."

"Searching out the competition?" Selina might have been teasing her, but her curiosity was piqued.

"No!" Virginia spoke louder than she had planned. She covered her mouth and returned to whisper. "No, I want to know who came to my ball."

Selina nodded sagely. "And you know everyone else?"

Virginia shot her a look, and Madeline jumped in before more could be said. "I shall let you know."

Virginia hugged her friend. "If anyone can find out about people, it would be you. You have rare skills in that area."

"I shall assume that is a compliment." Madeline giggled, but in truth, Virginia could tell the other girl was pleased with Virginia's words. Madeline had made quite a study of the ton. She was quite fascinated by the gossip and had a keen ability to ferret out the secrets others would rather keep.

The music came to an end, and some couples left the dance floor; others took their places. Her father found her, accompanied by a man old enough to be *his* father.

"My dear," her father said loudly enough to make it clear his words and the ball he paid for was not for the sisters who fled. "May I present, Lord Promington? Lord Promington, my daughter...."

Another dance, another introduction, another dance. The men were all the same. Virginia found something wrong with each of them. They couldn't dance. They smelled wrong. They talked too much, or they did not talk at all. The next half dozen dances were a blur of average faces and sore toes from clumsy but apologetic partners, whose only endearing quality was the sum of money at their disposal.

Begging for a moment to catch her breath, which was sorely needed, but impossible to accomplish, Virginia retreated again to the punch bowl. Selina was dancing with a young man who had taken Virginia on her second... or was it her third dance? All she could remember was that he had very sweaty hands.

"Psst." Madeline sidled up beside her. "It really is a lovely ball." She sounded almost wistful. Virginia scanned the guests, but Madeline touched her arm. "He left. During the last dance."

"Did...did Lady Roswell leave with him?"

"I do not know for certain. They left about the same time, though. I have been watching them both and had to turn down several invitations for dancing." The look she gave her was wounded. Had Virginia not known how much Madeline enjoyed subterfuge, Virginia might have felt guilty.

Virginia hugged her all the same. "If they are gone, then your work is done for the night. Go. Have fun."

Madeline smiled and gripped her hand momentarily before heading back to the dance floor. It was not long before a charming man swept her up for a waltz.

"Virginia!" Her father snapped at her, clearly put out at having to track her down once again. "You have had sufficient time to catch your breath. Come with me. I have someone for you to meet."

Virginia sent a heartfelt apology to her feet and followed her father dutifully onward to the next dance partner...and the one after that.

Chapter Six

Spending time in the carriage with her friends was agony. Madeline's eyes brimmed with impatience, and she practically bounced on the seat beside her. She had discovered something about her quarry, the beautiful Lady Roswell, and could not wait to report.

The agony was in the personage of Miss Albright. She was serving in the capacity of escort, or rather as watchdog. Virginia did not wish to even guess what it had cost her father to keep the woman from leaving outright. He had told her rather sharply though to behave. Virginia suspected the same message might have somehow been conveyed to her friends, for they had been quite subdued, all things considered.

Of course, Madeline would not dare spread gossip in front of the woman's intimidating gaze. All three young ladies had learned their lesson. Whatever she had discovered would have to wait for the moment. The waiting was agony itself.

Virginia had organised this little shopping trip just to hear what Madeline had found out, if anything. She had argued with her father that she no longer needed an escort, but she might have been trying to cajole a statue for all her progress. If nothing else, she did manage to cause him to laugh, albeit at her expense.

"The three of you unescorted?" He looked at her as though she had suggested London did not actually exist. "Good heavens, the mind quails at the very concept!" After his mirth died down, Virginia acquiesced to the idea that the redoubtable Miss Albright would indeed view each and every purchase with the same disapproval as she used for poorly cooked meat or Virginia's sense of humour.

If indeed "former" was the correct word, the former governess, considering her duties had not changed overly much, had officially forgiven the girls for the theft of her personal correspondence. Still, there was a chill between them all, which lingered and seemed insurmountable. Virginia was thankful she no longer had to put up with lessons from the woman.

The first shop was a preliminary stop. Though the fabric and the lace were lovely, the invented errand was merely a way to create a little distance between the friends and the governess. They walked through the local stores, leisurely looking into windows and speaking in inanities, the report behind Madeline's teeth hanging with them as they waited for the governess to wander into the next shop.

Virginia had to credit the woman with that much. She did allow the girls a certain amount of privacy once she was convinced they were not suddenly going to run wild and burn the city to the ground. The more they acted like "proper" ladies, the more room she allowed between herself and her charges.

"What did you find?" Virginia hissed at her friends while pointing to a hat on display behind a glass window. Miss Albright was far enough ahead she should not be able to hear. Hopefully, the gestures indicated they were discussing the merits of clothing.

"Lady Roswell." Madeline whispered in a breath that could have been heard for miles, "Is Earl Roswell's daughter."

Virginia did not recognise the name, though an Earl was a higher rank than Viscount Braithwaite and would be a good match for him. Her heart sank. What hope could she possibly have to gain the attention of a man such as he when she was up against someone of such standing?

She no longer anticipated Madeline's report, but for the sake of having complete information, she dared not interrupt.

Madeline cautiously monitored their escort, who was looking their way with a raised eyebrow and her scowl seemed to deepen. "She and Viscount Braithwaite were engaged."

"Were?" Virginia echoed, her eyes still on the governess.

"He broke off the engagement," Madeline smiled and nodded to Miss Albright, "months ago."

Selina choked back a laugh. "Does *she* know that?"

"A question I have been asking myself since." A familiar voice behind them froze them in place. Looking at the reflection in the glass, Virginia saw Lord Braithwaite standing behind them, looking rather bemused.

"I believe Miss Albright is summoning us," Selina squeaked and nearly bolted to where the woman stood patiently waiting. Madeline made no excuses; she simply followed her sister as quickly as possible, leaving Virginia alone with the young man.

"You must forgive my friends," Virginia turned slowly and faced Lord Braithwaite. Why was it every time he was near, she was blushing?

"Quite understandable." Braithwaite waved off her concern. "It was entirely my fault. I did come up upon you rather unannounced, insinuating myself into your conversation. I know that is improper, but I assumed that an expert opinion would not be unwelcome, since the conversation was indeed about me."

"I do not understand, Sir, how it is that you continuously catch me at all the worst times. I have often behaved well enough that my...escort has approved my actions, which is no small accomplishment. Yet, the only times I slip or am in error, you are there to witness it."

"Then allow me to find you at your best. Would you permit me to call upon you?"

Virginia forgot to breathe for a moment. She wanted to ask him to repeat that statement, not because she had not heard him, but because she wanted to hear it again. And again.

"I...I would enjoy that." She bit her tongue and tried again. "I mean. That would be acceptable, Sir."

"Excellent. Perhaps then, the day after tomorrow."

"Yes. Fine. Good." She clamped her teeth tightly to keep from spilling more words. The heat in her face grew. Lord Braithwaite tipped his hat and said something about anticipation. Virginia could scarcely hear him over the pounding of her heart.

~

The ride back to the house was a different sort of agony, though the cause was the same. Virginia had to report the essence of her conversation to Miss Albright in a sober fashion when all she wanted was to squeal and fly off the sidewalk and swing herself from the gaslights lining the way. At her announcement of his intention to call on her, Madeline and Selina showed no such restraint until they were called to order by their escort.

Coming into the house, she felt as though she could fly. Her feet never touched the steps; they must not have, for she floated up the staircase to her rooms. Even when her maid readied her for dinner, her mind was far away, basking in his attention.

"I see you enjoyed your time out." Her father chanced a grin as she came to the dinner table. Eloise did not try to hide a smile at Virginia's good mood. Even the absence of Eloise's husband away on business and her younger siblings, who were visiting friends, could not dampen her spirits.

"Yes, father." Virginia grinned back at them both.

"Well, we have other good news for you." He looked at Virginia's older sister, clearly passing the conversation to her.

"We have been talking on your behalf." Eloise took a deep breath. "We are aware that your coming out ball was arduous for you, and we both regret having pushed you so hard. I believe that you were not ready for such stress. Therefore," she held the pause as one would dangle a sweet before a child, "we have contacted Penelope on the Continent. You will spend the rest of the season with her and Mark. You leave in the morning. We can revisit the idea of finding you a match next year. After all, there is no rush. Isn't that wonderful news?"

Virginia felt as though she had been kicked in the stomach. The food arrived just then, the footman quietly setting a plate in front of her. It looked horrible, and the thought of eating was abhorrent.

Tomorrow? Lord Braithwaite would call on her, and she would be a million miles away. She might as well be on the moon for all it mattered.

"You...you cannot mean it."

Obviously mistaking her reluctance for excitement, her father nodded. "It has all been arranged and the tickets purchased. Penelope will meet you at the station when you arrive." He speared a large piece of meat and stuffed it into his mouth.

"HOW COULD YOU!" Virginia stood, her chair rocked on its rear legs before the butler caught and steadied it. She fled from the room feeling as though the weight of the world was suddenly thrust upon her shoulders.

"Oh, for heaven's sake." Her father swore colourfully in her wake, his voice tinged with annoyance. "*NOW* what?"

Chapter Seven

Selina came and sat next to her and wrapped an arm around her shoulders. "We shall miss you terribly."

Heartbreakingly, Virginia embraced her friend and then rose to embrace Madeline. "I will miss you both as well."

"It's only for the rest of the season," Madeline sounded like she was trying to convince herself, not Virginia.

"You must promise to write," Selina spoke up.

"I shall," Virginia promised. "You must promise to do the same, both of you."

"Why not tell your father or Eloise that you have a caller? Or that you do not want to go, or...tell your sister, and she can intervene on your behalf, or...." Madeline grew flustered and seemed to run out of ideas all of a sudden.

"My maid Bonnie is coming with me." Virginia turned to the fire and stared at the flame as if all the answers were hidden there. "And so is Miss Albright."

"Why?" Selina asked first, but her sister was hard on her heels with the same indignant question.

"Because my father still believes me to be a child, and apparently, my sister agrees with him. All because I did not properly enjoy myself at the ball. He suspects I might still need more lessons in becoming a Lady. He even said he would find a different governess for my siblings, so their learning would not be interrupted." She returned to the divan. "Right now, Anna is packing my things and her things, and Polly is helping. I don't even leave until morning, but I'm to go early and...." She stopped there and stared at something far away, the memory of Lord Braitwaite's face set behind her eyes. She had memorised every feature, every hair upon his head.

"And Lord Braithwaite?" Selina finished for her.

Virginia nodded sadly and heaved a heavy sigh. "And Lord Braithwaite. There was no one else at the ball. I danced with bad illusions and sweaty non-existent boys." She ignored the gasps that statement provoked. "To tell the truth, I cannot remember a single face from the dancing other than his."

The fire crackled and spat in the ensuing silence. "Then write *him* a letter," Selina said quietly.

Virginia gasped. The idea was an audacious one, hardly proper at all. "I doubt that Penelope or Mark would allow me to post a letter to a strange man, especially one so far away. Besides, what good would it do? I would still be far beyond his reach."

"No." Selina shook her head. "I mean, write it now. Not to send, but set down your feelings and say everything you would not dare say in person. You do not have to give it to him; you can toss it into the flames. But say it, get it out and onto the page. It might help you to...well, feel better about going. Less like things are being left unfinished."

Virginia contemplated the idea. It would be good to exorcise that demon; to vent in such a way might provide relief from the grief she felt. She turned to the desk and pulled a sheet of foolscap and a pen. She dipped the pen into the inkwell and poised it over the blank sheet. "I have no idea what to say."

"Start with 'Dearest Phineas'."

Virginia gave Madeline a scandalised look. "That is a *bit* familiar, don't you agree?"

"What difference would it make to the fire?" Selina teased her.

Virginia nodded and took a deep breath. She charged the pen again and put it on the page.

Dearest Phineas,

I will not be here when you arrive. I know it is unaccountably rude, but it is not my choice. When you asked permission to call on me, I was thrilled and excited. I was happier than I had been in a very long time.

Are you surprised by this confession? Honestly, even though you must think me very foolish and childish, I find that I really am happiest when you are near me. Now, as I am faced with the prospect of never seeing you again, I cannot help but wonder what might have been had you been able to call upon me. Would we have eventually courted? Or dare I say it, become something...more lasting?

Perhaps this is for the best. I doubt you wish to be saddled with such a flibberty-gibbet as I. We met while I was climbing a tree looking for apples, then I fell into your arms, and you caught me gossiping... I genuinely regret having given you such a poor impression of me.

She dipped the pen again. It was going to the flame; what did it matter if she was indiscreet at this point? She was already feeling somewhat better.

The fact is, I find you charming and handsome, and I shall always wonder what we could have had. I shall remember your ready smile, the way your eyes flash and most importantly, the warmth of my heart when I am with you.

May you have the most remarkable life. Please try to remember me in as good a light as you might summon.

Yours

Miss Virginia Gillingham.

"Pardon me, miss." The butler tore her attention from the message she had only just finished. "Your father requests your presence in his study."

"Yes. Fine." She rose with a satisfied nod at her friends; she crumpled the page into a ball and threw it into the fireplace. She watched curiously as it landed in a corner, began to unfurl from the heat, and wondered what it would have been like to post such a thing.

"Thank you," she said to each in turn. "Shall you stay? I can find out what father wants and return...."

"We should go anyway," Selina said, with a sharp glance at her sister. She hugged her fiercely, as though loath to let her go. Yet when the hug was over, Virginia felt as though it couldn't last long enough. It would be nearly a year before they saw each other again. Far too long.

Madeline likewise held her for a long moment and sniffled when they parted.

It felt awful saying goodbye to her best friends. Virginia turned and headed to the study and her father, her footsteps lagging. In truth, he was the last person she wanted to see right now.

Chapter Eight

I t was a carriage like every other carriage Virginia had ever been in. Yet her family might as well have placed ostrich plumes on the horses' bridles and given a bed of feathers to her trunk to make this a true funeral procession. Such maudlin thoughts were unfair, especially as she knew her father and sister meant the best for her. Still, they seemed unable to grasp her pleas to stay.

Virginia had even gone so far as to admit she had been wrong on the night of the ball, that she *did* enjoy herself, though it was a small lie. She *should* have enjoyed herself, but she was too obsessed with one young man to notice any other. That part she did not confess. Nor did she confess that she felt like a child acting like an adult. After all, her father and sister were convinced they had introduced her too early; to admit her childishness would only prove them right.

She had begged, but that too was childish. When she was asked why she wanted to avoid her sister and brother-in-law, she could not answer, as her quandary had nothing to do with either of them. She came close to mentioning Lord Braithwaite's interest in her, but she was not convinced that he *had* an interest in her. It might be a misunderstanding, or perhaps Lord Braithwaite was flirtatious and only wanted to please her by feigning interest.

If she had claimed a suitor where there was none, she would be shipped off for more than the rest of the season, she would be confined to her sister's house until she matured or until age claimed her and she reached spinsterhood.

The door to the carriage stood open, the bags tightly tied to the rear, and Miss Albright and Anna were both seated and awaiting her arrival. The sounds of the streets of London broke through her thought, and carriage wheels and horse's hooves echoed off the stone wall as though the city itself was saying goodbye.

Selina and Madeline had not arrived to see her off. After all, they had said their goodbyes the night before, but she had hoped for one more hug before she was exiled.

"Father." She turned from the carriage, ignoring the impatient eye roll of the governess. "Please, may I speak to you?"

"You have a ship to catch," her father reminded her. "You cannot dally long."

"I...I..." What? She could not think of any argument she had not already used. "I do not wish to go."

"I understand," her father said warmly. "It is frightening. But once you arrive, you will settle into a rhythm, and you will find...."

"No, father, that's not what I mean, I...." Distant hoofbeats pounded out the moments she struggled to explain herself. Distant hoofbeats grew louder as the rider approached, making it impossible to speak. Some messenger? She frowned. Not now, not when there was still so much to explain...

"Lord Gillingham!"

Virginia spun. It was him. Lord Braithwaite. He vaulted from his horse when it stopped and talked to her father, hand extended.

"Lord Braithwaite." Her father took the man's hand. "Forgive us; we were just saying our farewells to...."

"Lord Gillingham." Lord Braithwaite interrupted, "with your permission, I would like to call upon your daughter.

Her father blinked, and Virginia could see the thought processes behind her father's eyes. Braithwaite was a good match. He was also wealthy. He looked at his daughter as if seeing her for the first time, and perhaps he was. Eloise came and set a hand on the young Lord's arm in the stunned silence.

"Would you do the honour of taking tea with us, Lord Braithwaite?" She grinned up at him, eyes full of hope and speculation.

"Yes." Her father seemed as though he was coming out of a dream. "Yes, of course, you must come and take tea." He led Eloise to the door, giving the servants instructions to unload the carriage and unpack his daughter's trunks.

Stunned at how quickly the single action could change what a hundred pleas from herself could not, Virginia watched Lord Braithwaite with wide eyes. She started forward, ignoring both maid and governess as they dismounted from the conveyance. She paused just short of him, again struggling for what to say.

Lord Braithwaite gave her a conspiratorial smile as he paused to catch Virginia's hand. His grip felt solid and sure, as though he were trying to tell her she could count on him to make things right.

Virginia squeezed his hand in response, finding she didn't need words to say the perfect thing.

"Before we indulge," Braithwaite called after the retreating forms of her father and sister, "perhaps we can allow your people some time to readjust and unpack." He cleared his throat. "I might even be so bold as to suggest your daughter, and I might enjoy walking in the garden to get me out from underfoot?"

"I hardly think that..." her father stopped as Eloise poked his side.

"I believe that to be a splendid idea." She smiled graciously, "Sadly, Lord Gillingham and I will be required to stay and supervise the servants, so the two of you might as well proceed without us."

"Supervise?" her father looked lost. The carriage had already been relieved of the baggage, and Anna took charge of the bags. Another poke in the ribs, and her father seemed to catch on finally. "Yes. Good idea. Take your time. The tea will be kept hot."

With a giggle of relief that she could not entirely suppress, Virginia led her suitor off to the gardens before things became even more awkward. Honestly, she did not know if that were possible, but she had no wish to find out.

"How did you know I was leaving?"

He took her hand and tucked it into the crook of his elbow. It was an intimate gesture, yet it felt right, like being home. In answer, he reached into his pocket and produced a slip of foolscap. The edge of it was burned. Virginia gasped. "Your friends told me when they handed me this."

Virginia remembered the emotions she had put into the letter, intending that it never be read, and certainly not by him. She groaned and hid her face in his sleeve. "You must think me such a fool. And deservedly so. As I have said before, every time I am around you, I prove again and again how ridiculous I am."

He stopped walking and cupped her cheek in his hand. They were in a secluded copse of trees, where they could not be easily seen from the house. "It is the laughter and light that I love. Never change. Promise me that."

Virginia's eyes widened. "Love?" It came out as a whisper.

"Love." He took a breath as though preparing for some grand gesture. "Lady Gillingham, I think I may be about to kiss you."

Virginia smiled shyly. "When will you be sure?"

"Now."

And there in the garden, Lord Braithwaite showed her that he was very sure indeed.

Epilogue

For a simple wedding, it was quite elegant. The Bishop recited the vows and, on Christmas Day, announced for the first time, Lord and Lady Braithwaite. Lord Gillingham's chest was so inflated with pride. Penelope later confessed she feared his buttons would fire into the chapel like many cannonballs.

Virginia forestalled him as the ceremony ended, and Lord Braithwaite was about to take his bride in a welcomed kiss. She reached into the folds of her wedding dress. With a great flourish of pride, she produced a single red apple and offered it to her new husband.

Madeline and Selina exploded into laughter, closely following Phineas's own outburst. The Bishop seemed shocked, and her family was quite confused, but that did not matter a whit. Virginia and her groom understood, and that was all that mattered. It was not merely an apple; it was a pledge, a promise that some things would never change.

After all, she had given her word.

The End

Beholding The Lady

THE LADY SERIES BOOK TEN

Prologue

Duke Albion Weatherwax tried not to grind his teeth. If he were still a boy, he likely would have been entranced with cloak and dagger secrecy, like he had been skulking about in a dark and pungent alley, waiting at the servant's entrance like some itinerant drifter. It would have lent itself to some romantic ideal. But that child was grown and the man he'd become grew more and more irritated as the night wore on.

Somewhere, a dog barked. Cats chased rats around the shadows. The utilitarian side of the great house was built to be hidden from the grand, sweeping entrance of the main estate, and from the footmen in their pressed livery awaiting orders. The chill night air seeped past his overcoat and turned-up collar. Instead of keeping the breeze off his neck, it only seemed to catch the chill and funnel it downwards.

He cursed himself once more for being there. No, for the weakness he exhibited by agreeing to meet like this. He was a Duke, a strong, capable man who was used to commanding men of rank and commerce. And yet, here he was, with his Achille's heel. His own vulnerability demanded that he hide in the dark at the servant's entrance, and he hated himself for it.

He had decided on leaving. Not for the first time – his good sense told him, before he even got here, that this was a bad idea. He'd ignored these thoughts at first. But no longer. This time, he forced his feet to begin their journey back to his carriage and to his own warm home on the Square, when the door to the kitchen finally creaked and the flickering light of a single candle bravely shone out through the opening.

"You received my note." Her voice was the dulcet sweetness that wove its way into his mind and turned off his resolve.

He stamped down his reaction. It was no longer proper to have. "I am not in the habit of standing in alleyways in the middle of the night." He knew he was taking out his frustrations on her, but she *was* the cause, so he couldn't feel overly guilty about it.

"I know...my Lord." She wore a cloak with a hood, pulled up over her head. Had he not recognized her voice, he would not have known her for the Lady of the house. That was likely the point. She was protecting herself, a skill she had developed well since he had come to know her. "Thank you for seeing me. I would not have asked you here..."

"Asked?" Duke Weatherwax sniffed at the word. "I believe the word you are seeking is 'summoned'."

The hood dipped a bit as she lowered her head. He could imagine her biting her lip. It was something she did, one of those little habits no one would ever notice, unless they had been staring longingly into her face for a considerable time. "I fear discretion is a higher priority than politeness, my Lord. And in my case, desperation." She raised her head a little, enough so he could look into her eyes. The deepest blue that caught the glow from candlelight. She had captured her lower lip between her teeth and now regarded him with naked fear. "Please, my Lord. I need your help, or I shall be ruined."

"And you ask me to risk my own ruin to save yours?" Weatherwax took a deep breath. "If I am caught, the scandal would not be survivable. My family name would be taken through the mud, and the disgrace..."

"I know I have no right to ask it of you," her hand, that wasn't holding the candle, slid out from under the cloak and alighted on his chest. It was pale and delicate, long fingers splayed over his coat. At one time, he would have longed for the material between them to be gone, to feel her light touch on his skin. "But I ask it anyway."

Weatherwax opened his mouth to tell her that she was where she had led herself, it was no one's fault but hers, that maybe she *deserved* the situation in which she found herself. But somewhere, the words twisted, and he found himself trapped under that light touch.

"There is a ball..."

"Yes, although...under the circumstances, I have not had a formal invitation."

"I should think not." The Duke paused. As soon as he committed, her hand would be taken away and he would be in the cold and dark once more. "I will devise an excuse. Are you sure of its location?"

"I am told. My lady's maid has befriended a footman there and..." she let the rest drop off as her hand fell. His chest felt hollow, as though she had taken some part of his heart with her.

"I will inform you of my success." He nodded to her, "or the ton will speak of my failure. I expect your husband, my *dearest friend...* would have words as well."

She smiled then, a radiant smile she reserved for those occasions when she got her way. She smiled that way often. She stood on tiptoes and kissed his cheek. It was warm and soft and moist, and he lay his hand over it to keep the night air from erasing the feeling. "I shall make this up to you," she whispered.

She had used desire against him once. He would no longer allow it. Not at the risk of Doringham's happiness. He reminded himself the only reason he had come on this errand was for him. Not her. Never her.

He took a step back, ignoring the softness of whatever was beneath his bootheel. "The hour is late, my Lady." His voice sounded thick and heavy, as though every word had to be wrung out. "You should return to your husband."

She pulled the hood over her head again and turned to the darkness of the doorway, then slipped through. The door closed behind her, isolating him in the darkness as the only light was taken away.

I am a great fool.

Duke Albion Weatherwax began the long walk back to his estate.

It was going to be a chilly night.

Chapter One

The music swelled and dropped and rose again. Gentlemen in tails escorted ladies in brilliantly coloured dresses in a promenade across the dance floor as they spun and swirled. Rustling of skirts were like whispers, which spun moments after their dancers did. Anna Gillingham smiled from the edges of the throng, loving the multicoloured display and the music, even if the night was proving to be trying in other ways.

With little else to do than watch, she listened to the gossip, for what would these affairs be without the stories passed from one individual to another? Such things appealed to her romantic soul and became the inspiration for the stories she penned in secret for her own amusement.

Tonight, the conversation among those who talked rather than danced was almost entirely about the unexpected appearance of one Duke Albion Weatherwax. Apparently, he had attended, though Anna had not seen him herself. It was a rare occasion that was graced by his company, and she was eager to get a glimpse of the most eligible bachelor of the ton.

Unfortunately, there was little else being said. Boredom threatened her evening. The true focus of the ball was lovely, and the movement and music filled the hall, and for a time, Anna lost herself in the motion. Her dance card had but a single entry and that one was already done. It should have been enough to watch, there was an appealing ascetic to the motion, but Anna was ill-suited to being a wallflower. It was no help that she had three sisters who were all contentedly married and the burden of a finding suitable match now hovered over her.

Her oldest sister, who had brought her out, was most insistent that she mingle, dance, and find a match, but what was she to do? Was she expected to ask a man to dance with her when no one seemed interested in asking her himself? Was she expected to declare herself to a gentleman? This was beyond her control, was it not? If she was somehow invisible, no one saw her, it was not because she tried to blend into the walls.

Not for the first time, she wondered if she was simply not pretty enough. As evidenced by their matches, her sisters were, but looks often skipped someone here and there. She had excelled in social graces, her musical acumen was accomplished, but none of those qualities would be seen unless a suitor inquired, and so far none ever had.

"You are too retiring..." her sister Virginia would tell her, but that was all well and good for someone like her older sister, who craved excitement and drew adventure around her like a cloak. She had never wanted for partners. Ever. Much like that of her beautiful mother who Anna barely got to know before she died. She had heard enough stories about her mother who had been much sought after in her youth. And though they didn't particularly want partners for a time, her sisters seemed happy now.

Enough. You cannot be them, any more than they can become you. Perhaps a breath of air, then try again...

It was a rare moment where she had some time to herself. She found herself away from the close disapproving scrutiny of her sister's eyes and slipped back behind some potted plants near the large doors leading to the gardens. She considered making a journey to the punch bowl, but that was where she was caught last time and thrust into the single dance she had so far. Apparently, her sister considered it important that she be seen dancing. But to be on the floor with a young man of little rank and a habitual sniff seemed worse than anonymity in Anna's eyes.

It would not be long before either of her sisters would spy her quietly hiding and force her back into the ball. She looked for an escape, but leaving the room entailed interacting with servants, explaining oneself. Furthermore, where would she go?

The view from the doors behind her spoke of trimmed gardens and ornate benches. Anna gradually backed to the door, her eyes resolute on the dancers, she watched carefully for some well-meaning soul to ruin her escape. She felt the knob in her back and reached behind her blindly. The door was unlocked! She slipped through into the gathering darkness and closed the door quietly behind her, fearing the whispered *click* as the latch caught would attract unwanted attention.

She ran from the door, lest she be found so close to her escape. Once free of being seen, she leaned against the stone wall and listened for a moment to the strains of the music from afar.

The night was becoming chill as the heat-soaked ground cooled. Anna began to feel better between the darkness and the cool, at least marginally. She took herself in hand and braced her shoulders. It was time, more than time, to re-join the festivities. Even should she remain invisible, she must at least be able to truthfully tell her sister that she attempted to be cordial.

She stepped back through the door, taking care to not be seen on the wrong side of the glass and twisted the knob. To her horror, it refused to turn. She was locked out in the garden. To tap on the glass and await some kind soul to allow her back in was, to say the least, embarrassing. Though, she feared, perhaps it might even be considered scandalous if speculation about her activities or certain trysts should arise.

It was far safer to find another entrance. If memory served, there was another set of doors on the west end of the ballroom.

Sadly, she couldn't tell which way was west. The sun had set, and from where she stood in the garden, it was difficult to see any landmarks to indicate direction. Those doors were either to the left or right from where she stood. It should be easy enough to ascertain. One only needed to pick a direction.

She backed away from the door and headed to the right, assuming that was as good of a guess as any. An unbroken stone wall was her guide as she ran her fingers over the rough surface. Her dancing slippers were hardly the best choice for walking across the lawn, but her hand soon found another glass door and after a moment, a knob. The window was covered by a drapery of some sort, but she could still faintly hear the music. Perhaps the drape had been drawn to block out an unpleasant view or the setting sun's glare? No matter. This one turned easily.

Only this door wasn't leading into the ballroom. It seemed she was in a study of sorts. There was little light, only the fading glow from a banked fire. She was about to head out of the room and return to the ball, claiming she'd gotten lost when a tearing sound caught her ear.

She followed the sound to another room, an Annexe or closet to the study, some sort of more private chamber she supposed. There, under the light of a single candle, a man dressed like a gentleman had a knife to a painting. He was not defacing it, so much as cutting it free of the frame and rolling it up. Anna only saw a glimpse of the picture, but what she saw was quite revealing.

This was very definitely a private chamber, not meant for the ton's prying eyes.

"I beg your pardon," she spoke without thinking, she was so startled to see him there.

The gentleman spun, the knife in his hand. She gasped in fear, but he quickly held up the knife and set it on a nearby table. "Forgive me Lady, you but startled me. I mean you no harm."

Anna's heart raced, but he spoke well, and he had disarmed himself. "What..." she fought to regain control of her speech. "What are you about, Sir?"

"I..." He looked at the roll in his hand and the candle burning on the table beside the glow of the knife.

"You...you are Duke Albion Weatherwax." It wasn't a question. She recognized him from the whispered gossip that had accompanied him into the ballroom. But the question of what he was doing there, with *that* painting, was yet to be answered.

He seemed to draw himself up as if naming him had startled some inborn pride. "I have that honour," he answered stiffly. "And may I ask the pleasure of your name?"

"Anna...that is, Lady Anna Gillingham."

They stared at one another.

"I confess that this does not look good, m'Lady, but I assure you there is a noble cause behind my actions." She cocked an eyebrow and waited. He sighed and partially unrolled the painting. A beautiful woman stared back at Anna, her expression one of resolution and a touch of haughtiness. Her shoulders were bare, Anna had caught a glimpse of the woman in the painting before the Duke rolled it up. She was wearing very little indeed. A diaphanous drape of thin fabric carefully placed over a few areas was the extent of her modesty. He rolled the painting again.

"I am acting in the best interests of the Lady in question. In her youth, in an act of rebellion and fuelled by bad advice, she posed for this portrait, and now..."

"...now she wishes to erase that mistake?"

He nodded once. "Indeed. And I seem to have been elected to be her champion. Our good host has secreted this away upon future maliciousness. So, I have become..." he shrugged as if looking for a better term and not finding it, "...an art thief."

The words brought images to Anna, aromatized accounts of daring-do with rakish gallants who charm those from whom they steal. She looked over her shoulder briefly, half certain that a crowd had already gathered. To be caught with a man unchaperoned could ruin her, but to be so caught with a thief would destroy her and her family. She had no business being here, and if she had any sense at all, she would flee now before it was too late.

To her surprise, something quite different slipped out when she spoke. "How can I help?"

He shook his head, but before he could deny her the opportunity to play in the world of intrigue, she ploughed on. "You are the topic of conversation at the ball. All eyes are fixated on you. Do you honestly believe you can simply walk out with that large flag under your arm unnoticed?"

"In truth," the Duke said slowly, "I had planned on leaving the way you came in."

"And walk around the house during a ball without being seen?" Anna scoffed. "Please, Sir. Leave it to me. I will see to it there is sufficient distraction, that you might make your escape in true safety."

He stared at her for a long moment, the length bordering on rude, before he asked a single word, "Why?"

"Because..." Anna thought for a moment. Perhaps the real reason was that the Duke was devilishly handsome and seemed to have charm. Some of the reason was because he was risking his good name for an honourable act. Mostly, if she was honest with herself, it sounded like great fun, the sort of adventure one read about in stories. She wanted to live a tale for once, instead of read or even write one.

"For the Lady's sake." She pointed at the painting in his hand. "And because I do not like the idea of anyone using a moment's regretful mistake against her for who knows how long." She held up her hand. "But mostly Sir, because you have little other choice."

He actually smiled at that. "What have you in mind?"

She turned and crossed the office to the door. Cracking it open, she turned to see the Duke behind her, candle extinguished, painting crushed in his hand. She whispered, "a footman is standing at the door to the ball room. Once he heads into the room, you can be assured that the others will be otherwise occupied. That is when you must make your exit."

"But..."

Whatever protest he had was lost on her. Anna was no longer listening. She returned to the door she used to enter the room and followed the wall again, retracing her steps.

She came back to the bright light door and the music leaked out from within. She tested the knob again. As she thought, it was still locked. She took a deep breath. *You can do this. Be more than an observer of the stories. Become part of one.*

She screamed. Loud. Agonizing. As blood-curdling a scream as she could manage.

Anna Gillingham fell against the door, her body weight pressing it closed, and pretended to faint.

As the guests and the servants rushed to her aid, she pictured the Duke's exit. It would be a triumph of deceit and derring-do. A single figure walks through the house, a canvas roll under one arm. And no one else would know but her.

Chapter Two

"How embarrassing." Virginia tutted from the settee. "Fainting, I suppose I can understand, but the scream? Whatever on earth?"

"As I said, I was certain they had released the dogs."

"During a ball?" Eloise graced her with an arched eyebrow, indicating her idea of such a thought. "You must not have been thinking clearly."

"Leave your sister alone," their aunt said reprovingly, though she did not glance up from the needlepoint on her lap, which she had brought for her visit. "She has been through a great deal and needs her rest."

"I apologize." For her part, Virginia did sound contrite. "I should have panicked myself too, were I under the impression that I was to be attacked by dogs. But what was it you saw that convinced you that they were at large?"

Anna shrugged. "I cannot say, not for certain. Something was moving in the shadows. Perhaps it was a stray dog? I cannot be sure, I only know that my mind put me in mortal danger."

"Good thing you weren't," Eloise shook her head. "When you fainted, you fell against the door. A footman had to run around the house to get to you as you had sufficiently blocked the door."

"I regret being a burden," Anna couldn't keep the bitterness out of her voice, "or an embarrassment." That last was directed at Virginia.

"Nonsense, dear. I have heard little but sympathy for your plight. No one is holding it against you." Her aunt set down the needlepoint to address her directly. "It might, in fact, be helpful in the long run. You currently have the ton's attention, in a good way, I mean. We must use this time to make a good match for you, while you are still..."

"...visible?" Anna finished for her.

"I was about to say, 'popular'," Lady Gillingham said quietly, "but, yes, I suppose 'visible' might be accurate. You've made a practice out of hiding, don't deny it. The efforts are quite obvious."

Anna felt her back going up, but she held her tongue and tempered her mood down harshly. Perhaps her aunt's words would not have upset her had they not been so spot-on.

Her mind found refuge in the memory of the previous night. The Duke, standing in the dark room, the single candle brilliantly illuminating his eyes. His square jaw, wide shoulders, and somewhat heroic intentions. He was handsome to say the least and moved with confidence. She had seen him enter the ballroom at the beginning of the evening, it was as though there was little enough room for him even in the largest spaces.

His smile, on the other hand, was self-effacing and generous. It was no wonder he was the talk of the town. Every mother at the ball had aimed their eligible daughters at him, and the young ladies, by and large, had no objection. He had title and wealth and was devilishly handsome.

The fact that she had been able to lend him some assistance, no matter how slight, felt as though she and he were a team for a moment. It was as close as she was likely to get, but it was a memory that she could cherish for a lifetime.

As much as her family considered her actions during the ball remarkable, the ton spoke of little else but the rare appearance of Weatherwax and his even stranger disappearance later that night. It seemed he left without saying a proper goodbye to his host, a generally rude gesture, but for a Duke, some niceties are forgiven.

It was assumed that he left during the excitement, that is to say, Anna's demonstration. Perhaps he simply was lost in the excitement of the evening, and he had made his goodbyes. Still, others were too preoccupied to have noticed.

On the other hand, Anna could not imagine a world where someone such as Weatherwax could be forgotten. Anna Gillingham might have been invisible, on the edge of the dance floor, along with an empty dance card, but the Duke? Unlikely.

In the moment of silence, a footman entered the room discreetly, a silver tray in his hands.

Anna could see the form of a letter set on the tray and breathed a sigh of relief. A letter with other news might be just the fodder her sisters needed to drop the topic and allow Anna a moment's respite from their matchmaking efforts. It might also give her sisters someone else to talk about. Whomever the letter concerned, its appearance meant her cross-examination was over. But her eyes grew wide with surprise when the footman walked past her aunt and both of her sisters and presented the tray to her.

Laying in the middle of the tray, the bright white envelope held but three words in a flowing hand that was as eloquent as it was legible: *Lady Anna Gillingham.* She broke the wax seal and unfolded the parchment carefully.

"Well?" Virginia's inquiry made Anna suddenly realize that she had been staring open-mouthed at the letter for too long. "He...he wants to call on me." She reread it for the twentieth time thinking there had to be a mistake.

"WHO?" Virginia gasped and snatched the paper from her sister's hand. Anna was still in too much shock to object. "Oh my goodness! It appears that Duke Weatherwax has developed an interest in our little sister." She waved the paper towards Eloise who snatched it to read it just as carefully.

"So it has. Aunt Alicia, it would seem as though fate has taken advantage of the moment, as you said." She looked to Anna with a certain amount of respect, something her little sister had never seen in a glance from her before. "He says he's coming today. This very afternoon!"

"Anna!" Her aunt shot to her feet, the needlepoint clattering to the floor. "Quickly, go up and change."

"Change?" Anna looked down at the dress she wore. It was a bright, powder blue and though not fancy, it was serviceable, why would she...

"Come along!" Virginia grabbed her hand and dragged her from the room, giggling like she were a girl again, and not a married woman who was about to become a mother.

"What is happening?" Andrew stepped aside as his sisters nearly ran over him at the last moment.

"Duke Weatherwax is coming to pay respects to your sister," Aunt Alicia beamed, as though she had engineered the whole thing herself.

"Oh." Andrew shrugged and proceeded on his way through the house, clearly not caring.

"Well," Eloise giggled from the pianoforte, "that certainly puts the matter into perspective."

Chapter Three

The infamous Duke Weatherwax, the most eligible catch of the year, was actually sitting in her drawing-room with her aunt and sisters and looking as uncomfortable as Anna felt. He was gracious and charming, certainly, but he had the look of a man waiting for his wife to finish her dress fitting.

The tea was cooling on the tray, forgotten all but for an obligatory sip. The tray of cakes her aunt had panicked to be sure were served had been left uneaten.

Virginia had chosen the gown, a bright number that showed off Anna's complexion, and she also insisted on directing while her lady's maid styled Anna's hair. Then, it had to be redone as it looked too much of a styling meant for a ball, when she was supposed to have been lounging at home awaiting callers.

By the time her sister had declared her fit for company, the company in question had already arrived and was chatting in the drawing-room under her other sisters and Aunt Alicia's close scrutiny. Even Andrew had chosen that opportunity to prove he was grown up and no longer attended to frivolous games. Mainly, he wanted to hang about, eat cake, and wait to see what would happen next.

Anna was presented as she walked in, her aunt's smile seemed to be plastered onto her face. While she was genuinely pleased with such august interest in her niece, she was also confused at its suddenness, especially considering the report which she had been given regarding the previous night's ball. That was true for Anna as well, but smiling was not the first thing that occurred to her.

"Lady Gillingham." The Duke bowed as the introductions were made.

Anna curtsied and rose. He was as handsome as she remembered, even more so in sufficient light. "Lord Weatherwax," she breathed. "What...what are you doing here?"

"Anna!" her aunt sounded shocked and her sisters each tittered with nervous laughter.

"No, my Lady." The Duke nodded towards Aunt Alicia in reassurance that he was not offended, before returning his attention to Anna. "That is an excellent question and well asked. I have been out of the public eye for some time, and I have broken that silence with last night's ball. I can only assume that I would have called sooner if I had been so graced with meeting your daughter previously."

"Please," Anna waved to the setae he had just vacated. "Do not stand on my account." She dropped into a chair across from her aunt and the Duke. Eloise perched on the other side of him and Anna felt for the gentleman, trapped as he was between her inquisitive family members. There was a protracted moment of silence as they all waited for someone else to begin the conversation. Anna searched the Duke's face for some clue as to the reason he arrived.

Had they been found out? The painting missed? Had someone seen them after all? They were together in a dark room without an escort after all. Also, he was a thief, regardless of the nobility of the motivation, and she was his accomplice. It only just occurred to her that she risked more than a scandal. Her family really could be ruined if the events of the previous evening were to be made public.

"So, my Lord Duke." Her aunt broke the silence, "you say you have been absent. Do I take that to mean you have been away from London?"

It was a polite question only. The entire ton knew he had been away from London. What they did not know was why.

"Indeed." Weatherwax nodded stiffly. "I have spent some time in the

Americas. I have several interests there, including tobacco. I most recently stayed for a time in New York."

"That sounds...exciting." Virginia prompted. She sat on the edge of the bench at the pianoforte, which Eloise had abandoned as though she were waiting for someone to suggest she play. Anna said a silent prayer that no one would.

The trepidation was building in her until she thought she might burst from it. *Had* they been caught? To her knowledge, there was no report of a missing painting or any other theft, for that news would have gone through the ton like wildfire. She imagined all sorts of tragedy: the owner finding out and blackmailing them both, the Lady in the painting having been found out. Would she blame Anna for talking? Would she blame her for being exposed? Anna winced, *Perhaps there is a better word I should use instead of 'exposed'?*

"I do not believe you have answered my inquiry, my Lord." The words burst from her of their own accord. Had she kept them down, she would have choked on them. They would have poisoned her with fears both real and imagined. It was, perhaps, unfortunate that they came forth, as Virginia spoke of their older sister Penelope and her husband's more recent journey to the Continent.

"Anna," her aunt said through clenched teeth, "I believe the Duke has answered the question." Her tone was a warning, one she felt Anna needed to heed.

"To be blunt then, Lady Gillingham," the Duke smiled in a way that he meant to be reassuring, "I have come to call upon you today, because, frankly, I have been quite captured by you."

"Do you mean 'captivated by her charms'?" Eloise said in such a salacious way her aunt's shocked expression turned from Anna to her.

"Forgive me," the Duke interrupted smoothly. "I fear I have spent too much time on the Continent. I seem to have forgotten much of the common courtesy and manners, not to mention proper verbiage."

Much to Anna's shock, the look in his eyes suggested that he meant exactly what he said, and little else. Was that true then? He found her attractive because she had screamed and fainted? Was their little shared deception somehow attractive to him?

For the first time since sitting down, she began to dare that his visit was just as he suggested. That he was indeed calling on her as a gentleman...as a suitor. She sat in silence for the end of the interview, too stunned to speak.

"Anna!"

At her aunt's crisp call, Anna snapped back into the present. She realized she'd missed most of the conversation. "I'm sorry?"

"I was saying it would be my honour to offer you a ride tomorrow afternoon. I have an open carriage. Perhaps through the park?"

Anna looked from one face to another, wondering just how she was expected to answer this unexpected invitation. "Thank you, my Lord Duke. I would enjoy that." Of course. That would give them enough privacy for him to talk to her about his *real* reason for calling on her, away from the probing ears of her family. So, it hadn't been because her breathless beauty infatuated him. She snorted at her own naivete for believing otherwise.

Weatherwax politely and firmly refused to stay for a meal and left the women to themselves. As he was escorted out, her aunt and sisters turned to her as though their heads were all connected to the same control. Weatherwax hesitated in the hall for a moment long enough to catch sight of Anna. When their eyes met, her heart skipped a beat.

"Andrew," her aunt said without looking at the young man. "Leave us."

Andrew knew when he was outnumbered and fled, though he was too much of a man to show it. He strode quickly from the room with a defiant swagger. Anna would have laughed if she had been less under scrutiny.

"Well?" Virginia asked.

"What?"

"Do not feign innocence, dear sister," Eloise taunted with a shake of her head. "Just what was all that about?"

Chapter Four

"I must say, I have seen buzzards with a warmer smile," Duke Weatherwax mumbled to himself, as he shuffled in his seat under the close scrutiny of Anna's maid. Even from the length of the drive, he could feel the woman's gaze bore into his carriage. *Then there was Anna*, the Duke smiled. She looked so lovely and kind beside her maid, like the first welcome songbird of spring. Having an escort seemed foolish to Anna. After all, they would be in public, an open carriage, in plain view of the entire city. What could be a better escort than the entirety of London?

Well, Mrs. Wallace was certainly intending to do her duty as chaperone. She was indeed a formidable presence. She stared out at the scenery, her expression much like a guard dog who must accept a stranger in her midst. She'd taken on that look after Anna had told her in confidence about her role in the theft at the ball. A decision she knew would be kept safe in the clutches of her trusted confidant. But a decision Anna instantly regretted as the old woman now looked at her charge with the same peptic disapproval, as she saw the Duke's carriage approach.

The Duke held out both hands to welcome his guests.

"Do not worry about Mrs. Wallace, she is in my full confidence. We can speak plainly between ourselves," Anna said as she settled into her seat.

The Duke looked startled at that proclamation. He regarded Mrs. Wallace with some trepidation but was only answered with another sour glare. "Effective chaperone," he nodded and touched the brim of his hat to the maid. To Anna, he added in an undertone, "I suggest we not speak overly freely. Unlike the redoubtable Mrs. Wallace, my driver is *not* fully in my confidence. Anna glanced at the man who deftly guided the horses into the park and nodded. She would be careful.

"So tell me," Anna asked in a low voice once they were underway. "Why *did* you come to call on me? I am certainly no great beauty to be won."

"Quite the contrary," he said, a bit stunned. *Did she not know her own beauty?* "You are inarguably beautiful. Though you are correct in thinking there is an ulterior motive." He considered her watchful stare. "Quite frankly, Lady Gillingham, I owe you."

Anna waved that off. "I enjoyed the performance."

"But you risked much. I owe you for that."

"'Owe me', Your Grace?" The phrase left her uncomfortable. She was not sure she liked the idea of a Duke owing her a favour.

"I have done some...research on you and your family since..." he looked at the sour continence of Mrs. Wallace and continued under his breath, "since that night. You come from a moderate if well-respected family of middling prospects."

"Oh really?" Anna shifted in her seat. Her initial wonder at being shown off for all to see in the Duke's carriage was wearing off, and she was sorely tempted to join in Mrs. Wallace's opinion of the afternoon's proceedings. She had two sisters who had made quite a success in the matches they'd made. 'Middling prospects' felt somewhat unfair.

"Meaning no offence, of course," Dyke Weatherwax continued blithely. "Certainly, your sisters married well, and your father is by no means poor. But even you have to admit that your venerated family has done nothing to stir in society, which is precisely why you have a perpetually empty dance card."

"Driver, take me home!" Anna snapped at the driver. Mrs. Wallace was looking less sour and more like a guard dog who was going to slip its leash and take a good chomp from the Duke. Anna could even fancy she heard the woman growl.

"Miss Gillingham," the Duke lowered his voice, "do not be upset. There is no shame in being average and I certainly do not mean it as an insult. But the fact that you are without many prospects, despite your noble and notable family, cannot be denied. However, what is it every man wants?" He paused for effect, but as Anna refused to face him or involve in such speculation, he continued. "He wants that he cannot have. Your prospects should increase exponentially, to be publicly seen with me, with me calling on you."

"Indeed?" Anna's voice could have frozen open flames.

"It is the nature of the ton. This is not arrogance, this is reciprocation. You have done a good turn for me, and I do one for you in return."

"By *allowing* me to be seen in your presence." Anna stared at him in disbelief. "By *pretending* that...that you could be interested in someone so...non-descript? How noble."

"You seem to not understand, my Lady. I mean no insult to you or your family. Nor do I set myself to such lofty standards. It is an indisputable fact that..."

"*TAKE ME HOME!*" Anna bit off each word, doing all she could not to scream the words. Mrs. Wallace shifted in her seat and Anna leapt to sit beside the older woman. Duke or not, the maid looked as if she would gladly tear into the man with little or no provocation.

"Miss Gillingham..." The Duke looked as though she had spat in his face, and she was sorely tempted.

"After all we have been through, the risks shared, you think that it will all come out even because you were kind enough to give me a *carriage ride*?"

Duke Weatherwax continued in silence. He stared at the passing rows of houses and the finely dressed crowd promenading on the paths, enjoying the warm spring air. "You are correct, I suppose." He seemed to be speaking to himself more than to her. "A single carriage ride is not likely to change much, though I daresay there will be some new attention." He tried to ignore the glare from the maid, though Anna did see him do a double-take, seemingly shocked by the intensity of the glare. A hundred years ago, looking at a Duke that way could have gotten her jailed. Even now, she certainly risked her job if she insulted him so publicly.

"I am sorry if I have misspoken, but you cannot deny any of the salient points in my argument. I have only recited facts, and those that are well known. I am offering my assistance in your case, Lady Gillingham, this is not charity if that is what bothers you. I do owe you a favour."

"You owe me *nothing*, Your Grace." It was difficult to talk over the pressure behind her eyes. The tears were desperate to fall, but she would not give him the satisfaction.

"I can see your point, however." The Duke continued as if he had not heard her. "A single ride in a carriage, no matter how public is not sufficient for our purpose. Therefore, I shall ask your permission to court you, at least for appearance's sake. That should enlarge your prospects a great deal." He felt a new sense of excitement and purpose at this idea.

"I must ask, Your Grace, is there room for anyone else to compliment you?" Anna penned aloud. "Or have you taken all the accolades for yourself already. I daresay you deprive us mere mortals unable to fit an accolade in with your ego. I do not know where you have found this enlarged perception of yourself, but let me assure you, I have neither need nor desire for your assistance in finding someone who would accept the likes of *me*!"

"That is not..."

The carriage arrived at the front of the house and Anna practically leaped out, alighting before the driver or a footman was there to offer her hand. Her maid followed with all the speed of her mistress if not the grace. The Duke remained half seated, a look of pure confusion on his face at how exactly this turn of events had come about. He would not have been more shocked if Anna had sprouted wings and flown away.

Anna ran up the steps, barely clearing the door as she lifted her skirts, up the steps, and headed to her room.

"Anna?" She ignored her aunt's concern and flew into her room and fell upon her bed. The tears she had been holding back with such great effort burst from her eyes, and she gulped air between sobs.

Her aunt came in to comfort her but could get no sense from the distraught girl. Mrs. Wallace assured her that Anna was neither harmed nor molested but admitted that the ride had not lived up to Anna's expectations. She refused to elaborate further, proving Anna's confidence in her.

It was nearly an hour before she could gather herself and rose again, exhausted and drained. It was near time for dinner, and she would have to explain to her aunt what caused the tears. Anna pouted at her table, idly tossing aside brushes and combs.

"You are awake, my Lady." Mrs. Wallace breezed into the room. She walked to her charge without preamble and began fixing her hair. Her own maid was slightly better at hair, but Mrs. Wallace was a comforting presence and her touch was soothing.

"Thank you," Anna said softly. "For everything." She stared at her reflection, at the heightened colour in her cheeks. Even now, he left her an unseemly mess. "The arrogance of the man!"

"It did sound that way, didn't it?" Mrs. Wallace took out the remaining pins from Anna's hair and grabbed the brush.

"You did not think so?"

The older woman shrugged as she concentrated on Anna's hair. "There is modesty and false modesty, my Lady. He might have a high opinion of himself, but that does not mean he is wrong. It does seem that interest generates interest. Perhaps he has a point?"

"What? That we are, that *I* am...average?"

"That is not an insult, my Lady. You come from an honourable, respectable house." She set down the brush for a moment. "With all due respect," she hesitated, "though I know it is not my place, but I know that your father puts some pressure on you to find a suitable match. You might take advantage of the Duke's offer."

Anna turned around to stare at her.

"Now, do not give me that wounded look, my Lady. I know he was rude and he vexed you. But consider that perhaps it is a little different from your aunt's efforts or your sisters. And a Duke should know some very fine prospects indeed."

"And if he thought so much of my chances, why..."

Mrs. Wallace nodded sagely. "I see. Turn around now and I'll finish your hair."

"What do you see?"

The brush caressed her head again and the tender grasp on her hair soothed her once more. "You are most upset because none of the prospective suitors are the Duke himself."

Anna tilted her head to allow the long strokes on her hair. "Maybe." It was true. Maybe, what upset her most was the business-like arrangement, so callous and cold. Yet, if the Duke had no romantic interest in her, assisting in a good match that would please the family was actually a decent thing.

Anna looked into the mirror and the resolve she felt stared back at her.

"Very well," Anna said softly, though she could not have said if she were talking to her maid or her reflection.

Chapter Five

"And where is your formidable maid?"

Anna felt a chill down her spine. Could she go nowhere without running into Duke Weatherwax? This was a tea, a handful of people, most of whom she did not know, but it was a small, intimate gathering, not a fancy ball. Yet, the one person the ton had written off as a recluse was here as well. She realised he was here for her sake, paying off his imaginary debt for the spectacle she had made of herself that night at the ball.

She turned and sure enough, he stood behind her. His eyes scanning the grounds as the guests walked among the flowers. It was an excuse to be seen, to be noticed. It told the rest of high society that one was still viable and still important. It also allowed the ladies to show off their new dresses and occasionally new suitors.

That was the one thing Anna had no interest in, parading before the ton.

"I did not expect to see you here today, Your Grace."

"If we are to cause a stir, then we must be seen, and often." The Duke nodded to her as if he were absolutely delighted to be in her company. "Unless you were in earnest about refusing my assistance?"

"Upon hindsight, I believe that I will accept your assistance, Your

Grace." She paused for just a half-second before adding, "Whatever it might be worth."

The Duke grinned at the jibe. "Some would say it was worth a great deal."

Anna walked a few steps and turned. "Are you coming with me, or is this a fake long-distance relationship?"

Weatherwax happily caught up to her and they began a tour of the garden. Oddly enough, she began to enjoy herself.

Anna had been raised on flowers and blooming plants. It was the basic education for a well-bred young lady, but she had expanded her knowledge far beyond such frivolity. While the Duke was rather less educated in flora, he was exceedingly well-read and very intelligent. Anna fell into the conversation, ranging from politics to business to exciting scientific advances reported in the papers.

It was simply easy to be with him and they seemed to fall into a pattern. Even their silences were compatible.

"I suppose that a false relationship should include false escorting," Anna said as they took a turn in the pathway and were momentarily alone. She slipped her hand into the crook of his elbow.

Weatherwax glanced at her hand and smiled, lifting his arm to cradle her hand. His eyebrow shot up at the gesture and if he was about to object or approve, he did not get the chance before a soft, lilting voice called, "My Lord Duke. How pleasant."

Anna fought the urge to unhand him, as if caught with her hand where it should not be. It was, after all, the illusion she was here for was it not? She turned to the sound of the newcomer and nearly swallowed her greeting. She recognized the face of the woman in the painting. She was as beautiful as the painting would have her. No. In fact the painter did not do her justice. It was difficult to not see her draped in a soft diaphanous fabric and for balance she squeezed the Duke's arm to steady herself.

"Lady Doringham. May I present Lady Gillingham." The Duke seemed to be embarrassed as well. He placed his hand on Anna's as if they were having an intimate moment. Anna could see the reaction in the widening of Lady Doringham's eyes, though she did her best to remain cordial.

"Duke Weatherwax, you remember my husband, Lord Doring-ham." The bold gentleman with her thrust out his hand and the two men shook.

"Weatherwax," Doringham smiled, "My wife tells me you have recently come from New York."

"Indeed, Sir." The Duke was cordial but stiff. It was like watching two roosters in a farmyard, though Anna could have sworn there was a familiar tone to their conversation, as if they knew each other quite well.

"I hail from Boston, recently converted to this country by way of a distant relation who left me an estate here along with some nuisance of a title. Abigail here wanted to live in London," Lord Doringham said to Anna, including her in the conversation.

"You will have to forgive me, but I do not remember your family." Lady Doringham turned an upraised eyebrow, not to Anna, but to the hand that held hers.

"Forgive me, this is Lady Anna Gillingham," Weatherwax said. "The daughter of Lord Theodore Gillingham. Her sister Virginia recently wed the Viscount Braithwaite. Lady Gillingham, Lord and Lady Doringham are dear friends of mine. Lady Doringham is the daughter of Earl Weston."

Lady Doringham blinked as though the phrase 'dear friend' was not entirely that which she would have used to define their relationship. If anything, she seemed as though she might argue the point, were she not in her husband's company.

Well. Obviously, I am doing the Duke a service as well, this season. He appears to be wishing to make the Lady jealous. Anna wondered how she felt about that.

Still, Anna wasn't above playing a part. Had she not already proved this? She leaned into the Duke's shoulder as though the two of them had an arrangement. The move was not lost on Lady Doringham.

"You must come by sometime and tell us about your travels," Lord Doringham was saying, "I have not been to New York in a long time and I would love to hear how it is now."

"Yes..." Lady Doringham tore her eyes off of Anna and set her gaze on the Duke. "Both of you must come to dinner. I insist." The tone belied the words, but her husband seemed oblivious to the intonation.

As the Doringhams wandered off, Lady Doringham threw a look over her shoulder at them. Anna smiled and grasped the Duke's arm tighter and stared up into his face longingly just to make the point. It was a ridiculous pose but served the purpose well, for the Lady's face darkened with barely suppressed rage.

"What are you playing at?" The Duke hissed.

"Me?" Anna purred with the smile plastered hard on her face. "I am not the one with the noble goal of making a married woman jealous."

"How dare you!" The Duke would have made to pull away, but Anna held on.

"I mean no offence, this is just verifiable fact. I am here to help you as you have helped me."

Weatherwax was silent for a moment and when he spoke it was with a heavy voice. "I suppose I am a great fool. There was a time..." he stopped himself and shook his head. He covered her hand with his again and led them down the path, following the Doringhams.

"Tell me," Anna asked quietly. "Where is the painting now? Has Mr. Doringham seen it? He might actually enjoy it, as it is a remarkable likeness."

"That is none of your business. And no, he has not. Nor shall he."

"So," Anna laughed as though he had just said something entertaining. "Despite all your protestation of assisting me to make a match, you are using me to make her, a *married* her, jealous."

His grip tightened on her hand, he looked at her painfully. "I have kept my word. Have you not found yourself fielding multiple requests from eligible members of the ton who had not previously noted your existence? In the course of the last week, I would suspect you have had several invitations by now."

Anna walked in silence for a few steps. It was true. There were invitations and requests from several young men who had previously ignored her. Admitting it to herself was bad enough, but to confess it to the Duke...no.

"How long must this charade last?"

The Duke released her hand, but kept his elbow in place for her to hold. She stretched her fingers. "You may end this charade at any point you choose." They walked a bit further, neither of them wanting to release the other. "But perhaps it would be advantageous for you to wait until after next month's Grand Ball?"

They walked on in silence for a pace while she considered it. "And what do we do until then?" she asked finally.

"I have arranged for several instances where we can be observed to the best advantage. There is a lecture on Greek history, some chamber music I understand to be quite accomplished."

"Yes. I think I can manage that. As you say, my calendar is quite full but I will find time for you."

It was perhaps an unfair statement, but in the last week she'd rather liked having the attention of the Duke and it piqued her to no end. Anna found she did not want to take her hand back. Why was he so fascinating to her?

They continued the promenade in silence. Anna began to warm to the idea of their false relationship, until the delighted gleam in her aunt's eye sent a chill against her ardour.

A pretend relationship means I must spend more time with him and learn who is truly is.

To her surprise the thought was rather...enticing.

Chapter Six

T he music was lovely, that she had to admit. Eloise and Jackson took the seats in the back of the Duke's box and allowed Anna to sit in the front with Weatherwax. There were some sly looks and suggestions that they might be more attached than were letting on, but it was meant in good fun, and Eloise did enjoy embarrassing her younger sister from time to time in the manner that older siblings did.

The musicians struck a sad tune. Sad, but very sweet, a song of unrequited love, if memory served. Anna watched them pull harmonies from their instruments with interest, but her mind quickly began to wander. She had to remember that she was there on a business arrangement, nothing else. The fact that the Duke was easy to be around, not to mention rather pleasing to the eye, was helpful for the sake of the false relationship. But things could not go further than this.

It was something she tried to remind herself of every day.

Even sitting next to him now was like sitting next to an open flame in the middle of winter. He was warm. Exciting. She could feel him beside her, as though he radiated his presence. Fake relationship? Perhaps, but she was beginning to understand that the emotions she was feeling right now we're certainly not false.

If anything, she had been looking forward to this night, in the way she looked forward to every outing they had been on. She thrilled at the touch of his hand upon hers. Even just sitting together as they were now, a sweet torture. She was so attuned to everything about him. From the scent of his shaving powder to the way his hair fell over his furrowed forehead entranced her.

It was maddening. Thrilling. Exhilarating.

She was in love with him.

She couldn't breathe. *My goodness, I am in LOVE with him.*

She took a deep breath and turned to regard his strong face, the square jaw, the fiery eyes. His eyes, however, were fixated elsewhere. He was looking across the theatre at another box. Anna turned to see what he was looking at so intently.

Lady Doringham was seated in a box further back from the stage. It was dark, and the forms there seemed difficult to make out, but yes, that most certainly was her. She wore a bright pale blue dress that shone in the shadows. The gentlemen around her wore dark coloured coats and kept to the back, giving her a darkened tableau to shine against. That there were three of them was apparent. That none of them was Lord Doringham was equally as obvious.

Duke Weatherwax was staring into the darkness of that box as if he had just discovered mould on his shoes. His face collapsed into a frown and his hand gripped the arm of the chair until his knuckles turned white.

Anna turned back to the stage, staring resolutely at nothing in particular. The music took on a sour tone, a subdued *wrongness* that had little to do with the musicians. The evening had become nearly unbearable. Anna concentrated on breathing. On telling herself it didn't matter. She would sit in her chair and wait the concert out. Eventually it would be over and she could go home.

She did not dare look at the Duke again.

Was he one of them? One of the men that fawned and prostrated themselves in front of Lady Doringham despite the fact she was married? Was he angry that she had other men there, or was he envious and wanted to be among them?

And why were there so many men showering their attention upon the Lady? Anna did not know what it was about Lady Doringham that made her so popular, but judging from what she saw in the box, it certainly wasn't fidelity.

When the concert ended, she pretended a headache and begged her brother-in-law Jackson to take her home. While it was her own fault she had fallen for someone who thought so little of her, that didn't mean she had to stay a moment longer than necessary.

He had seen to his side of the bargain. The pile of invitations in the morning mail had proven that. As far as she was concerned, their bargain was over and done with. He had repaid her tenfold whatever he felt that he owed her.

Chapter Seven

"Of course you must go!" Virginia was shocked. "Why would you not?"

"Do you not want to dance with your Duke? He is quite handsome," Eloise pointed out.

"Leave her alone, if she chooses to play difficult, it may whet his appetite all the more," Penelope chimed in.

While it was good to have her sisters around her again, Anna fervently hoped that they would change the subject. "I simply do not wish to attend," Anna said and busied herself at the writing-table.

"It is the biggest ball of the season!" Virginia cried.

"I have convinced Jackson to go," Eloise said, in that wheedling tone Anna knew only too well. "If no one asks, you may dance with him. At least you will have a dance!"

"That might make your Duke take notice!" Penelope teased.

"He is *not* my Duke!" Anna spat the words and tempered herself. "By that I mean... I believe he fancies another."

"Who?" Eloise reacted as if she had found the Duke to be a criminal of the lowest sort.

"I...cannot say." Anna would have to leave it there. To answer would only raise too many questions.

"Then there is but one thing to do," Penelope said, rather determined. "Fight fire with fire. You are going to make him notice you. Come, there is no time to lose. This calls for a new dress. Completely different hair..."

"Wait!" Anna interrupted the list before it could grow too long. "What if he is simply not interested in me?"

"Then he is a fool," Virginia started, but Penelope held up a restraining hand. "That is not the question, dear sister. The only question is...are *you* interested in him?"

In the silence, Anna finally admitted to her sisters what she had not wanted to admit to herself. "I am. I think I have fallen in love with him."

"Then the man will not stand a chance! Come sisters, we have much to plan!" Eloise squealed and grabbed Anna's hand. She began dragging Anna out of the room. "There is still time for the dress to be made, but we must visit the modiste immediately!"

Chapter Eight

"**M**y feet are aflame." Anna limped over to the punchbowl and gratefully accepted a cup. She drained it greedily, forgetting for a moment, proper manners that a lady were called to *sip* the punch.

"A far cry from the last ball, daresay." Virginia grinned and pitched her voice so only Anna could hear her. "You have danced every dance thus far."

Anna held up the card in her hand. "Thus far? Sister, my dance card is full. It was filled the moment we arrived. It was almost as though they were lying in wait for me!"

"No doubt." Eloise searched the room. "There is a great deal of whispering about and it all centres on your not-my-Duke."

Anna stared at her. "I do not understand."

"They want to know who it was that was able to drag the Duke back into society and what powers you have over him. The gentlemen seemed determined to find out for themselves."

"I did no such thing..."

"And..." Eloise continued, "I heard something else about your... about Duke Weatherwax. Apparently, it was a woman that caused his self-imposed exile in the first place."

"Really?" Virginia was all ears. "Do tell."

"From what I gather," Eloise paused to be sure she had their full attention, "he was infatuated with a woman who refused him. She threw him off for someone who was not even of the ton. An American who had inherited a title and has not the least idea what to do with it."

Lady Doringham. Anna clutched her chest. *She is speaking of Lady Doringham and that...husband of hers. And Weatherwax is still affected by her, enough to risk scandal twice over for her.*

"Who?" Virginia demanded.

"I did not hear." Eloise sounded frustrated. "It happened discreetly, but word soon got out."

"And now, I must burn the bottom of my feet in the endless dance so these..." Anna left the word out, "so that I can be measured, judged and what? Am I supposed to tell what I do not know to people who do not care?"

"Anna," Virginia set her hand on her sister's arm, "you know that the ton runs on gossip. While it is in your favour, use it. You are wearing the loveliest dress here. Father nearly died at the price."

Anna looked down at the folds of silk and satin and ribbons. True, it had cost a King's ransom and it was indeed beautiful. By the time her hair was done and she was dressed, the elegant woman staring at her, in shock and awe from her mirror, was someone she didn't recognize.

"You are lovely, Anna," Eloise confirmed. "That is why the young men wish to dance with you. Not for your connection to your...to Lord Weatherwax."

Anna appreciated her sister being supportive. But the truth was that getting noticed had suddenly come much easier since the Duke started this sham of a relationship. If getting prospects was her goal, then that was reached and certainly the charade could truly end, just as she thought. That was all she wanted. Was it not? Let the besotted man grovel at that another woman's feet. What was it to her? If a man wished to make an ass of himself, who was she to interfere? She was only the youngest daughter of a dependable, unexciting family.

On the other hand...her thoughts were interrupted when the musicians struck up a lively tune. "I believe this is my dance?" Another eager young man appeared beside her. They were all eager young men and their faces had begun to blur in her memory. She might have the dance card, but by the end of the night, the names would be meaningless to her, as they were all a mere blur of eager young men.

She accepted his place in her card and joined him on the floor. It took no time at all before he was eager to talk about Weatherwax, as though somehow *he* could find the scandal behind the Duke's interest in her. Anna supposed she should be offended, but she turned the conversation around and pulled from the young man what he knew.

It had been love, not infatuation. The Duke did love the woman, deeply, or so it seemed. She had apparently broken his heart in the crudest way possible. She had thrown him over for...well, that's where the young man fell short of the rest of the story. While it was true the American was wealthy, Weatherwax was as well. The American held no title other than what he'd inherited, and she certainly didn't honour what it meant to be part of the ton, leaving him out of many of the social events of the year. Therefore, it was not rank that the woman craved. So why she should release a Duke for...well, him? The young man could not understand.

And that was the quest behind the gossip seekers. If the Duke was calling on Anna, surely, he would have told her.

The thought that she would then tell everyone else was horrifying. What they must think of her to attempt to pry such information from her...

She nearly walked off the dance floor then and there, but that too would have caused a scandal and apparently, being associated with a rejected Duke was risky enough.

Love. How does one compete with love? Did he still love that woman? Of course. Look at the great lengths he'd gone to in order to save her honour. It was still love and she was still using his emotions to control him. Anna's heart sank. Weatherwax was indeed one of the men who draped themselves over her, as she had seen in the box at the theatre.

Anna smiled and pretended to listen intently to the young man whose name she did not remember. Eager young men cared little for a woman's thoughts so long as she smiled and seemed to hang on their every word, so it gave her room to think.

It was she who was the fool. Weatherwax had clearly stated the terms of their contract before being seen with her and he had fulfilled his end of the bargain. It was she who allowed emotion to enter the agreement. *Very well, then. I have reaped the benefits of the lie we sowed. I have become the talk of the ball. I shall then enjoy it.*

The music drew to a close and the dancers retreated to the sidelines to await the next. Another eager young gentleman approached her. Anna could see the nervousness in his steps. As she watched him approach with something akin to resigned dread, a body stepped in her line of sight. She looked up in shock and stared into the face of Duke Weatherwax.

"This is my dance."

"But..." Anna glanced at the eager young man who seemed confused. "My dance card..."

The music began and Weatherwax took her hand and pulled her to the dance floor. "This is *my* dance."

They began the steps to a quiet, sedate rhythm. "I have watched you dancing all night," the Duke growled after several silent moments, during which he seemed to do little but glower at her.

She blinked in surprise that he should have noticed her at all. "That was our agreement, was it not? I was to pretend you were courting me so my prospects would increase?"

"I confess that allowing myself to withdraw has not been as easy as I might have once considered it to be." He looked into her eyes. Anna nearly fell into them.

The past two weeks of their 'false' courtship ran through her mind: the carriage rides, the concerts, all of it had somehow become more vivid, more bright in her memory than the season leading up to these moments. She might have been the one who violated the unspoken agreement, but that did not negate the feelings she had.

In his arms now, looking up at him, she saw him as a man, not a Duke. She realized she was in love. With him. Not with the title, not with what he could do for her. She loved Albion. It was that simple.

"I...cannot!" she turned and ran as fast as her skirts would allow. She left Duke Weatherwax standing alone on the dance floor, wondering what just happened. Let him ask the gathered ton for a clue as to what had just happened.

She imagined they would have several theories on the matter.

Chapter Nine

"What did he say to you?" Virginia sounded as though she were ready to attack the Duke with her bare hands. Anna had found an empty room, a library of sorts and she hid in a corner, the tears running freely down her cheeks. "Nothing!"

"Anna..." Eloise began, but the door flew open and Duke Weatherwax stormed in. "I would speak with your sister." It was no request, but Anna's sisters waited until she nodded. They floated to the corner of the room so the Duke and their sister could speak privately,

Anna gathered herself and dried her tears before turning to confront him. "And what is it you require from me now, Your Grace? Is there another painting to steal? Another Lady to make jealous? What will you have me do?"

"Our...agreement..."

"I am well aware of our agreement, Your Grace." She spat the words. "And it was to end here. Tonight."

"I do not wish it to end at all, Lady Gillingham." He rushed the words as she took a breath. "In truth, I no longer wish to pretend or play children's games. These past few days have been among the happiest I have ever been."

Anna felt as though she were hanging over the edge of a great precipice. She searched his eyes for any hint of betrayal, unwilling to believe her ears, not daring to think he felt the same about her as she felt about him.

"What about...Lady Doringham?" That spectre rose between them. "You will always be in love with her."

If she had suddenly produced a live fish from her reticule, Duke Weatherwax would not have had a more shocked expression. "Lady...in *love*? Are you *mad*?"

"You do not love her then?"

"No! Most emphatically not. In fact, it was I who introduced her to her husband." He shook his head, "Our families were well acquainted and there was some hope that she and I would wed, but..." he looked to be sure Eloise and Virginia could not hear, "...but that painting was not a single incident of her...indiscretions. I would not speak ill of a Lady, but she is a bit of a...flirt."

There came dual snorts from the corner, proving her sisters could hear quite well when they put their minds to it. In truth, she was sure the gross understatement had barely begun to tell the tale.

"Why should it have mattered to her then, what happened to the painting?" Anna asked, truly curious despite herself.

"After having met her husband, she regretted some of her choices. I imagine that was the indication of true love. She claimed she wanted to be better for him. Alas, I fear she still struggles with her old ways though." The Duke's voice was filled with contempt.

"At the theatre...when you could not keep your eyes off of her."

"It was the company around her. I feared she might have been reverting to her...rebellious ways, but apparently her husband had been detained and was sitting in the back, having arrived late. You see, he is the one who found me the tobacco investment in America. He has created an impressive revenue stream for me, and he is my good friend. I was worried on his account."

"Then..." Anna was trying to process all of this. "...then you do not love her?"

"I have never loved anyone," Duke Weatherwax took her hand gently in his, "until I met you. And now, I find I cannot get you out of my mind. Your courage and bravery in assisting me that night revealed to me what a unique young lady you truly are. Our conversations have impressed me with your wit and intellect. How could I not have fallen for a Lady so intriguing, so utterly amazing!"

It was all she needed to know. Brazenly, she grabbed him by the lapels, and then, standing tiptoe, brought her lips to his and held him in a long kiss.

"Anna!" Virginia sounded shocked, but the warning held an under-current of humour.

"I think it acceptable," Anna whispered to her sister, though she never took her eyes off of that of Albion. "After all, we are to be married. Are we not, Your Grace?"

Albion touched her face as if in wonder, his voice was husky with a note of awe. "Lady Gillingham, I have seen the world through your eyes and it is a wonderful place. I cannot imagine and do not wish to experi-ence the world without you. Indeed, I could not have said it better myself. I do rather wish to marry you."

"There you have it!" exclaimed Anna in satisfaction. "My dear sisters, how long do you suppose it takes to plan a wedding?"

Epilogue

D uke Weatherwax looked fierce, but Anna knew enough of him now to know that it was nerves which gave him such a foreboding mien. He stood at the end of a long walk and fidgeted. As the doors opened and he turned to see his bride, the scowl vanished like the sun coming out after a storm. He seemed...pleased. Happy. Anna found she could not stop smiling, for she knew exactly how he felt.

A year ago, on the very day he had asked for her hand in marriage. It had been the greatest year of her life but awaiting this day had been a sweet form of torture.

The ceremony took very little time. It seemed to fly by so quickly. And then she was Duchess Weatherwax. She passed through the church in a daze, hearing the congratulations of her family and friends only dimly. Her eyes were only upon her Duke.

They entered an open carriage, one more ride around the park to commemorate their beginnings before heading to the wedding breakfast, which had been planned at his estate.

Something occurred to her as they travelled, thus, enjoying the feel of holding her husband's hand. "My love, whatever became of the painting?"

It took him a moment to remember what she was talking about. When he did, he laughed.

"I fear that met with a tragedy." The Duke sighed dramatically. "Somehow, it burned completely. I have no idea how that might have happened. The strangest things catch fire sometimes."

She giggled and curled up in the crook of his arm. "What a shame."

He handed her a card.

"What is this?" She opened it to look inside. His name was written in the card, a dozen times, one after another.

"It's your dance card for every ball from now on." He smiled. "It will never be empty again. For as long as we both shall live."

"I do love you!" she exclaimed and laughed, for she had truly found the happiest of endings for her own particular story. Oddly enough, it also felt very much like a beginning of a whole new adventure.

She rather liked the idea of that.

The End

Loving The Lady

THE LADY SERIES BOOK ELEVEN

Prologue

Andrew Gillingham had been on the run since breakfast.

Of course, when you're eight, the general idea is to just keep moving. It is much harder to coerce one to stay in and do lessons when one cannot be found. With this in mind, Andrew had escaped to the garden in the moments when his governess was preoccupied with his sisters. And thus far, he had done a fairly passable job of keeping out of sight from everyone save the gardener. Not that he would tell. The gardener and Andrew were old friends, of a like mind that there was more to be gained in a day spent free of encumbrances of the female variety. Better to spend one's time outdoors.

Andrew wanted to be a gardener when he grew up. Nanny called this foolishness, as Lords were not gardeners. Though Andrew could really not see the logic in that. It seemed a Lord could do anything he liked, so why not gardening?

It was these kinds of heavy thoughts that tripped Andrew up from time to time. He had been so worried over this puzzle that he quite failed to notice that he was no longer alone. Only the hand that reached out to snag his sleeve was not his governess, but someone far worse.

Amanda Abbott. A tiny head with blonde hair so white it might have been spun from cobwebs. She grinned now, blue hair ribbons dancing about her face in the breeze as she shifted eagerly from one foot to the other, as though ready to dart away at a moment's notice. Annoyingly, though she was nearly two years younger than him, they were of the same height, meaning he was looking into those startling blue eyes of hers, which missed absolutely nothing. Which was very likely how she had found him. He *had* been hiding after all.

"What are you doing?" she asked, tugging at him, trying to draw him out from what he'd always considered his secret space between the garden wall and the tool shed. "Come play with me. My Father is talking about..." she frowned over the word, carefully sounding it out, "in-vest-ments. He will be absolutely forever and said that we might play."

Andrew sniffed. It was more likely that her father expected Amanda to be trailing around after his sisters. Ignoring her, he bent and picked up the small wooden box he'd had tucked into the shade. "I am otherwise occupied," he informed her primly. He had heard the phrase just this morning over breakfast when the servants were talking, and he had rather liked it. It felt good to already have found the perfect occasion to use it.

Amanda's brow furrowed and her lips moved as she sounded out the words. "O-ther-wise-oc-cu-pied. What does that mean?"

He drew himself up, haughty now. "Busy," he said and stomped past her through the bushes and into what would have been the wilds of the garden had they not been so well-tended.

He really didn't expect her to follow. He had to half-crawl through the wisteria which tugged at his clothes. His shirt snagged on a branch and tore, not that it bothered him any. Amanda's delicate dress surely would not hold up to such a wild passage. It was like crawling through a jungle. For a moment he imagined that he was. He wondered if there were jungles like this in India.

A yelp behind him and a wild rustling of branches told Andrew this was not the case. Amanda was right behind him, gamely crawling in his wake.

In desperation, Andrew shoved his way through the rosebushes, despite the way the thorns scratched. A moment later he came out on the banks of a small decorative pond in the middle of the garden. He had a long scratch on the hand which still held the box, but it was of no matter. What was a scratch? He sat down on the bank and pried at the lid of the box which was stuck tight.

Amanda appeared behind him, minus her hair ribbons, her hair a tangled mess about her face, a twig dangling over her left ear. Her blue dress had a long rent in the skirt, and her face looked as though she had done battle with a wild beast and lost, with several scratches marring her skin. She was grinning, as she plopped down on the grass beside him. "Found you."

"Go home, 'Manda," he muttered, digging his fingernails under the lid of the box and pulling upward. When that didn't work, he shoved his hand in his pocket, trying to find the fishhook he'd brought just for this occasion. Maybe he could hook the barbed metal under the lid and pull it open.

"I am home." Amanda looked about her in contentment. "My father said so. He told your father that if I would marry you when I grow up it would..." She paused and thought her way through the words. "U-nite our families and for-tunes."

Andrew looked up from what he was doing. "No you are not." He growled the words, his eyes narrowing as he studied the little girl with growing dislike.

"So, when I marry you, this will be my home," she finished in triumph. "So I am right. Kind of." She stuck her tongue out at him.

He scrambled to his feet, to tower over her. "Take that back! I would not marry you if you were the last Lady in the whole wide world!"

"Will too. I love you, Andrew Gillingham!"

Andrew was so mad at this that he dropped his box, which hit a stone bordering the pond. The box sprang open, and a mass of worms fell out, scattering over Amanda's shoes. She looked down and screamed, stumbling backwards.

The only problem was that there was no "backwards" to stumble into. Amanda tripped on the rocks surrounding the pond. She teetered at the edge for a moment.

Andrew was grinning by the time she hit the water and sat down hard in the mud. He wasn't exactly too worried, even when she started screaming like a stuck cat. The water was only about six inches deep. She wasn't hurt any. She also wasn't talking about marriage anymore.

Andrew stuck his tongue out at her and seeing his governess already running down towards the pond with a few other people from the house, Andrew decided it was time to make his escape back through the bushes. All the while he was thinking how nice it was when things just had a way of working themselves out sometimes.

Chapter One

"Dash it all, Gillingham. I tell you I saw an angel and you seem to not even be listening!"

Andrew Gillingham cracked an eye open to study his friend's face briefly before closing it again, with every intention of returning to his slumber. "My dear fellow, I am simply fashed and here you are going on about some skirt you saw at the theatre—"

"Skirt! My God, man, this was a Lady. A representative of the Ton, a debutante without equal. To refer to her as a 'skirt' is a gross insult, one worthy of a duel!"

"Have you even been introduced to this paragon of virtue?" Andrew asked, sitting up and giving up all pretence to sleep. The club was too noisy by now anyway. If he wanted slumber, it would be better to return to his Mayfair apartment and get it there.

"What difference does that make?" Laurence du Campion looked so put out, that Andrew could only laugh.

"Quite a lot, if I am to die at dawn for the sake of her honour."

Laurence subsided, sinking into the wingback chair so sullenly that he was near invisible to outside observers. From where Andrew was sitting, somewhat sideways to his friend, he had a good view of the top of Laurence's head and his feet.

Andrew relented. "All right, tell me who has captured your heart. Mayhap I can get you an introduction if that's what you desire."

Laurence sat up and levered his boots against the floor, his body turned his chair so he could face Andrew fully. "What makes you think you could accomplish such a feat?"

"Many sisters," Andrew muttered and shrugged. "Truly, there is not a Lady of the Ton that they do not know. Not one of them would miss an opportunity to see me wed. I suspect they would get me an introduction to any young Lady who is available just to settle me 'appropriately' as they call it."

"Which gets *you* an introduction, but not me," Laurence mourned, plaintively.

"Truly Laurie, you are an idiot. I can introduce you once I have been introduced."

Laurence brightened momentarily. "Pass off the introduction. A clever plan. Except..." he gave Andrew a look, "...once you see this Lady, you will undoubtedly wish to keep her for yourself. Truly, there is none other like her."

"It is a risk I am sure," Andrew laughed, gaining another evil look from his friend. "Oh, go on with you. What kind of friend would I be to tear a lovely Lady away from a man such as yourself? Who is she?"

"Where do I begin? Her hair was so gold that the sun itself must have lent her a portion of sunshine to create the silken strands. Eyes as blue as a summer sky. She is newly returned from the Continent. She was away...some school or another... Her Father is a Baron I believe. I heard someone call her—"

"Amanda. Miss Amanda Abbott," Andrew murmured with a shudder. "Tell me she is not the one you have been mooning over.

"Yes, Amanda! How the deuce did you know?"

Andrew's flesh crawled at the thought of her. He had earned a whipping once on behalf of the chit when she was but a child. And she had never let him forget it. No. It was not the whipping she had refused to let him forget, but the plans she had made for the future. Plans involving him. He had endured much over the years regarding this single-minded threat. Even a dunking in pond water had failed to chill her ardour.

Granted, she had been six at the time.

Still, he had been enjoying the reprieve while she was away at finishing school. He had not seen her for several years now, though he had not forgotten her. How could he when she had written him relentlessly for several years, letters he had burned rather than open, until eventually they had stopped.

She had likely been lying in wait.

He shuddered again. "She will be at the ball tonight that my family is giving. I just know it," he moaned. Now it was he who tried to disappear into his chair.

"Then you can introduce me!" Laurence exclaimed, all smiles now that the matter had been resolved so easily.

"Trust me you would not—"

Andrew stopped himself. Wait a moment. What if he DID introduce the Lady to Laurence? Laurence and his family were newcomers to the Ton, which would give him a certain exotic allure. The fact he was half-French would not be a thing that would bother the Lady, having just come from France herself. In fact, the common ground might prove interesting enough that they could, in fact, find quite a bit to talk about.

It was not altogether impossible that the Lady in question might find Laurence quite fascinating indeed. Meaning her attention would be elsewhere tonight.

Not upon him.

Of course, he had no way of knowing if her silly schoolgirl infatuation with him was over. He certainly hoped so, for the girl talked far too much and was much too...well...cloying in her attentions. He could only imagine what she was like now that she was properly out in Society.

He shuddered again.

"Yes, old chap, I would be positively delighted to introduce you. First thing. Why, you would be doing me a favour actually, by taking her off my h— I mean, in helping to introduce her properly into Society. Her having been away for so long and all."

"You mean it?" Laurence's eyes grew distant, even misty as though he were overcome with emotion. "*Mon ami*, I should be in your debt!"

"*Au contraire*. It is I who would be in yours," replied Andrew, positively preening at how easily he had dealt with the problem altogether.

Chapter Two

"**S**on! There is someone I want you to see!"

Lord Gillingham was quick to catch his son's arm the moment he set foot into the ballroom. It was almost as though he was...lying in wait? Andrew gave his father a sharp look. The old man had a canny look about him. That settled it. The man was up to something.

Quickly, Andrew's eyes tracked their trajectory. He was being expertly steered towards where a pair of ladies talked idly. One was in some kind of yellow dress, which seemed fashionable of late. The other in a magnificent blue.

That blue...something about the colour triggered a memory. A very unpleasant memory. There was only one young Lady to dare wear so rich a colour in a sea of pastels, for the blue matched her eyes...which were fastened quite squarely upon him.

Dash it all, he was about to be foisted off on the very young Lady he had been hoping to avoid.

Except...Miss Amanda Abbott was not the same girl he'd last seen when he was fourteen.

Oh, there was no mistaking it was her. Her hair was a deeper gold, which suited her immensely. Her perfect complexion, a worthy canvas for pink, luscious lips, and those...amazing...eyes.

Andrew skidded to a halt. THIS was Amanda Abbott? His brain finally made the connection. This amazing, beautiful young woman who moved with such grace, laughing gaily at something Laurence said.

Laurence?

How the deuce had Laurence been introduced already?

"Son, you are making a scene." Lord Gillingham was not pleased to be thrown off balance by his wayward son, especially since they were standing together in the middle of the dance floor, like some dreadfully mismatched couple, as the first dancers were taking their places.

"I am...sorry, Father. I am coming. Right behind you."

He was babbling, but still, Laurence's description had left him unprepared. He had thought that perhaps Laurance had overstated things. He was wont to fall in love easily and tended to see his ladies through...well, eyes which were perhaps easily made blind to a Lady's flaws.

Not that Amanda Abbott was flawed. Not in any way.

Dumfounded, Andrew somehow made it across the ballroom without tripping more than two dancers in the process. He murmured apologies, oblivious to the destruction in his wake, as one of the dancers bumped into another pair and precipitated a chain reaction that left the entire chain of participants stumbling for several beats.

Oh sure, he heard the cries, the exclamations, the outbursts of anger and surprise. He just didn't realize they were meant for him. His eyes were entirely upon Amanda...and her suitor.

"Miss Abbott, a delight," Andrew said with a bow as he drew even with the group. "du Campion, I see you had no need for an introduction after all."

"Lord Gillingham," Amanda acknowledged him with a curtsey. "I am afraid that you must blame me if I ruined your intentions for the night. You see, I positively begged for my mother to find someone to introduce me to this fine gentleman. He caught my eye at the theatre last night and I could not sleep for regret that I did not make his acquaintance."

Laurence positively blushed under these fine words. Andrew could only stare. "I see."

Amanda's smile was that same mischievous one he remembered

from when they were children. Nothing else about her reminded him of that girl. As a child, Amanda was forever tripping over her own feet it. She'd talked incessantly. This refined young Lady was everything the young Amanda was not. It was quite a transformation.

"It is good to see you whole and without injury though. I am pleased with it," she continued, a dimple appearing at the corner of her mouth at her amusement.

"Well?" he asked, somewhat stupidly. It seemed he was having trouble forming full sentences.

"Why...I had imagined you must have lost a hand at the very least, to account for your lack of common courtesy." Her eyes, those infernal eyes bored right into him. "It is considered quite rude to neglect one's correspondence, would you not say, my Lord?"

Andrew blinked. "I..."

Laurence only shook his head, tsking quietly. "Mademoiselle, it would be a shame to dwell in the past on such a night as this. I believe I have the next dance. If I might escort you to the dance floor?"

"Andrew! Explain yourself!" Her father was turning various shades of purple as he stared after the couple. "I brought you over here in hopes you would honour the agreement I made with her Father, God rest his soul, ten years ago. Tell me you have not bungled something so simple as a simple conversation with the girl."

Andrew stared after them, not altogether sure of what had just happened. As his father's words sunk in, he felt his mouth go dry. "Wait...you did *what*?"

Lord Gillingham only shook his head. His eyes were filled with disappointment for his youngest child, his only son. It was a look Andrew had seen often. "Fix this, Andrew," he muttered and turned away.

Andrew stood where he had been left, not altogether sure of what exactly he was supposed to fix. Not that he was about to marry just anyone his father told him to. Still, agreement or not, nothing was going to change one little fact. Miss Amanda Abbott might have loved Andrew once. But from the look in her eyes, he was sure that she positively despised him now.

Chapter Three

"So many callers!"

Amanda's sisters were beside themselves with wonder and joy. Sometimes being the eldest had its disadvantages. Now was one of those times. Her sisters had been hovering upon the landing where they could watch the arrival of each gentleman who'd shown up in the course of the day. By the time these callers had left, they had already discussed, quite avidly, each bouquet of flowers, every beribboned package that they'd witnessed coming into the house and had chosen their favourites by far.

Now, with Amanda all to themselves, they had plenty of observations to make while the only thing Amanda wanted, more than anything, was to hide in her room and cry.

"Now girls, your sister is a bit overwhelmed. She's only just come out and truly, today was a touch...unexpected I think," their mother interrupted, nodding to the maid to pour tea for each of them.

Theresa sighed prettily. She was coming out next year and was already quite beside herself with plans for her own debut. She was the sort of girl who liked planning everything down to the last detail, yet romantic enough to be quite smitten with soft words and boxes of chocolates. "Amanda, did you not think Lord Taylor was most elegant?"

"Lord Taylor? Baron Rothschild was much more dashing," Felicity exclaimed, with a shake of her head. The youngest of the trio, she was the one with the most set ideas of what a romantic hero should be. Of course, her observations were mostly culled from the novels she tried so hard to hide from their governess, which might have given her a somewhat biased opinion.

"There is more to a marriage than soft words or a well-cut figure," their mother said with a laugh. "Though in truth, I was rather surprised to not see Andrew Gillingham in attendance."

Amanda flushed and busied herself with her teacup. "I expect he had better things to do," she murmured, thinking that perhaps she shouldn't have been quite so cutting at last night's ball. "Laurence du Campion was quite nice..."

Felicity sniffed. "He is foreign, is he not?"

Therese giggled. "He is French," she said decidedly, as though this was something far worse than being foreign.

"Half-French," Amanda corrected them, idling, watching her white cat who had come into the room and was winding around the table legs purring.

"But a middle child with such obvious imperfection of breeding..." her mother commented, taking a sip of her tea. "I can see where you might be quite taken with his manners, for he was quite charming. But really Amanda, you must give more thought to whom you allow to court you. The wrong sort could discourage what might be a better match."

Amanda stared at her mother, appalled. "That is a terrible thing to say! Mr. du Campion was quite lovely." She set down her teacup hard enough for it to rattle against the saucer. "Besides, did I not just arrive back from school in Switzerland? There were many French girls there who I quite thought of as friends."

"Well, one does what one must in such situations. I am sure they were very pleasant, but you must put such things behind you. We sent you there that your manners might grow more refined, more polished." Lady Abbott's smile was kind. "In truth, they did a marvellous job. Why look at you! I can hardly get over the change! You were quite the hoyden once."

Amanda frowned, for if she had changed, it had been her own

doing, not the school's nor her teacher's. It was she who had decided to pursue the path of becoming the sort of Lady who might one day...well, what did that matter now? She bent to pull the cat into her arms, ignoring her mother's look of disapproval. Merriweather purred louder and bumped his head on the underside of her chin.

She sighed. The problem was, she'd only changed outwardly. And her hoydenish behaviour had only ever concerned one specific boy who had brought out the worst in her. Or the best. For Amanda had been a shy child, a late bloomer. Only with Andrew had she been relaxed enough to play, scream, and have fun. To be herself.

Was it any wonder that she had loved him?

But he had betrayed her. In the end, he had proved cruel like so many others. Cruel enough that she had become furious at him. As one letter followed another, all without reply, she had resolved to change, to become the sort of Lady he could not possibly ignore. Last night had been a success in that regard. Why then, did she feel so empty and hollow inside? She buried her face in the cat's fur. She no longer wished to think about any of this.

"Amanda? Amanda, are you listening to me? I was asking if you had said anything to Lord Gillingham last night. He seemed rather put out..." Her mother was frowning at her. Her sisters were watching, wide-eyed and delighted as though their sister's discomfort amused them.

"Mother, you must excuse me. I think the excitement of this all has rather left me tired." She set the cat down and stood up, a trifle uneasily. "If you will excuse me, I think I would like to lie down before dinner."

She did not wait for a reply. Perhaps in a sense, it was true that she was fleeing the room to avoid a conversation she had no wish to engage in. But could she be blamed? For so long, she'd plotted Andrew's downfall. It had been so simple. She would get his attention, and then she would snub him in a way that would hurt him the most. Judging from his expression while she had been dancing with Laurence, she had quite succeeded.

Why then, was she the one hurting right now?

Chapter Four

"What in heaven's name are you doing in here? When I asked Preston if he had seen you, little did I expect him to point me *here*!" Virginia stood in the doorway, arms crossed over her stomach, something she was doing more and more of late regarding her younger brother.

Andrew waved her off. "I am in the library. I have every right to be in the library. It is part of the house where I live."

"I cannot help but notice it is also quite full of books. I thought you broke out in a rash every time someone tried to expose you to the printed word."

"I am merely allergic to reading them," Andrew muttered, his eyes darting back to the window, which gave him quite a clear view of the Abbott House next door. "What in the devil do you suppose is the draw?" he asked as yet another carriage came rumbling to a halt at the front door. "All week long, they have been doing that."

Virginia came into the room to look over his shoulder, trying to ascertain what he was looking at. "The carriage?" She straightened and shrugged. "I expect those are callers."

"Callers!" He grimaced at the word.

"Yes. You must be familiar with the practise. It is when one might expect company to show up and make nuisances of themselves until they are either rousted out or asked to stay to tea, or better yet, dinner."

"Theresa and Felicity are not out yet, are they?" he asked, already knowing the answer.

Virginia's eyes widened, and she might have muffled a laugh, which she very hastily buried in a poor rendition of a cough. "No, not yet. Only Amanda as far as I know."

"As far as you know." Andrew stared at the house next door as though he could see through the walls or draperied windows if he only glared hard enough. "Their mother is a widow though..."

Virginia barked a laugh and pointed at the next carriage that was arriving. "I hardly think Lord Taylor is interested in Lady Abbott. Why, he must be half her age!"

"That doesn't stop a man from calling upon a girl who is half *his* age," Andrew muttered, pointing at the next carriage. "Lord Folsom...?"

Virginia smothered a gasp as she peered past him. "I should hope he is calling upon Lady Abbott given his advanced years, but somehow I do not think so." She shuddered delicately. "I have been most fortunate in my own match, I must say. I am thankful to not be in such a position as Amanda is right now."

Andrew groaned and covered his eyes with his hand. "Do not say such things."

"Why, brother dear, do you mean to say that you have been mooning all this time over our Amanda? The girl you pushed into the pond when you were eight?"

"I did not push her," he said, dropping his hand that he might glare at her properly. "She tripped. There is a fine distinction."

"You also left her there."

There was nothing to say to that.

Virginia sank down into one of the leather chairs near the fireplace, her hand upon her gently swelling belly. She was visiting before her time for lying in came upon her, and lately, she had been resting more and more. This did not prevent her from involving herself in her brother's life at every opportunity, this being one of them. Her eyes upon him had a distinctly speculative look.

"Do not say whatever you are about to," Andrew said, surging to his feet so he might be better prepared to flee if necessary.

"Oh fiddlesticks, you are the most prickly thing, Andrew. Sit down and listen to me."

Reluctantly, he sat. Though he perched upon the edge of the chair.

Virginia sighed. "My dear brother, you do not need to look so much like I am about to eat you. Though I must say, my appetite has been much improved as of late. Be a dear and pull the rope. Perhaps Preston can bring tea."

"You only just told me to sit."

"And now I am telling you to stand. Honestly, Andrew, must you argue about everything?"

Grumbling, Andrew went to pull the rope.

"As I was about to say, if you are this bothered, the only true solution would be for you to go over there."

"Go over where?" Andrew wasn't sure which conversation they were having anymore.

"Go over to the Abbott House. Call upon Amanda. The way a Gentleman calls upon a Lady. With flowers perhaps. Or some of those little cakes the cook makes so well. Oh, be a dear and ask Preston if there are any of those cakes. I just want one. Or two. Maybe a dozen. Yes, have him bring a dozen cakes. For me. Not Amanda. She can have something else."

Andrew stared at his sister. "You want me to call upon Amanda. Whyever for?"

"Well, obviously, to get to know her better. In case you might wish to make her your wife?"

That did it. "*Wife*? I was only looking out the window and noting an abundance of carriages. You are as bad as Father, having me wed to her before I have said so much as two words to her!"

"Well, you are obviously interested in her!"

"I am not!"

It was such a blatant lie, that there was nothing she could say to that. Surprisingly, neither could he.

"She would not make a suitable wife. Her mother counts every coin in a man's pocket to determine his worth. Her sisters are absolutely impossible. And she...she would not know the first thing about managing an Estate this size. I am, after all, our Father's heir. It would fall upon my wife to..." He gestured at the room around him. "Do whatever it is mother did before she died."

"She is quite intelligent," Virginia said softly. "I have spoken to her, and I see much to be admired in her conversation."

"But she is quite frail."

It was true. She had become quite ill from falling into the pond. It had been far too cold. Even now, her delicate features, her slender form spoke of a fragility that gave him an intense urge to protect Amanda at all costs. His own mother had died under the strain of being Lady Gillingham. It had not been an easy position to hold.

"It would be different for her, with you as her husband."

"And if I am like our Father?" he snapped.

"If you mean you are being too logical, too mathematical in your decisions, then yes, you are." Virginia's shoulders slumped, her disappointment clear. "Father has always counted what would be the best for the Estate over what would be best for him. Or for us."

"What else is there?" he asked, almost shouting.

She rose, her expression was sad. "There is love," she said softly then noted the butler waiting at the door.

"You wanted something, my Lady?"

Virginia seemed to be blinking back tears. "Never mind, Preston. I do not feel quite so hungry as I did a moment ago. Thank you."

Andrew watched her go, not sure which felt worse. Her disappointment in him, or his disappointment in himself. Either way, he wasn't fit to call on anyone.

Not that Amanda would have let him if he'd tried.

Chapter Five

Enough was enough. The next morning Amanda declared that she was indisposed and fled to the garden with a book. Nothing her mother or sisters said could dissuade her. She was tired of courtships, and constant invitations to balls and musicals. She's seen enough plays to last a lifetime and taken more rides around the park than she cared to remember.

She truly had *tried* to allow herself to be courted. None of it was quite satisfying though, and while many of the gentlemen had been quite kind, the only one who had been worth her time was Laurence. But even they had fallen into more of a quiet comradery, such as a brother and sister might share. There was no spark, no real love there.

Not the kind of thing she'd felt once for Andrew.

Of course, she didn't feel such a way *now* towards Andrew. She was only thinking about him in terms of comparison. This had nothing to do with Andrew. She hadn't even talked to him since that awful ball two weeks ago.

"Argh!"

She threw her book down in consternation. There was no way she could read when her mind kept going around in circles like this.

"Does the book deserve such treatment?" a voice asked from nearby.

She glanced up only to find the subject of her disquiet mumbling peering at her over the garden wall.

"Garden walls are dangerous. Do you not know this?" she asked primly, picking up her book and shaking the leaves out of it, for it had fallen into a flowerbed.

"How do you come to that conclusion?" he asked, frowning.

"Did your sister not wind up marrying a man she spied over a garden wall?"

"That was on the other side of the house altogether," he said, pointing. "And she was on his side of the wall when she met him."

"Well, it is a good thing we are on opposite sides then," she said and opened the book as if to continue reading. Never mind that the book was upside down in her hands.

There was a long silence. In the distance, they heard the sound of a door slamming from somewhere in her house. Her mother's voice called her name.

"You could try to escape," he said, clearly reading her absolute abhorrence towards what was surely coming next in her eyes.

"Where? I can hardly climb into my book and disappear." She looked sadly at the pages. How many times had she wished that she could?

"The garden gate would be much easier, I expect."

"I would be alone. In a garden. With you."

"My sister is right in the house. I can fetch her, and she can chaperone if you feel uncomfortable with being seen with me."

Her mother was calling to her from the door. In a moment she'd come out into the garden to find her.

"Agreed."

In no time at all, he had the door between the gardens open. She was giggling as she passed through. It was almost like old times.

Almost.

"I will fetch my sister."

A moment later Virginia was waving from the Verandah. "I will have Preston bring out tea. And little cakes," she called, obviously delighted by their afternoon guest.

"I would not count on getting any of the cakes," Andrew advised softly.

Amanda laughed.

"Just tea will be fine."

Andrew relayed this to Virginia who, oddly enough, seemed not quite so inclined to talk.

"I am absolutely exhausted of late," she said, with a pleased look at her expanding waistline. "Perhaps Andrew would like to take you around the garden while we wait on Preston to serve."

Andrew had, rather, taken on the look of a startled deer, as if at any moment he would bolt. Feeling a little wicked, Amanda slipped her hand into the crook of his elbow. "That would be delightful."

Virginia seemed pleased as they started off. Andrew rather scowled the moment his back was turned, and his sister could no longer see his expression. "That was cruel," he muttered.

"So were you."

He drew her out of earshot of his sister and paused under a tree, as though showing her some particular specimen of plant growing in the shade. "I was wrong," he said, with a wary glance back towards the house. "This is not the best place for apologies perhaps—"

"Then find a better place." It was a challenge, but she was in no mood for half-meant apologies. If he wanted to be sorry, then he could do things properly.

They started walking again. It took her a moment to realize where he was taking her. She stared at the small pond at the edge of the lawn. "It seems smaller."

"Most things do, when you're grown."

"It felt like a lake to me."

"You were in the middle of it."

She stifled a laugh. "Well, you are blunt at least."

He shot her a look. "You make it seem as though it were an admirable trait."

"I am tired of petty compliments." She looked back towards the garden wall, where her house could only be seen in the stiff peaks and dormers of the upper floors. "It is a cage of sorts."

"You were relentless," he said suddenly.

"What?" Amanda gave him her full attention. "Relentless?"

"In the way you pursued me. You were always there. Right behind me. Telling me..." He faltered here and she nodded. She knew what she had told him.

"We were children," she said, trying hard to be gentle, but her eyes pricked with tears. "But when I left...I was alone. I needed...I needed a friend."

It was his turn to shift uncomfortably. "I did not know."

Amanda gasped as realization dawned. "You never read my letters." She stepped away from him. "I should have guessed. You never even read them."

He only stared at her.

"I poured my HEART out in those letters."

"THAT was the problem!" The words seemed to explode out of him. "You were always pouring your heart out to me. You loved me. You wanted to marry me."

"I was a CHILD! Besides, my letters..." she choked back a sob. "My letters were nothing like that. I was lonely. I was scared. I needed a friend. That was all I was looking for!"

"But what you did—"

"What I did? When I was six?" She shook her head. "This was a mistake. I thought there could be a truce. That maybe we could be friends. You used to be someone I could talk to."

"You only ever had one thing in mind." He too had drawn himself up, his back rigid and straight. "You talked of nothing but being mistress of this house."

She sucked in a breath.

"I would thank you not to remember that," she said as icily as she could manage when her heart was aching with a pain she thought she'd resolved long ago. "Please convey my regrets to your sister."

With that, Amanda turned and walked away. She was almost running by the time she reached the gate.

Chapter Six

The next day, Amanda was scheduled to go riding with Laurence. It was almost a relief to be away from the house, away from her family who frowned so much over who she chose to spend her time with. As though Laurence was unworthy of her attention, when right now he was the only person that she could stand to be around.

"I could almost marry you," she shouted as they cantered through the park together.

Laurence almost fell off his horse. She took pity on him and drew her mare up to wait for him upon the hilltop. He came, half out of the saddle, trying to regain a stirrup at an uneven trot. "That was most unexpected," he complained as he readjusted himself in the saddle. "You made me look quite the fool."

"You do that quite well without my help," she retorted, and he laughed.

"Now, what was this you were saying about a potential betrothal? Because I warn you, my Mother has been eagerly awaiting an announcement."

"I was saying I could almost marry you."

"Almost." He sounded almost hurt as he repeated the word.

"We both know I cannot."

He was silent for a long moment. His horse took the opportunity to nip at her mare. She smacked the stallion's muzzle with her riding crop, nearly unseating Laurence again. "How long have you known?" he asked, as he settled his mount with a steadying hand upon its neck.

"Long enough to know that you are not in love with me, but too polite to say so. There is someone else, though, is there not?"

He was so shamefaced that she would have laughed had the conversation not been so serious. "She is not...free to return my affections."

Unrequited love. Amanda knew too much about that.

"Speaking of...what the devil is going on between you and Andrew?"

Amanda winced. "How did you...?"

"Perhaps we are both a little too observant...?" Laurence asked. His smile was sympathetic.

Another couple was approaching. Amanda nudged her horse into a walk. Together they meandered along the path while talking, lest they cause gossip from merely sitting like this. After a bit, she spoke up. "I listened to my Father."

"Is that a bad thing?"

"Probably." She thought about how jolly her father had always seemed to her. How much he had doted on her. He had only ever asked one thing in return. "From the time I was small, he told me I would be mistress of the Gillingham Estate. That I would marry Andrew. I grew up certain in this knowledge. He had talked it over with Lord Gillingham and I...being a child...had assumed it all to be true."

"Andrew was not amenable with this plan?" Laurence asked, frowning.

"I honestly do not think he ever knew. He only saw me chasing after him, talking about when we were wed." She laughed a little. "I thought it fantastic fun. I loved Andrew. He had the best ideas. We were always in trouble. I could never understand why he was so set on denying what I knew was the simple truth. The more he denied it, the more I told him."

"Good Lord." Laurence drew up his horse so abruptly that the couple behind them almost ran them over.

Once all the riders had sorted themselves out, with Laurence and

Amanda yielding the right of way to those behind them, they resumed their ride. "By the time I went away to school, I knew. I still pestered him about it. I was hurt though, and still very young. I was fourteen when I went away. I used to tease him about us marrying just to watch him stammer and blush. But I was also mad. Not at him, but I think at my father for being wrong about all of it. Only I no longer had a father to blame by then." She bit her lip. "I did not really have anyone to talk to. Here I was in a strange new place with no friends, with sisters too young to understand and no real friends I could write to about this. So, I wrote to the one person I thought might still be my friend. Only he never read my letters at all."

"Which explains the absolute lack of delight in seeing him at the ball. Yes, I noticed," Laurence's voice was gentle. "It would have been hard not to." He paused. "I take it you still have feelings for him?"

She laughed at that. "Would it matter if I did? He has no interest in me. He has made that clear quite a few times over the years."

They rode in silence for a bit.

"We are quite the pair, are we not?" she asked Laurence with a wry grimace. "It is a shame we are not suited for each other. It would solve so much."

He was thoughtful. "What if..."

"What?" They were riding abreast. She pulled up now, waiting for him to do the same.

Only he didn't stop. Rather, he kept riding, speaking over his shoulder for her benefit. "No. It is foolishness."

She kicked her horse that she might catch up again. "Stop and talk to me!"

He grimaced but did as she said. "'Tis foolishness."

"You are repeating yourself. What are you thinking?"

"The Lady in question..."

"Yes?"

"Ladies talk to one another, do they not?"

She laughed. "Sometimes."

"Well, the Lady in question rather likes rakes."

She stared at him. She could immediately see the problem. Laurence was about as far removed from being a rake as he could be.

"If you were to perhaps...spread a bit of gossip perhaps. A few words in the right place...?"

"My goodness." Of course, she quite liked Laurence, but this was a rather large favour he was asking.

"I would help you in return. With Andrew." He spoke in a rush. "I am not sure how, but perhaps there is something I could do on your behalf...to return the favour."

It was brilliant. It was daring and probably quite foolish. "I cannot promise it would work," she said after a moment.

He shrugged. "Nor could I promise you the same."

It was a wicked pact, one a properly brought up Lady would never consider. Still, what was the alternative? A life of Andrew's hatred? A marriage to someone else?

Faust they would not have made such a deal.

"Agreed," she said, and reaching across the space between him she took his hand, to shake in the way men would. "Let us do it."

Chapter Seven

Another ball. There was always another ball. How many had he been to so far this Season? Had there not been so much pressure from his father, Andrew would have avoided every last one of them. He'd even tried as much, but his father had tracked him down at White's and forced the matter by threatening to cut off his allowance.

His orders were clear. He was to find a bride and produce an heir. The sooner the better.

Unfortunately, his father still had one very particular bride in mind.

Unfortunately, so did Andrew. The Lady in question thought otherwise.

At the same time, somehow their paths never crossed. Many times, Andrew saw Amanda from a distance. He would memorize her profile from across the room, thinking how terribly lovely she was. He would spend an hour working up the courage to approach her and she would disappear. To complicate matters, she seemed to be spending an overabundance of time with Laurence. Which made him feel like a perfect heel for being jealous of his friend's good fortune.

As if summoning the very spectre of his friend, Andrew caught a snippet of conversation from two men heading towards the library to smoke.

"du Campion? The middle boy is rather a rake, is he not? Surely, I would not allow my daughter to be seen with such a man."

"Agreed!"

Andrew was already sprinting after him. "By any chance were you just discussing Laurence du Campion?" he asked, his mind reeling from the chance comment.

It did not take long for the gentlemen to give him a good accounting of the wild ways of du Campion. Several of the stories told were clearly embellished. Andrew himself had been with Laurence upon the dates mentioned and knew for certain these events had never happened. The rest though...could it be possible that his friend had fallen into bad ways? Gambling? Chasing after light-skirts?

Chasing after...Amanda?

Andrew's stomach lurched. No, surely not. He had intended to introduce Laurence to Amanda himself. That he hadn't had the opportunity, meant nothing. The intent was what mattered. It was as if Andrew had handed Amanda into the cad's hands himself.

Andrew clutched at the doorway, needing something to hold himself up. Two ladies passing by gave him a wide berth, no doubt thinking he was well into his cups. He groaned. Let them think what they would. He needed to find Laurence to get to the bottom of this matter.

No, he needed to find Amanda. To protect her. Even if the stories were not true, the very fact of their existence would hurt her reputation. To be seen with such a man...!

Thankfully, Amanda was not hard to spot. Her hair shone like a beacon, making a soft halo around her head. An angel. Amanda was an angel and did not deserve a man such as Laurence.

Tonight, there was no waiting. Rage gave him the courage to cross the ballroom, to come to stand in front of her, to take her hand and pull her out onto the dance floor though it was not his dance. She protested, but she could hardly pull away without making a scene. Instead, she laughed as though this was all a great joke upon the man who had been about to escort her out to dance, while he could see the anger in her eyes. Such fire promised retribution.

"My dear Sir, I do not believe you were on my dance card," she said as they stepped into the first paces of the dance.

"I needed to speak with you in private."

"This is 'in private'?" she asked, laughter quirking her lips in such a way that he was reminded anew just how beautiful she had grown.

"It is about Laurence du Campion. Blast it, you know who I mean!"

"Your language!" She stepped back and away in time with the music, giving him time to compose himself until she was within reach again.

"I promise to speak civilly," he said as they joined hands and turned first one way, then reversed to move in the opposite direction.

"Then speak." Her words were as crisp as her movements.

He had no time to find the right words. Best to get right to the heart of the matter then. "You have been seen in the company of a rake—"

To his surprise, she laughed. In fact, she was laughing so hard that she stopped dancing altogether, causing no small amount of consternation on the part of the other dancers. When it seemed that she had no intention of starting to dance again, the others moved awkwardly around her. Andrew stared, unsure of what to do. Finally, he grabbed her gloved hand in his and drew her from the dance floor entirely, starting an entire spate of new gossip, he was sure.

"You find this amusing?" he asked once he had her as far away as he could get from any who would listen, which took quite some doing in the crowded ballroom.

"I am hardly worried about a little idle gossip."

"It is hardly gossip!" he flared. He was not about to name names, but the gentlemen he'd talked to were above reproach.

"Miss Abbott, are you well?"

It was the devil himself. Laurence insinuated himself into their company. His brow was creased with worry. Andrew saw Amanda's mother approaching, and his own father. Things were quickly devolving. He had very little time to make his position clear. "I absolutely forbid you to see Miss Abbott!" he said, turning towards Laurence as being the one most likely to agree. They were friends, after all.

Or had been.

"What?" Laurence seemed confused.

"You do not have the right to make any such demand!" Amanda said at the same time.

"Andrew, what in the world are you doing?" His father had gotten there first. In fact, a lot of people had shown up suddenly. Someone grabbed his arm, pulling him away from Amanda whom he desperately needed to keep safe. Why did no one understand this?

"Laurence! You will not see her again!"

Laurence wasn't listening. In fact, he seemed to have his arm around Amanda and was guiding her away. His *arm* around her.

Andrew pulled away from those who would have held him back. In a moment he was on Laurence, his fist finding the other man's nose with uncanny aim.

Chapter Eight

"I never thought I would raise an idiot."

Andrew winced. Well, he'd been expecting a lecture, hence the careful retreat to his club rather than home. Of course, his father had known where to find him. The only surprising thing was just how long it had taken for him to show up.

"Go away," he muttered, taking another long drink from the snifter he cradled in his hand. The alcohol went down like fire, burning away the past few hours of his life. Maybe if he drank enough, he could reset his life back to where it was before Miss Amanda Abbott came home.

"Fine words for someone who just did you a favour." His father settled heavily in the wingback chair next to him and motioned for the steward to bring him a drink as well.

"A favour? I do not recall any favours. The only thing you have done is to shove me relentlessly at the only debutante of the Ton who would not have me."

His father started at that. "You have a rather high opinion of yourself."

"Is it not true? I am in line to inherit the title, the estate...which is worth quite a great deal of coin by any estimation. You have done quite well for yourself."

"It was not always so." His father frowned into his drink, swirling the contents of the glass idly. "There was a time when we were not so well off. When I rather pushed your sisters to make good matches—"

"Which they did." Andrew shrugged. "There is no harm in wanting your children to marry well."

"I tried to do the same for you."

"I take it Amanda has a considerable dowry?" Andrew shook his head. "I never cared for any of that."

"She is from a good family who has done well by her," Lord Gillingham agreed. "But more than that, there was a promise made. A binding of empires, if you will. Two families with much to gain from a simple alliance. I never told you, but Lord Abbott and I had an agreement regarding our children. I never told you about it. Perhaps I hoped if I pushed the two of you together, you would...well, find each other without my needing to resort to...well, never mind. He is long dead, and the agreement has no need to be bound. I just thought since the two of you got along together so well as children—"

"She was a torment!" The words exploded from Andrew without his meaning to say them. He flushed. Well, it was true. But she was no longer.

His father only chuckled. "I recall the way she prattled on about marrying you. I suppose her Father must have told her."

Her father had told her. Well, that explained a lot. Andrew groaned and motioned for the man to refill his glass. "Well, it does not matter now. I suppose du Campion will call me out to a duel. Whatever dreams you had for me, end here, old man. There will be no one to leave your empire to." He raised his glass in his father's direction and was about to take a drink when the snifter was snatched from his hand.

"You fool!"

His father stood over him, fury written all over his face. "Do you not think I have already fixed all that?"

"Your 'favour'?" Andrew shook his head, trying to clear it. "What have you done?"

"I have saved you from disgracing our entire family. You would have been the ruin of the Gillingham's and the du Campion's both if I had not intervened. You left poor Laurence in a dither. Do you have any idea what it would be for a Frenchman to call out an Englishman in a duel with the current political climate? Yet honour would hardly dictate otherwise. Instead, I managed to convince those who were nearest to swear the two of you have both been drinking and had been playing at being the fool to impress a girl. It has cost me a great deal to save you from this mess you have created."

"Wait—" Andrew held up his hand to stop the flow of words. Why did the room have to spin so? "You mean to say you made us both into the laughingstock of the Ton?"

"Better that than dead," his father snapped.

Andrew sank deeper into his chair while he forced his muzzy head to think. "I owe Laurence an apology."

"You owe Laurence an apology. Miss Abbott you owe a great deal more. I would suggest rectifying this entire mess as soon as possible, before the gossipmongers turn this into something far worse than it already is. Her reputation is on the line. Would you ruin her chance at future happiness?"

Andrew sat up quickly. "I should say not!"

"Then fix this, Andrew. I have done what I can for you. The rest is up to you." Lord Gillingham turned to go, taking his hat and coat from the servant standing ready at the door. He paused there, on the threshold. "One more word of advice, Andrew..."

"Yes?"

"The next time you start getting all worked up about just who a young Lady is spending time with, you might want to try talking to the girl and seeing what she has to say before engaging in fisticuffs."

With that, he tipped his hat to his son and left.

Chapter Nine

Normally, boating on the Thames with her family would be considered an enjoyable pastime, especially in the company of Laurence who always found so much to be enthusiastic about. They'd taken a few such outings in recent weeks, ending always with a picnic upon the riverbank. Today though, the day had been soured from the outset. No one was enjoying themselves. The sun was too hot. Her sisters were bored. Laurence looked a mess between his broken nose and dejected attitude.

Not that Amanda was making any of this any better. She too was out of sorts, especially given the way her mother kept making noises that she felt her eldest daughter was taking too long to decide upon a suitor.

"You must make a match at some point," she said, with a quelling glance at Laurence who was showing Felicity how to hold a fishline, making it clear he was not included in this whispered conversation.

"I fail to see why there is such a rush to send me to the alter."

"After last night's scene, you dare to say that? It will be any wonder if you have any suitors left after that disgraceful display from that Gillingham boy. And that du Campion is no better. Why I heard—"

"Oh, for heaven's sake, mother." Amanda stood up and brushed off her skirts. She had had enough. The rumours she'd started had clearly worked all too well. Not that it had done any good. The girl he'd been trying to impress had absconded to Gretna Green just last night, thankfully taking the attention off the drunken antics of a pair of rakes at a fairly unimportant ball.

Thank heavens it had been a small affair last night and that both men had been credited with drinking heavily beforehand.

Fairly well put out by all of this, she walked down to the riverbank to watch Laurence in his attempts to fish. What she needed was some peace and quiet to sort out her thoughts.

What she found was that someone had gotten there before her.

"Andrew!" Amanda started in surprise, turning to a dreadful suspicion that things were going to escalate the way they had last night. She could well picture Laurence landing in the river the way she'd landed in the pond so long ago. Evidently, Laurence was thinking the same thing, for he scrambled to his feet.

"What do you want, Gillingham?" he asked, his voice cold, his hands already fisting at his sides.

Andrew put his hands up in a placating gesture. "Please, hear me out. I came to apologize."

Laurence and Amanda exchanged looks.

"I am listening," Amanda said finally as Laurence nodded. She nodded that they should walk together, creating some distance between her sisters and hopefully out of range of her mother's sharp ears.

Andrew looked from one to the other as though trying to figure out how to begin. Amanda crossed her arms and waited, not about to make this any easier on him.

"You see, I know both of you very well. Which I know makes no sense given how I have been acting, but...Laurence, I know you. There has never been a man who is less of a rake. How those silly rumours got started—"

"Um. That was my fault." Amanda blushed. "I know how rude it is to interrupt but...I started those rumours."

"To help me. To...er...win a Lady."

Andrew seemed to have stalled out. He looked from one to the other in consternation. "But I thought..."

Despite herself, Amanda began to giggle. Laurence looked at her and his lips twitched until he too was laughing. The problem was, the more they laughed, the more put out Andrew seemed to become.

"Right. I can see I am a fool." With that, Andrew turned to leave.

Suddenly, everything wasn't quite as funny as it had been a moment before. Amanda took a step after him, but stopped, unsure. To her surprise, Laurence was right there, pushing her gently forward.

"Go. I think it's time a few things were explained."

He was right. If anything, she should have just talked to Andrew from the start. "Lord Gillingham. Wait!" She dashed after him, too fast, for she wasn't even looking where she was going.

Which was how she tripped on a rock, stumbled, and somehow pushed Andrew right into the river.

Chapter Ten

The chit had tried to drown him!

"Oh, get over it already. The water was shallow where you landed. At least I was nice enough to help you out, and not leave you sitting in the mud. Unlike some people I could mention," Amanda said, quite ignoring her mother's screams as she wrung out the edge of her dress.

Normally he might have been more interested in the proceedings, especially giving the brief tantalizing glimpse this afforded of her rather shapely ankles. But Andrew was still rather put out, for shallow water or not, he was quite drenched.

Darned if she wasn't cute when she was giggling like that.

Then Andrew was laughing right along with her, though why exactly he could not say, except she'd come after him, even if he'd landed in the river.

"What happened to us?" she asked when she could speak again. "We used to be such friends. "

"Speak for yourself," he answered then ducked his head when he realized what he had said. "We were children," he corrected himself. I will admit I was not always on my best behaviour."

"Nor was I." She glanced over her shoulder where he could see Lady

Abbott arguing with Laurence who was quite clearly trying to keep her from rushing over.

"Perhaps you had best speak quickly if you have anything to say," she suggested.

"I thought you were the one with something to say. Given you were rushing after me," he pointed out.

"I did not know what I was going to say," she replied, lifting a hand to brush the hair from her eyes, leaving a streak of mud adorably upon her forehead. "I only knew that I did not want you to go."

He caught his breath. "I am not well-versed when it comes to expressing my feelings."

She looked again towards her mother. "Then you had best learn quickly. Here she comes."

"I love you. Amanda Abbott, I love you and want to marry you!"

His exclamation coincided with Lady Abbott's arrival. In her wake came the other girls and Laurence, along with no small number of bystanders who had stopped to either render assistance or to watch the show. More likely the latter.

"Well!" Lady Abbott paused in whatever she had been about to say.

"Well," Amanda echoed the sentiment.

Andrew started to smile. "Besides, you already claimed the house as yours. You might as well marry me. Given you proposed first."

Lady Abbott's mouth opened and closed with no sound coming forth.

"Yes, I suppose I should honour my earlier such...proposal," she replied, her eyes twinkling.

"As soon as possible," he added, taking a step towards her.

"Absolutely," she agreed, taking a step towards him.

"By special license?" She was within reach. He could almost taste those luscious lips.

"Are there circumstances requiring them?" she asked breathlessly.

"There are about to be..." he said and might have taken her into his arms then and there had Lady Abbott not fainted, with Laurence catching her.

"Well, I say!" Laurence exclaimed, sounding very British for once, while behind him, the girls tittered.

Epilogue

The wedding was everything they could have imagined. While the ceremony was intended to be kept small and intimate, Andrew's sisters showed up with husbands and children in tow, making the whole thing quite an affair. It was splendid to be all together again in the home where they'd grown up as children.

Lord Gillingham looked on in satisfaction. He drew Andrew aside as the group went in to enjoy the wedding breakfast and asked after Andrew's plans.

"I am taking her to the Continent for a honeymoon. We shall travel all the way to Rome, perhaps even to Venice."

"Venice." It was Virginia who overheard the word and gasped in horror as she considered him from across the table. "Where the streets are made of water."

Amanda laughed. "Perhaps not Venice. Given our past...difficulties," she said between giggles.

Andrew reached across and took her hand in his. How soft and delicate it felt there. He lifted her fingers to his lips that he might kiss them. "Dry land," he agreed. "We shall endeavour to stay upon dry land."

"After we cross the Channel," his wife reminded him.

Andrew blanched. "After we cross the Channel."

She giggled. "I do love you," she said, and squeezed his hand.

Phineas leaned in to whisper to Virginia, "Am I missing something here?"

There was no explaining it. Instead, there was only time for joy, and for each other. Andrew reached for his wife, happy to find Amanda already reaching for him. There, in front of everyone, they kissed. Who cared if this was not proper etiquette for a wedding breakfast or not? He only knew he needed her as she seemed to need him.

So, they kissed, ignoring cheers and good-natured teasing from those who loved him best. His entire world was in his arms, and he didn't care who knew it.

The End

Retiring with The Lady

THE LADY SERIES BOOK TWELVE

"Well, I suppose that is that." Lord Gillingham watched as the carriage trundled down the street carrying his youngest child, Andrew, and his new bride off on their honeymoon. While he was happy for his son, there was something that felt sad in the hooves clattering on cobblestones and the creak of the carriage. It was a lonely sound. One that signalled the end of a very significant portion of his life.

His family was gone.

Not gone. Married. Happy. Starting their own families. It was the way of things, something to be expected. Besides, Andrew would be back after his honeymoon. He and his wife would settle into their lives again here in London in due time. As Lord Gillingham's heir, he still had much to learn about running the Estate. In time, they would act together as partners, preparing the young man to someday take his place as Lord in his own right.

In the meantime, in the weeks they were away touring the Continent, the house felt very empty. His daughters had not stayed long when last they came, having their own lives to attend to. Of course, they would visit. But in the meantime, he would...

Well, he would come up with something. Now that he didn't have to squire offspring around to balls and the like, keeping a weathered eye on their prospects, something they had never considered near as much as he had; now he had time to do other things.

"So, he is off then?"

Startled from his reverie, Lord Gillingham looked around to find the intruder. He was deeply annoyed that he should be caught standing in the street and ruminating about the past like an old man with nothing better to do. One of his neighbours, Lady Pelbrook, stood near at hand. Her maid was beside her, carrying a hatbox of all things.

"Oh, er, yes they are." Lord Gillingham looked for a hat to tip and found he was not wearing any. Put out that he should be caught bare-headed and outdoors in such a way, he might have been a little brisker in his reply than intended. "If you will please excuse me, Lady Pelbrook. I am not quite myself." He nodded with as much dignity as he could muster and turned to go in.

Lady Pelbrook put out a hand to stop him. "Lord Gillingham, if I might offer a word..."

"I should say you already are," Lord Gillingham responded without thinking, and flushed, for it was quite ungentlemanly of him to say so. "Your pardon, my Lady. I truly am at a disadvantage. I can see you mean the best, but..." He cast about desperately for the polite thing to do. "Tea perhaps? Though I suppose you do not have the time given you are quite obviously returning from a shopping expedition."

Immediately, Lady Pelbrook's face blossomed into a smile. The look startled him, for as a man of fifty years, he had thought himself quite beyond noticing a Lady in quite this way. But Lady Pelbrook, a Dowager in her own right, was still quite attractive with honey-blonde hair threaded through with silver, and a face still quite unlined by age even if she was of his generation. "I would like that."

In no time at all, the Lady was seated quite amiably in Lord Gillingham's parlour, teacup in hand. Lord Gillingham, feeling more himself in this setting relaxed considerably. "You seemed to have something you wished to discuss with me outside?" he prompted as he accepted tea from the man serving.

"Quite. Though it seems rather bold of me now to have started this conversation."

"Are we not of an age where we can speak our minds? Lady

Pelbrook, I have known you since before you and I had our first Season together. You have been a neighbour to me for at least half of those years. I expect that we should be able to speak on just about anything at this point. If there is some problem—"

"Not a problem!" she interrupted, setting down her teacup upon the table. "It is just...I have had a concern for some time and now that your children have grown and set out upon their own adventures, I wished to...botheration, but this seems rather forward of me, prying into your life like this. But would you say that you are happy, my Lord?"

"Happy?" He stared at her. Of all the topics of conversation she might have brought up, this was not one he would have expected. "Of course, I am happy. Why look around you. The house is well-appointed, I am welcomed in the best circles—"

"Ah, as I have thought." Lady Pelbrook took up her tea again and added more sugar.

Lord Gillingham's eyes narrowed. He was fast coming to regret this hasty invitation. "What have you thought, Theodosia?" he asked, unconsciously calling her by her first name as he had when they were children.

"If you must know, *Theodore*," she responded, using his name with perhaps a little more force than was necessary, "It has been quite obvious you have changed. You have focused upon money and prestige to the exclusion of...well, what truly matters in life."

"Why?" Lord Gillingham snapped, getting up to place his teacup on the table next to him, though the movement was unnecessary. "Because I have wanted my children to marry well?"

"Do you think the Ton has not noticed?" she asked, her tone becoming gentler, her eyes softening as she watched him pace the room.

"I do not care what the Ton has or has not noticed." He drew himself up stiffly. "And I think it rather crass of you to bring up such a topic of conversation. It is simply not done, Theodosia!"

"I have overstepped myself." She rose too, exchanging tea for reticule and shaking out her skirts. "I truly meant no harm. I just...well I worry about you, Theodore, for I know your life has changed now. You are alone, as we are wont to find ourselves when we have reached this age. I went through this a year ago. And I found that what kept me grounded was being able to focus on the important things in life, the things that money cannot buy."

"There is nothing money cannot buy!" Lord Gillingham snapped.

The look she gave him was pitying. "What about happiness?" She tilted her head a little as she looked at him, as though examining him for something she could not see. "I rather miss the boy you once were, Lord Gillingham. As you said, we have known each other a long time. I had hoped..." She stopped herself with a shake of her head. "Good day, Lord Gillingham. It was kind of you to invite me in."

Whatever she had hoped was lost as she took her leave. Lord Gillingham watched her go, feeling almost like he was at sea as he had watched his son's departure only an hour before. No, this was worse somehow. For his son had left in happiness and joy while Lady Pelbrook had simply left, leaving him very little idea of what she thought at all, except that he was somehow a disappointment to her.

Why that should matter so much, he had no idea. After all, why should he care what *she* thought?

Chapter One

Had his personality changed so very much? In the days that followed, Lord Gillingham revisited this thought more and more. Worse, Lady Pelbrook had implied that he was greedy, thinking only of his coffers and not his children's happiness. It was a most unfair accusation and one that put his back up every time he considered it anew.

"Confounding woman," he muttered under his breath as he paced about his library. He was unable to even sit and enjoy a volume of history or poetry, pastimes he had always enjoyed but could find no pleasure in now.

Yet, all five of his children had married quite well. They were all also quite happy with whom they were sharing their lives. That the road had been rocky in getting to this state of affairs was hardly of any importance. Nor was the fact that he'd tried, on more than one occasion, to guide his offspring to matches he'd felt were more suitable at the time.

"I did nothing any other parent would do," he said as he came to stop at the window. It overlooked the square and, quite coincidentally, Lady Pelbrook's house a few doors down. "I only ever wanted to make sure their futures were secure. That they would want for nothing."

The fact that he had been able to leverage the fortunes of his children into investments, which had benefited him as well as them was a mark of astute business management. Nothing more. And everyone else seemed happy enough with this. So, if anything, he was quite justified in his actions to ensure his children married well.

Except...well, everything came at a cost, didn't it?

Lord Gillingham had noticed a definite decline in visits from his daughters. Though several were in London currently for the Season, now that Andrew and his wife were gone without expectation of returning for several weeks, if not months, they no longer seemed to have time to come around. It was as though they had been there more to visit each other than to visit him.

No. He had clearly deceived himself. They had never come to visit him, otherwise, they would be there now. Visiting.

"I was hard on them," he admitted softly, his words swallowed up by the cavernous room that held his priceless works of art, his tomes, and the bits and pieces he had accumulated since the rise of his wealth. Funny how the room felt cold now, even with the fire burning in the grate.

He rose, going to poke at it himself, throwing another log on. His back protested at the action, a reminder of just how long it had been since he had tended his own fires. It had been years now. The servants would be horrified if they realized he had done this himself.

The problem, he realized as he settled back in his chair, was that Lady Pelbrook had perhaps been more accurate in her assessment than he liked. What had she said? That he could not find happiness without spending money to do so, or some such nonsense?

"Botheration!" The word exploded from him even as the door opened to admit the butler who offered him a letter upon a silver salver. The man hesitated a moment, as though trying to figure out if this word had been meant as judgement upon himself or the letter upon the tray.

"I do believe it is from Lady Pelbrook, Sir," the man said somewhat hesitantly as he drew the tray back once the letter had been taken.

"Well double botheration then!" Lord Gillingham said, turning the missive in his hands as though suspecting it might hold some trap within for the unwary.

The man, if anything, seemed all the more uncertain. "I believe I was to wait on a reply."

"Triple it then!" Lord Gillingham broke the seal and unfolded the paper. The note was short and to the point.

"Lady Pelbrook requests the presence of Lord Gillingham for dinner tonight."

Lord Gillingham stared. How easy it would be to say no. He owed the woman nothing. At the same time, he admitted to certain curiosity. Lady Pelbrook had certainly spoken her mind, which was in itself refreshing. She had even been accurate in her assessment after a fashion. It made one rather wonder what damages she intended to inflict next upon his person.

"Perhaps she means to poison me directly," he murmured thoughtfully.

The man was startled. "My Lord?"

Lord Gillingham smiled. It was not a nice smile. "Send word I would be delighted."

Chapter Two

"I treated you unfairly."

Lady Pelbrook twisted her napkin in her hands. Her soup was growing cold, not that she cared. She had felt terrible all day thinking about how her mouth had run away with her, yet again, and how she had hurt someone she had known for years. Why? Because he did not conform to the standards she had set for herself?

"Truly, it was none of my business..." she continued, wanting to get the apology out of the way quickly before she talked herself out of it. "How you live your life—"

"You were right."

Lord Gillingham set down his spoon, which had been balanced aloft in his hand since she'd started speaking. "You were absolutely right, Theodosia. I have been a..." He frowned, as though he were having trouble finding a strong enough word.

"A nincompoop?" she suggested. "A miserly, miserable..."

The look he was giving her spoke volumes. Lady Pelbrook stopped before she got herself in any deeper. "Yes. Well." She cleared her throat. "If I might ask—"

"You might not."

"But you came for dinner nonetheless...?"

Lord Gillingham settled back in his chair, while behind him the servants shifted uncomfortably as though trying to figure out whether to bring in the next course or not. Finally, she waved her hand, directing them to take the soup and bring whatever came next.

"Lady Pelbrook, I will admit that coming to dinner tonight was an impulse born out of curiosity. You speak the truth, which is something that is rare enough in the Ton. At the same time, you made an assertion if you will. Something about," he paused and closed as eyes as though this would bring the words back to him with more clarity. "Money not being able to buy happiness."

She smiled. "Ah. I see. Perhaps if this seems unclear, it might do well to start with a definition. How would you list what is important in life?"

He stared, ignoring the proffered plate the footman had brought of fresh fish, sautéed delicately in butter. "I sense already a trap within the question," he muttered, taking a portion of fish with little grace. "You may as well tell me what you think is important in life and leave it to me whether or not I agree with your list."

She actually laughed at this. "It is not as hard as you might think." She ticked the items off upon her fingers. "Family, friends, health. Perhaps I would add living life to the fullest. Finding time for who and what is important to me and less on material things such as how much coin is at my disposal," she hesitated. "Love. I would add love to that list. Seeing the happiness upon your Andrew's face as he drove away with his bride nestled next to him. They were a perfect picture of everything in life that matters, would you not say so?"

She could see him struggling to find a way to disagree with the assessment. In the end, he concentrated on his fish in silence, his forehead furrowed as he thought about these things.

Ah, that he was at least *thinking* about it mattered so very much to her. He was listening and it did her heart good to know, for it had pained her how she and her friend had lost the easy companionship they'd once enjoyed. Marriage would do that, she reflected, wondering not for the first time why he'd never proposed to her all those years ago. They had been so well suited back then.

"How then would one..." He stopped, almost desperately reaching for the butter that he might attend properly to his roll. "If one were to..."

She understood only too well what he was trying to say. She remembered the emptiness of her days after her last child had married, the way the house had echoed. He needed something different in his life but had no idea just what that would be. It would take time, she knew, to settle into this new rhythm of life. He would need to explore for himself what life had to offer.

"Dinner!" she exclaimed, and he started, his knife nearly slipping from his hand, his roll half buttered.

"I beg your pardon?"

"We start with a dinner party. A few friends. People you already know, maybe a guest or two of my choosing to make things interesting. An evening in the company of friends."

"Friends." He set the knife down.

Lady Pelbrook stifled a sigh. "I am sure you understand the concept."

The look he gave added a few more volumes to the last such look. She would soon have an entire library of ill-tempered looks.

"When would this," his lip curled, "*dinner party* take place."

"Thursday." She chose the day quickly, wanting to establish something near enough that he would not forget his resolve to change, but far enough to give her time to plan something suitable.

"Thursday."

"The day after Wednesday," she supplied helpfully.

"Fine. Thursday." He seemed surprised by his own acquiescence. "But it will be a *small* affair."

"Only a few very close friends," she assured him. "It will be quite an intimate soiree."

He dug into his fish. "See that it is."

Chapter Three

He was in over his head.

It was an uncomfortable feeling. Lord Gillingham had always prided himself on being in control of what went on around him. Of course, his children had not always accepted his fatherly leadership, to the extent that they had each found their own mates without his guidance at all...

Well, maybe that wasn't the best example.

In his *own* life, he had been quite certain of himself. He had made decisions in his business, which had brought about excellent results because of that stern control. A fact which explained why this particular dinner left him uncertain and even...well, not afraid exactly. Full of trepidation.

It was for this reason that he had lingered for an uncommonly long period of time before heading in.

Perhaps if he hadn't been so preoccupied with this dinner, he might have noticed the uncommon amount of traffic on the street. *Someone, somewhere, must be giving quite the affair,* he thought idly as he walked the short distance to Lady Pelbrook's house. He was fortunate that he was so near as to not require a carriage for this dinner.

The house at least seemed quiet enough when the butler opened the door. This might well be because he was late, he supposed. He would be the last guest to arrive.

And the first one to leave, if I have anything to say about it, he promised himself as he handed over his hat and walking stick to the butler.

Indeed, he was later than he thought. The guests had only just gone in, the butler informed him quietly, as he ushered him directly to the dining room. Thankfully, they had not taken his place from the dinner table yet. The Lady had insisted they leave it, sure that he was coming.

Flushed and uncomfortable at being so unfashionably late, Lord Gillingham stepped through the doorway, excuses already upon his lips. He was brought up short by the sight of the dining table in full leaf with at least a dozen couples milling about as they took their seats. He looked upon the throng in horror. *This* was a small affair?

Rather put out by such blatant disregard for his feelings, Lord Gillingham might have left right then if Lady Pelbrook hadn't been so adroit at fastening her hand to the crook of his elbow, as though he were walking her in. "Right on time!" she sang out, though the lines about her mouth and eyes told of the strain he had put upon her by being late.

This, more than anything, made him feel as though it would be ungentlemanly to abandon her now. He allowed her to draw him into the room, and to his place next to hers, which was of no surprise. She had, after all, put this thing together on his behalf.

Still, he was not pleased by the arrangement of guests. Sure, they were an amiable bunch, well-titled and refined. Though she had added in some interesting personages to note. There was a poet across the table from him. A well-known scientist, who had come to London to lecture on the topic of primitive botany. An archaeologist who had recently been to Egypt. Had he not been so put out he might have been enthralled. Each person to whom he spoke was utterly fascinating, well-pleased in their chosen life's work, and with much to say on interesting topics ranging from music to art to history to science.

Lord Gillingham, his head in a whirl, spoke little.

Perhaps it was because he was overwhelmed by the sheer volume of choices that she had thrust upon him. They had, after all, talked of the emptiness of life with the children grown and gone. That the world held so many wonders was a new and startling thought. There was more to life than making money. This he was seeing very clearly. But did she have to present this information to him as though beating him over the head with it?

Would I have listened otherwise?

Feeling morose, he found it hard to listen. He had spoken hardly a dozen words all night and was aware that the other guests were casting looks at him, perplexed at his lack of response. He lingered at the end of dinner, while the hostess said goodbye to her guests before turning to him in utter exasperation.

"Why did you even come if you were not going to give the evening a fair chance?" she asked, her hands fisted upon her hips.

She was truly glorious; anger lending a flush to her cheeks, a brightness to her eyes. He had noticed this attraction to her before, the beauty of the woman when riled up. It made him wonder how she would look when other passions were aroused, a thought that was also startling, if not titillating.

And entirely not suitable to the occasion.

"I attended the dinner as you asked," he said a touch defensively though he well knew to what she referred.

"You were rude to my guests!"

"How was I rude? I never said so much as a single thing which could be construed as rude!"

"Your silence was remonstrance enough. It was clear you were bored silly and thought yourself above the entire affair!"

"Above? My good woman, I never put such airs and graces in my life."

Her eyebrows arched up in surprise. "I can name a dozen such occasions where you have acted as though you were better than those around you, each taken from the past few Seasons when your children were courting."

"That was then," he muttered uncomfortably.

"It proves my point!"

"I would say it does not, if you have to stretch to grasp an occasion of my supposed misbehaviour from a ball which happened a year or more ago!" he shouted in triumph, noting the butler hovering with hat and coat as though wishing to eject the Lord himself, though not quite daring to take the initiative without leave of his mistress.

Well, he could certainly prove his good manners by not lingering for a conversation such as this!

"I daresay there is nothing more to say if this is how you feel," he said stiffly and motioned for the butler to bring his things. "I thank you for the evening, My Lady. I will see myself out."

It was a beautiful parting show, only he ruined his exit entirely. He was in such a hurry to leave that his arms became tangled in his coat. Worse, he might have hit the butler with his walking stick on his way out. Entirely by accident of course. It wasn't like he was running away or anything.

Chapter Four

I owe her an apology.

Lord Gillingham sat with his aching head cradled in his hands. He might have overindulged a touch upon arriving home last night. Not that there was anything wrong with a whiskey before bed. It was the three snifters that followed which were problematical.

But the main problem was that he had acted like an ass last night. At the very least, he could have feigned some sort of enthusiasm. Or offered a comment with genuine interest to the scientist who had proved rather fascinating, especially when discussing the local mushrooms found in the area where Lord Gillingham had grown up. As a boy, he'd enjoyed picking mushrooms and bringing them to the cook.

The gentleman who was a poet had been equally as interesting. The man had been well-travelled and drew upon his experiences when writing.

No, the problem had been Lord Gillingham. He had been faced with something that he had not expected and acted in a boorish manner, only spiting himself in so doing. He had deprived himself of many such conversations. Why, the woman who was a professor at Oxford had been delightful really, seated upon his other side. He had not known any women who taught at such a level. She surely would have been interesting to talk to.

Theodosia might, likewise, prove interesting to talk to as well.

Yes, he owed her an apology.

He took a sheet of foolscap, intending to jot a quick note of apology, but the words would not come. Sure, he had done wrong, and a few words would have sufficed to make his excuses, but he was not satisfied with such a shallow missive. Did he not owe Lady Pelbrook more than this?

Indeed, he did. Which meant he needed to explain why he had acted so badly. If only he understood himself what had gone so wrong.

Perhaps it was the infernal list of hers from the other night. What was it she'd said? Family? Health? He cast about for the answer and came up blank. Unless...

He looked about his desk. He remembered sitting in this very place last night, whiskey near to hand and writing...something. Sure enough, there in the scraps of paper neatly bundled and placed where he might easily lay hands upon them in case the notes were of any importance was what he remembered writing. Well dimly remembered. And 'writing' might be putting too strong a word for it if these scribbles were anything to go by. Stick figures decorated one sheet, as though the page were an attempt at hieroglyphics for the Egyptologist. What was his name? Cummings?

Underneath was something a little clearer. He hadn't been so deep in his cups when he had written this particular note.

Family.

Friends.

Health.

Living life to the fullest.

Beneath these four items was a single word, circled several times.

Love.

Bosh. What nonsense. It was no wonder he had been so out of sorts. As if he did not have those things already.

Lord Gillingham looked at the apology he'd started and added to the end, a few choice words.

"...while I regret my actions last night, I still fail to see the point you have been making. Your list is utter nonsense. I have family and friends

aplenty. My health is fine, and I daresay how I live my life is my concern, not yours."

Well satisfied now with his response he called for his man and sent it off.

There. The deed was done. Let Lady Pelbrook chew upon that.

Only...

Well, how many of those things did he truly have? His family was scattered to all corners of London, or in some cases, to the world. His friends? While he had acquaintances aplenty, how many true friends did he even have? Who in his circle of friends would dare to speak to him openly, the way a friend would?

Lady Pelbrook. Is not Theodosia your friend, you old fool?

Well, maybe. But he had his health. That was something.

Even if his leg had been bothering him lately. And there were nights he had difficulty sleeping, so uncomfortable was he from the rich foods served at the balls he attended. His father used to complain of such discomforts before he died.

Lord Gillingham paled.

Well, what about living life to the fullest. He was...

He looked about the room. The same room he had been holed up in all week. Save for the nights at Lady Pelbrook's, when had he last left the house.

And as for love? Well, he'd had that once. His dear wife had passed, and since then...well. He had it once. That was enough.

Wasn't it?

He rang for his butler.

"The letter I gave you. Is it posted?"

The butler stared at him for a long moment. "It was for Lady Pelbrook, was it not?"

Lord Gillingham started. "Well, of course it was. Her name was written on the outside, clear enough."

"I had the kitchen boy take it over directly, on his way to the market for cook. It seemed the most expedient way to handle it."

Lord Gillingham swallowed hard. He tried to recall just what words he had used in his letter.

"Will there be anything else, My Lord?"

"If you would wait a moment."

Feeling a proper fool, Lord Gillingham took another sheet of paper and dipped his pen in the ink to begin again.

"Lady Pelbrook, I fear I owe you an apology for my apology…"

An hour later, a reply came.

"You might make it up to me by taking me on an outing to Vauxhall Gardens on Saturday next."

Lord Gillingham read and then re-read the note several times. Well, that was clear enough. His reply was a single word.

"Agreed."

Chapter Five

Vauxhall Gardens was for young people.

Apparently, Lady Pelbrook had not been satisfied with the idea of a simple outing. She was waiting for him to arrive with her own carriage ready, though he had made a point of bringing his own. "We shall need the extra space," she said to him as she greeted him herself at her door.

She disappeared momentarily to return not just with hat and parasol, which he expected, but with an absolute hoard of children and grandchildren. It seemed her entire family was visiting, and he was expected to escort the entire assemblage. They divided up into the two carriages, a noisy bunch of at least a dozen people, mostly under the age of ten. He went quite pale just thinking about what this would mean for the day.

He had his second surprise when they arrived at the Gardens, and he found he was not escorting the others at all.

"I only thought it would be more convenient than hiring a second carriage," she told him as the group disembarked, dividing naturally with her children rounding up their offspring, and setting off to enjoy the day, leaving Lady Pelbrook entirely in the care of her escort.

"You only thought..."

"Well, today is a day about budgeting ourselves," she responded quite cheerfully. "Why not use what we already have, meaning both our carriages, rather than hire a conveyance for the day, which would be parked in the shade for most of it?"

"There is an admission," he said, offering her his arm and escorting her towards the gate.

She sniffed. "A pittance. The price is set to a shilling that anyone might enjoy Vauxhall to the fullest."

He laughed at this, handing over his shillings with almost a smug satisfaction. "There are costs to the things within the Garden," he pointed out.

"Not with the day I have planned," she said rather primly and immediately nodded towards a meandering path near the entrance. "I understand this will take us on the loveliest of walks with no additional fee necessary."

"At least if we hide among the shrubbery, no one will see how ridiculous we look. Wandering about the Gardens at our age," he muttered, half under his breath, knowing full well this particular path was a favourite for young people hoping to steal a kiss.

She gave him a warning look, showing that she had indeed heard him. "We are here to enjoy our day to the fullest."

The reminder only served to worry him all the more. What precisely did she mean by enjoying the day to the *fullest*? Surely, not at their age...

Yet the morning passed rather pleasantly. There were benches enough where they could sit and rest whenever they felt like it. To his relief, she suggested these breaks often. His leg still troubled him, though the unaccustomed exercise had the added benefit of working out some of the knots. Maybe his doctor had been correct in saying he needed to exercise more after all.

Lady Pelbrook certainly seemed to delight in the greenery. She paused often to exclaim over a particular bloom, or to enjoy how picturesque their surroundings were.

Not once did she do anything so overtly flirtatious as to indicate she hoped he might take undue advantage upon this walk to steal a kiss. Not that he would have. Though as the morning wore on, he did consider the shape of her lips at one point and wondered, when she leaned against a tree ostensibly to adjust her shoe, she might have been inviting...

No, it was all in innocence. They were much too old for such things.

The trail ended at a small building where they might procure lunch for a fee. Lord Gillingham puffed himself up at the sight of it. "I suspect you would be interested in something to refresh yourself after such a long walk," he said with a certain satisfaction, already reaching for his purse.

"Indeed, I am quite glad I thought to make such arrangements earlier," she said and nodded towards where the tables were set out in the shade, to where her man was setting out dishes from a wicker basket while another servant assisted in laying out delectable bits of chicken, fruits, and cheeses, alongside several tempting cakes and other sweets.

"You arranged this," he said, staring rather stupidly at the picnic. Of course, she had. Why pay for an overpriced luncheon when one could bring a perfectly suitable one from home? Other people did it, for he saw several such baskets. Why would she not think to plan this much for him?

"Bravo," he said as he guided her over to a chair and helped her to settle in comfortably where the sun would not be in her eyes. "Well played. I shall delight in seeing what you are up to next."

"Up to?" She blinked at him with such innocence of expression he almost laughed.

"Up to." He repeated the words back and shook his head. "Never mind. I look forward to whatever you have arranged for the rest of the day."

After lunch, it seemed she had counted on spending time with her family. He had to admit, that as her grandchildren capered about, showing off this or that new wonder they had discovered, it was pleasant indeed. They marvelled at tightrope walkers. They explored the Turkish tent. There was no part of the Garden left unexplored. By evening, the party had again split up, the children going home with their nannies so as not to miss their bedtime routine. The adults stayed to walk under the glass globes that lit the Gardens at night making it a fairyland.

If it seemed fitting to steal a kiss, laying his lips gently upon her cheek under those lights, it was only because he was an old fool who could not be expected to behave himself at his advanced age. She blushed and her fingers tightened in his as overhead, fireworks filled the sky.

All in all, it was a very good day.

Chapter Six

It was Sunday. Lord Gillingham awoke feeling strangely refreshed despite the strenuous outing of the previous day. He hummed while he dressed, which disconcerted his valet. He startled the kitchen staff by sending them compliments upon a fine breakfast and even had a kind word for the driver and footman who both managed his carriage on the way to church. All in all, the day seemed bright and full of possibilities.

Arriving at church, he paused to greet several acquaintances as he made his way to the family pew. Here, he was put out for a moment at the sheer vast emptiness of the long wooden bench. He reminded himself that Andrew would come home at some point, and eventually, his wife and offspring would fill these empty spaces. In the meantime, he would manage quite well on his own.

He wondered if Lady Pelbrook felt similarly encumbered by the emptiness of her own family pew. But when he looked in her direction, he saw she'd found company for this morning's worship in the form of a young lady he remembered vaguely as her niece from the day before. The girl had recently been introduced at court and looked quite charming next to her aunt. Though in his opinion, Lady Pelbrook was the superior of the two, the lines of her form being more pleasing to his eye. He had no such use for spindly, fluff-headed girls who were barely out of the schoolroom.

As if discerning his thoughts, Lady Pelbrook glanced his way in that instant. Their eyes met. She smiled. He smiled. Indeed, from this point forward, he was hard-pressed to focus on the service at all.

I will talk to her afterwards, he promised himself as the homily was delivered. Perhaps I should invite her upon another outing. Boating on the Thames perhaps.

He felt quite young, or at least a bit younger than he'd been feeling for a long time as he navigated the press after the service. It took some time to get to her, hampered as he was by his cane and the sore leg, which wasn't as appreciative about his long day out yesterday. By the time he reached Lady Pelbrook, he saw she was talking to a circle of young men. Rather, she was supervising their interest in her niece.

Lord Gillingham frowned. Did he not know the families of several of the lads? None of them seemed worth much as far as fortune was concerned. If he were to classify their type, he would call them fortune-seekers. At least two had been in the ranks interested in his younger daughters in the last few years before they were safely married. Neither had been worthy of her.

Eventually, the girl moved away to speak to a friend. The flock of gentlemen moved with her, each vying for her attention, bolder now that she was in the company of a gaggle of brightly dressed young misses who giggled at everything they said from behind lifted fans. Lord Gillingham shook his head and addressed Lady Pelbrook more sharply than he intended.

"Have a care, Lady Pelbrook. Those rapscallions would have your niece's fortune in a thrice if you are not careful!"

Lady Pelbrook seemed somewhat surprised by the greeting. "Dare I say good morning, ere we fall into another argument? It is Sunday after all."

"Joke if you must, but that particular young man she is talking to now has no fortune of his own. He comes from a poor background. His father lost everything only last year."

Lady Pelbrook's eyebrow raised in a way that only could be termed 'dangerous.' "Do tell."

"I daresay he is after a rather fat dowry," Lord Gillingham finished in triumph as the second eyebrow joined the first.

"And you feel I am unaware of the situation and need warning?" Lady Pelbrook's tone had taken on a rather severe note.

"Well, is it not your duty to protect the girl from scoundrels in absence of her parents?"

"Have you proof that this man is a scoundrel?" she asked. There was something sad lurking in her eyes.

"His lack of fortune—"

"I thought so," she said, putting up a hand to stop his flow of words. "I will have to bid you good day, My Lord. I can see it is no use talking to you."

"No use talking to ME?" He looked about at the other members of the Ton standing around and talking after church. The day was quite fair and there were several conversations going on. So far no one had given them much notice. Thankfully. He was quite put out by how this conversation was turning out. "Whatever do you mean?"

She looked around too before speaking, showing she understood his desire for discretion. He was pleased by this sign, that she cared about her standing in the Ton and would do nothing to damage is, such as to create a scene. The next words out of her mouth caught him off guard.

"I shall have to say, I am fairly disgusted with you, Lord Gillingham."

He blinked. "How so?"

"The young man you question comes from a good family, which has fallen on hard times through no one's fault. They have been at the mercy of an unscrupulous man, a matter that has caused them no end of difficulty. They are well-titled, to be sure. But more than that, they are kind people. Intelligent, and well-worth knowing." She shook her head. "Truly, it is you who are disappointing to me, and if anything, further proof that I have been wasting my time with you."

"But..." He stared at her, remembering the feel of her hand in his yesterday, the quick peck upon her cheek under the lights.

"You see the world only through the lens of money and prosperity. I had hoped the outing yesterday would have been proof that one does not need funds to find genial company. In truth, I had thought better of you."

"Better of me." He was repeating the words, trying to understand them in his mind.

"I really must go. Lord Gillingham, while it was pleasant to reacquaint ourselves, I can see that if I am to still treasure the memories of the boy I once knew, I would do better to not know the man he became."

With that, she curtseyed and went to collect her niece along with the charming young man.

Lord Gillingham watched her go, a mixture of fury and dismay coursing through him. The day had gone drab, as though all the colour had fled from it. The walk to his carriage felt terribly long, and the ride home was very lonely indeed.

Chapter Seven

Lord Gillingham's blasted leg hurt more than ever, and he could barely walk. "Fetch the doctor," he snapped to the butler as he came through the door. "This awful leg will be the death of me."

The butler bowed and went to do his bidding. Lord Gillingham managed to stagger to his study with help of the footman, who helped make him comfortable upon his favourite chair. His aching leg was supported by a well-placed footstool, with a pillow upon it to make it comfortable.

When the doctor arrived, he clucked over the arrangement. "You would be better off in bed," he said, shaking his head.

"I will not be carried upstairs like a child!"

"Then I suggest you find a way to relax the muscle of the leg. You told me yourself you had an injury to this leg years ago. The spasms you describe can be attributed to tightness in the muscle, made worse by holding yourself so rigid. Even now, you are sitting so straight you make my back ache to look at you."

"I do not pay you to pass judgement upon my posture."

The doctor only laughed. "You do when your posture is affecting the rest of your body. Truly, you must not push yourself so hard if you want to keep use of the leg. This constant state of agitation will only make the pain worse. Quite naturally, if this happens, you will use the leg less until you are quite immobilized by it."

"And what of my meetings? There is business I must attend to this week. Investments that need my attention. A meeting with my bankers…"

"I would advise you to find someone else to manage your affairs for a time. Sit outside. Enjoy your family. Do things that give you pleasure." The doctor cheerfully packed up his bag to leave, pausing to put a stoppered bottle into Lord Gillingham's hand. "If all else fails, I would suggest this tonic. Take it as needed to…aid in relaxing the muscle."

Lord Gillingham pulled the stopper and took a cautious sniff of the liquid within. "Why, this is scotch!"

"And it will definitely relax you." With that, the doctor tipped his hat and took his leave.

Lord Gillingham was just exploring the idea of sampling some of this miracle 'tonic' when Virginia and Anna burst in, all smiles and laughter.

"We have just seen the doctor as we came in and he suggests we make things jolly for you. Would you care to go for a drive, Papa? Or shall we call some friends in and create a dinner party? Why, we have heard you are courting Lady Pelbrook. We could ask her—"

"You have heard *what*? Lady Pelbrook?" Lord Gillingham was so put off by this offer, he started to rise, forgetting his leg entirely until he put his weight upon it. Groaning, he sank back down into his chair. "You will NOT invite Lady Pelbrook anywhere, do you understand me?"

The girls looked at one another. "Oh dear," Virginia murmured.

Anna nodded. "I see."

"You see what?"

"That you are quite smitten. Oh Father, how lovely!" Virginia said when Anna couldn't seem to find the words to explain tactfully.

"Lovely? I tell you I do not wish to see her, and you call it *lovely*?"

"I see that you must be quite taken by her to be this upset. Oh Father, do tell us what happened," Anna urged, drawing a chair up to sit next to him.

"It might help," Virginia murmured, doing the same.

Lord Gillingham stared at his daughters in consternation. He started to put them off, to tell them to leave him alone. Then he thought back to Lady Pelbrook's assessment of his character. The importance of health – he glanced at his leg – and family.

He sighed. "There is hardly anything to tell," he muttered.

Virginia smiled helpfully while Anna reached out and took his hand. "Then it shall not take long," she said.

In the end, it took longer to explain than he had expected. It was hard to put his thoughts in order, especially when there were things he'd never admitted to himself until now. Like how much he had hurt his family with his actions.

"Your preoccupation with money did make some difficulties for all of us when we were courting," Virginia said and Anna nodded, twisting her reticule in her hands. There was much they left unsaid, but then, he already knew. He'd made them all miserable, trying to foist his own choices upon his daughters, despite the fine character of their chosen mates.

This was fast getting into areas he no longer wanted to discuss. "Why did you come here?" he asked finally. "I was not expecting either of you today."

The girls looked at one another. "But—" Anna started but Virginia shook her head.

"Let him think upon it, dear. In the meantime, there is no harm in letting you know about our original errand. There is to be a ball for charity, the Widow and Orphan's Fund."

"I knew it. You never show up without needing money."

"Father! After everything we have just discussed!" Anna protested.

Virginia's lips were pursed, as though she were trying very hard not to say something she might regret later.

"You might as well let it out, Ginny, before your face freezes that way," Lord Gillingham muttered.

"I was only thinking it is no wonder Lady Pelbrook wants nothing more to do with you," Virginia said primly, standing up and shaking out her skirts. "Anna, we might as well leave. We will get nowhere with him today."

"I will not be treated like a child!" Lord Gillingham burst out as they headed for the door.

"Then stop acting like one!" Virginia retorted and left.

Anna hesitated long enough to run back and hug her father. "She does not mean it," she murmured, though her words lacked conviction.

"She meant every word of it," Lord Gillingham said quietly. "And she is right. I will be all right, Anna. Just...Give me time to sort things out."

She nodded and left.

When he was finally alone, Lord Gillingham looked at the bottle of 'tonic' for a long moment. It was a tempting solution. Easier than that list he'd written the other day. Cautiously, he stood up and limped over to his desk. The paper was where he had left it.

Family.

Friends.

Health.

Live Life to the Fullest.

Love.

His gaze lingered on the last word for a long time.

Love.

He picked up his pen and dipped it in the inkwell. A moment later he put it down again. He simply couldn't find the words.

Chapter Eight

Lady Pelbrook paced nervously. Had she pushed Lord Gillingham too far?

She glanced out the window at the small garden behind the house where the children played in the sun. Her daughters sat in the shade, talking and laughing while watching the little ones play. Her niece Sophie was running with the little ones. Not so long from the nursery herself she sometimes seemed more child than woman.

Ah, the time would come when that would change. The girl would marry and take her place in Society and her childhood would be something to recall fondly. The way Lady Pelbrook recalled her own days of her youth.

The way she recalled Theodore.

"The old goat. What did he have to grow up and become so priggish for?"

It was a silly thing to be mooning about him indoors when so much awaited her in the garden. She should join the others. The girls would share the latest gossip. They would laugh over the antics of the children and talk about Sophie's upcoming engagement. There was something very fulfilling in such a life. She could be content with these things, could she not?

Except...

She remembered the brush of his lips upon her cheek, surprising her with his boldness. The way his fingers had felt safely twined through her own. Somehow, in her experiment to show her old friend a lack in his life, she had discovered a lack in her own. She had family and friends. Her health was still good. And certainly, she lived her life to the fullest.

But she lacked love. She had not thought such a thing was even possible. Not at her age.

Lady Pelbrook shook her head and started for the door. To her surprise, she ran right into Sophie, who'd just come in from outside, flushed and breathless.

"Aunt Theo, I was just looking for you. Come outside and play with us. 'Tis the nicest day."

Lady Pelbrook smiled and hugged her niece before falling into step with her. "I will come outside, but I find I do not have the heart for playing just now."

"Because of Lord Gillingham?" Sophie guessed wisely.

Lady Pelbrook stopped in her tracks to look at her niece in surprise. "What do you know of Lord Gillingham?"

"Only that you seemed quite happy to visit with him this last week. And you were glad to see him in church. At least you were before the service."

"Humph. You see far too much," Lady Pelbrook muttered, half under her breath.

"I notice everything," Sophie said in delight.

"Then you might have told me I was wasting my time trying to teach that old curmudgeon a lesson. You would have seen he only has a love for money, with no room for anything else."

"Aunt Theo," Sophie said, taking her aunt's hands so that she might look seriously into her eyes. "I told you I notice everything. What I saw was a man who was trying very hard not to fall in love with you." She leaned in to whisper, "I think he failed, for he seemed quite out of sorts when you sent him away."

"Sophie!"

"Well, he did!"

The two ladies looked at each other for a long moment before bursting into laughter.

"I perhaps owe him an apology," Lady Pelbrook said, letting go of her niece and heading back towards her writing desk.

"Or...you might meet him outside..." Sophie said with a nod to the window on the other side of the room, which overlooked the street.

Lady Pelbrook went to look outside. When she did, she started laughing. "Indeed, you notice everything." With that, she kissed her niece on the cheek. "Perhaps you can arrange..."

"I will make sure you are not interrupted." Sophie smiled and hurried outside where the others were still enjoying the afternoon.

Lady Pelbrook took one last glimpse up the street at the figure gamely limping for all he was worth down the walk from his house to hers. "You old fool," she said softly, but she was smiling as she hurried outside to meet him.

Chapter Nine

L ady Pelbrook's door opened in the same instant Lord Gillingham put up his hand to knock. Disconcerted, he half expected to see a footman or even the butler. Maybe a visitor just going out. The last thing he expected was to see Lady Pelbrook herself standing there, with a rather odd look upon her face.

"Lady Pelbrook, I was calling to suggest a...a...walk?"

She stared at him a long moment and then finally burst out laughing. "I would expect a spot of tea would be better," she suggested with a significant look at his bad leg.

Flushing now, Lord Gillingham had to laugh with her. "Perhaps so."

In no time at all they were settled in the parlour, a pot of tea between them, and a fresh plate of scones and tiny sandwiches near to hand. "Do you know," she said as she poured tea into a cup for him, having told the servants she'd rather pour the tea herself, "I have no idea how you take your tea."

"With just a bit of sugar," he said, nodding when she added just the right amount.

"The point I was getting at, is we barely know each other," she said, taking her own cup to sit next to him upon the settee.

"We knew each other well, once."

"Thirty years ago?" she asked and smiled. "I imagine we have changed since then."

"Is that not how we got into this whole argument," he asked somewhat sourly, not liking to be reminded of that conversation, even if it were the reasoning behind what brought him here to her now.

"I owe you an apology this time," she said, and shook her head. "We have been apologizing a great deal this last week, have we not?"

"It is a mark of being willing to work out our problems." He stirred his tea thoughtfully. "Some would call it a good sign in a relationship."

"Is that what we have?" She seemed surprised by the word.

"I think it is what we are trying to form." He considered this a moment. "Building an attachment to someone else can be a difficult thing."

"Especially when one of the two people forming the...er...attachment...is trying to teach the other a lesson." She bit her lip. It was a rather endearing gesture, distracting enough that he almost missed her apology. "I really AM sorry."

"As am I," he said, reaching out to take her free hand in his own. "I apologize for being so caught up in money that I have failed to see what is right in front of me. I suspect if I had not been so focused on position and prestige, I might have seen what was right there all along. What has always been in front of me."

She shook her head. "It is not your fault. We did not move much in the same circles after all. We almost always stayed at the Estate, avoiding the London Season. I came only sometimes, for a short stay, for many of the years since Harold's death."

"I am sure it brought back many memories."

"It did. But then my girls needed to come out and well...I found I liked London again. There were things worth staying for. Some...just right down the street from me."

The look she gave him seemed to be significant. Lord Gillingham's mouth went dry. For a moment he forgot how to speak.

"Shall we start over?" she asked softly.

Her hand was still in his. It felt very right. "And if we start over, then what? No...I do not want to erase this past week. I needed to learn a few things and I would be afraid of forgetting those lessons otherwise. But I do want to make things right."

"You do not—"

"I do." He brought her hand to his lips and kissed her fingers. "Let me think about how to do this. A grand gesture perhaps. A ball. The Charity Ball, in fact."

"The Charity Ball?"

"I should like to host it. That would help the Widows and Orphans Fund, would it not? Let them sell their tickets to raise funds, but I will pay for the ball itself."

She gasped. "That is quite a gesture, Theodore. Quite an expensive gesture. For charity no less."

When he looked at her, he was smiling. "You cannot make a grand gesture without doing something rather large, Theodosia."

Little did she know this was only the beginning.

Chapter Ten

T he ball was the grandest ball of the Season. Being meant for charity, Lord Gillingham went all out, hoping to draw the generosity of the Ton for the fund. Anna and Virginia enjoyed helping with the planning and with so many tickets sold, the affair was guaranteed to be an event people would talk about in years to come.

The splendour of the decorations, the sparkle of the champagne, and the intensity of the music were eclipsed though by the loveliness of Lady Theodosia Pelbrook. At least this was so according to Lord Gillingham who could not take eyes off the lovely Lady, who looked years younger in her happiness, for she held a secret she could not tell. At least not yet.

Instead, they put their focus on the ball and upon the fund it meant to benefit. Towards the end of the evening though, a small celebration broke out as a certain young man announced his engagement to Sophie Pelbrook, Lady Pelbrook's niece. Lord Gillingham, proving that indeed his character was changed for the better, at least in part, added the offer of a partnership to the young man. It was by way of a gift, to start him with a small series of investments to manage on his own as part of his apprenticeship at the bank where he would be working. That Lord Gillingham might have pulled a few strings to get the young man the position was something no one at the ball needed to know.

His daughters found out though and cornered him. As did Andrew who was only recently returned.

"Has Father grown soft in his dotage?" asked Eloise. She had been away and had only recently returned to London with her husband, Jackson, in tow.

"Do not ask me, I have been gone as long as you," Josephina mumbled while Virginia laughed.

"I think he is in love," she proclaimed, and Anna immediately seconded this. All eyes immediately went to their father who stammered and blushed, much as a schoolboy might have.

"Am I not so old that I can do as I like," he muttered and tried to shoo them away, but they would have none of it.

"You will ask her tonight, will you not?" Anna asked. And when the others heard the story, they too added their voices to this opinion.

Their father grew thoughtful. "This ball is a celebration of love it seems," he said, thinking perhaps of the engagement already announced that night.

"If you are going to ask me, the night is passing quickly, and I am not getting any younger," Lady Pelbrook said, for she had somehow slipped into this particular huddle without anyone noticing.

Lord Gillingham took her hand, drawing her over to him so that he might put an arm around her waist. He guided her away from the rest, though he knew his family was there watching to see what he would do. He did not care though, for the audience was only his family who loved him and wanted what was best for him. Besides, his focus was entirely upon this woman who stood so boldly in front of him, waiting for him to find the right words.

"Lady Pelbrook...Theodosia...I have known you my whole life it seems. For a time, we lost touch, but I have never forgotten you. You were my best friend, and even now, you are the voice of reason, guiding me aright. But more than that, it is you who makes me complete. When I am with you, I am at my best, and when we are apart my world comes to an end. I love you Theodosia, and I am asking you now, in front of these witnesses, if you would consent to become my wife?"

She looked at him a long moment before taking the hand that he was already holding and bringing it to her lips. "I will say yes on one condition."

"Anything."

"Answer me this. Why did you not ask me this question years ago?"

Lord Gillingham's eyes softened as he looked at her. "Because your father told me that I was not good enough for you. I was not well enough off, nor were my prospects good. He would not allow me to marry you because I did not have a vast fortune to keep you."

She moaned, the sound coming out a soft, "Oh..."

He looked at her sadly. "I never forgot his words, only somehow, they got mixed up in my mind. That if I ever wanted to find true happiness, I would first need a fortune."

She was crying then, but he was there to hold her, to kiss the tears away.

"Shhhh...do not make my proposal a sad thing," he teased. "It took a lot of courage to ask."

"Then I shall answer you with happiness," she said, and indeed she smiled. To Lord Gillingham, it was as though the sun came out.

"Yes, I will marry you," she said and this time when he put his arms around her, she was already there, and kissing him for all she was worth.

Epilogue

L ord Gillingham and Lady Pelbrook wasted no time in getting married. They wed as soon as the banns could be posted and married while their entire families were still in London. It was considered the wedding of the Season, in part because it was such a grand affair. But there were many such grand affairs every Season. No, what made this particular wedding so special was the love the couple obviously had for each other. Though advanced in years, Theodore and Theodosia had a passion that anyone who saw could see, just in the way the couple looked at one another.

As they came down the aisle after being pronounced man and wife, they were welcomed into the arms of their families. Friends were eager to sing their well-wishes, so thrilled by the couple that the wedding breakfast had become quite a large affair in its own right.

Lord Gillingham took Andrew aside not long after the ceremony.

"Son, it seems rather odd that the moment you came back from your own honeymoon, I should leave on my own. I trust you though, with the running of the Estate. You have been ready to take on this position for some time now. In the last year, you walked with me through my daily life and saw what was needed to be done to keep the Estate and help it to prosper."

"Thank you, Father. But surely you will not be gone for so long as to give me such a dramatic speech as you leave," Andrew exclaimed, with an uneasy glance towards his siblings who had likewise gathered around.

"You are all grown and have married well. You already manage your own families. I expect you can manage the Gillingham Estate without me. Andrew, you will take the reins as my heir, but you have good people around you who can advise you if I am not here. My wife," here, he paused and smiled fondly at Theodosia who was waiting near the door for the time when they would leave. "My wife and I intend to take our time before returning. There are funds enough for us to enjoy together, whatever time we have left. We would like to see the world and just to enjoy living life to the fullest for a while."

At this, Theodosia clapped her hands together, barely suppressing her delight.

"But will you return?" asked his children and he smiled, putting his arms out so that he might hug them all at once, even if they were adults.

"God willing, we shall return. For family is one of the best things in life, as are our friends." He looked fondly out over the gathering. "But the greatest of these is love, and for the time being, I want to spend every day making Theodosia the happiest woman on earth. Just as she makes me the happiest man on earth."

His children were moved by this speech and hugged him hard, each in turn. Then the time came to leave. Lord and Lady Gillingham said their goodbyes to London and got into the carriage, already headed to their next adventure. The world was at their feet, just waiting to be explored together.

The End
Did you enjoy *The Gillingham Collection*?
Please consider rating it on <u>Goodreads,</u> <u>Bookbub</u> or your favorite retailer. Reviews help me reach new readers.

Read ***The Blackmore Collection,*** the next collection in The Lady Series.

Join my Newsletter for updates, sales and giveaways!

Glossary of Regency Terms

Adventuress – a woman of loose morals, wild

Almack's - Private, very exclusive balls were held there each Wednesday night of the Season. Only those approved by the patronesses were allowed to attend.

Apoplexy – a fit

Bag of moonshine - a lot of nonsense

Bit of muslin - a woman of easy virtue

Blue devilled - depressed

Bounder - a man of objectionable social behaviour

Cad - a man who doesn't treat women proper.

Canterbury tales - lies.

Chatelaine – the keeper of the keys, ruler about who went where

Chit - a saucy, forward girl

Coming Out – A young lady's first entry into Society. Presented first at the Royal Court to the ruling monarch, a ball was later held in her honour. She is hereafter free to attend social events and seek a husband.

Countenance - a person's face or facial expression

Dalliance – courtship, relationship

Dash it – to Hell with it

Devil's own scrape – terrible trouble

Devil to pay - trouble
Doing it much too brown - overdoing it so that it is not credible
Dressing down – telling off
Flush in the pockets - rich
Fustian – rubbish, nonsense
Gammon - lie or nonsense
Get on – manage, run
High dudgeon - very angry
Hogwash – nonsense, rubbish
Hoyden – A mischievous, spunky girl who is felt to lack decorum.
Incomparable - a female of the ton without rival, match or peer.
Kick up a lark – get up to mischief
Libertine - a person, especially a man, who freely indulges in sensual
pleasures without regard to moral principles
Loose in the haft - has many vices and little respect for proprieties
Make a cake of oneself - make a fool of self
Not a feather to fly with - to have no money
Not care a fig – not care at all
Purse-pinched - have little money
Raising a breeze – up to mischief
Reticule – handbag
Ride roughshod over – bend to your will
Riding habit – the clothes women wore for riding; a skirt, jacket,
hat, boots and often gloves
Romp – fun, joke
Shockingly loose in the haft - has many vices and little respect for
proprieties.
Stirrup-cups – shot of alcohol to keep riders warm
Toilette - outfit
Ton – high Society
To go about – to behave
To be a goose – be silly
Throwing a rub in the way - spoiling the plans